ST☆RCHILD PUBLISHING
PRESENTS

D0993086

BAPTISM BY
FIRE

PART II: BACK FROM HELL

A NOVEL BY

MICHAEL STANTON

PUBLISHING

Starchild Publishing
PO Box 6068
Newark NJ 07106

Manufactured in the United States of America.

For more information regarding special discounts or bulk purchases, please contact Starchild Publishing/special sales at 973-494-0868 or star@starchildpublishing.com

ISBN: 978-0-9793820-2-4

WORDS FROM THE AUTHOR

I wish I could find the words to tell you how much love I received since I wrote *Baptism By Fire Part I Empire*. I did not know you would thoroughly enjoy the story I needed to tell. I have met so many good people who cussed me out to get back into the lab to give them the rest of the story. You remind me of the little Boy and the Bum (SMILE).

My stories read like the truth because I write from in depth experience. I do not write to glorify the life I lived, but to better explain its circumstances on an emotional level. Many will never be able to grasp it in its entirety.

I have been in the street life since I was 13 and since the age of 15, I have never had less than a hundred grand in the stash. Although money was being made, it did not stop the loss I have experienced as I gained so much from the streets. My friends were dying around me, or getting life in prison.

It took me reaching the lowest point in my life to figure out I am at my strongest when I am on my knees giving glory to God. He has saved me from myself and I am so grateful to Him for loving me that much to do so. I know death was about to claim me if I did not change.

You just don't know how good it feels for you to tell me how much you enjoyed what has been manifested out of my imagination. This is what has given me my self-worth. Not the pure drugs I sold and the addicts who chased me down to buy my product. It was you who chased me down to buy Part II of my books. This writing has taken me on a journey and exposed me to me. It showed me a gift I did not know I had.

When I said writing is far cheaper than therapy, I meant that. I was going through a process of elimination and removing the things in my life I did not need and embracing what I needed.

I prayed to God to show me a better way and to help me change the things I have yet to acknowledge. I was reading the Bible and came to Luke 3:16 and this is why I titled my first book *Baptism By Fire*. A lot of the people in the urban genre told me this was a risky title, but I was determined to stick with it. It has not been easy, but this is all a part of God's plan. How can you have a testimony without a test?

I used to think God was a spooky being. I now know the God I serve is LIFE. It just took time for me to sit down and figure out what has been in my face all along.

Don't get me wrong, I am still a little rough around the edges, but now I have limitations and boundaries I will not cross for any reason whatsoever. It was you who told me I was a writer and now I am perfectly sold on that idea. I just want to say thank you and please reach out to let me know you are a part of this movement. I love to speak with those who can finally see the good in me. Tell someone about these books and let's Baptize this world by FIRE together!

Truly yours,

Michael Stanton

PROLOGUE

Cleveland Ohio:

The branches from the massive oak trees swayed back and forth from each gush of wind. Since early this morning the atmosphere was humid and stifling hot. A marginal breeze danced on the leaves and brought a moment of relief to the people in the park.

In the center of the park, a dog was chasing a tennis ball being thrown by his owner. The dog chased each ball as if he did not have any inclination of the heat wave cooking the flesh of everyone under the beaming sun. The dog was furry, but ran like it was the dead of winter.

The little Boy sat on one of the benches quiet and in deep thought about some of the things the Bum had said to him yesterday with regards to the life and death of Don Starchild.

He had been sitting here for nearly an hour. Reaching the park was the first thing to come across his mind as soon as his eyes focused on the light of the dawning of the new day.

The Boy's eyes were scanning every inch of the park for the Bum. When he did not see him anywhere in sight, a wounded look crept deep into his sullen eyes. He thought he would never see the Bum again and this would prevent him from knowing whether Don Starchild was dead or alive. Every passing second made him feel like hope was passing along with it.

The Boy rolled the brown paper bag tightly in his hands. This was to prevent any chance of the air spoiling the sandwiches he prepared for the Bum and himself. He noticed the Bum eating a turkey and cheese sandwich.

Three long doubtful hours had gone by and the Boy was still patiently waiting. He felt his heart roughly leap from his chest once he saw the Bum stroll through the front entrance of the park. A huge duffel bag was draped over his shoulder.

The Bum walked directly to the bench he occupied every day in the park since the Boy first saw him sleeping. He placed his bag on the bench. The sound of the zipper broke the silence between them. The Bum removed four packages of raw meat.

The Boy leaned over to see what was making the thin high pitched sounds inside of the bag. The head of two baby panthers came into his view. Their yellow eyes were set inside the limits of their rich black coats. They both meowed like kittens into the Boy's eyes.

Before the Boy could ask a question, he saw the Bum toss one of the packages of raw meat into the trees. It landed in the mouth of a large Black panther poised on one of the sturdy branches like the Queen of all Panthers.

The Bum continued to throw the meat up to the panther until she devoured all the packets of meat. This was just a snack to hold her until nightfall. Once she noticed nothing else was coming,she climbed up higher into the oak trees and disappeared from sight.

"Are you afraid of animals?" the Bum asked.

The Boy shook his head no with a triumphant smile. "I love animals." He reached to pet one of the baby Panthers. "Where did you get these from?" he asked, "the zoo?"

The Bum removed one of the panthers and handed him to the Boy. "This little fellow likes to be held." The panther hissed as he was removed from the bag and into the waiting hands of the Boy.

The Boy ran the palm of his hand across the smooth coat of the panther's head. "He looks like a black cat." He brought the face of the panther closer to his. "Cute little fellow."

The Bum removed the other panther from the bag. "This is the girl. Both of these little things will be dangerous when they grow up."

"Where did you get them from?" the Boy asked for the second time.

The Bum glanced upwards. "That's their mother up in the tree." He spoke like he did not hear the question. "She has to stay up there until the darkness can hide her on the ground. I don't want her scaring everybody."

"Why do you have them here anyway?" the Boy asked.

The Bum continued to stare up into the trees like he had not heard the Boy's question. "What brings you here so early." The Bum reached into the bag and handed the Boy one of the little bottles of warm milk. "They have not eaten since last night. Feed him until he has had enough."

The Boy was starting to get used to the way the Bum did things. He did not like to have to answer too many questions. He only wanted the Boy to know what he wanted him to know. He would eventually tell him all he needed to know without his having to inquire.

"I came here to speak with you," the Boy replied. "When I did not see you, I thought it would be best to wait and see if you would show up."

The Bum pressed his back firmly on the bench. "I guess you want to hear the rest of the story about Don Starchild."

The male panther wrapped his paws around the Boy's hand while he fed him the bottle. Normally, the Bum would allow the panthers to feed from their mother. It was day time and she had to remain in the trees until the sunset. The Bum did not want to alert or alarm anyone of a full grown panther parading around the park as he did not want any attention brought to himself whatsoever.

"I have a question for you I have been thinking about all night and . . ." The Boy stopped in mid sentence, because he was about to ask the Bum a question.

"You want to know my name? "the Bum finished.

The Boy lowered his head, his features were remarkably composed and angelic. He nodded his head yes and did not bother to turn towards the Bum to see if he noticed his gesture of yes, as he could feel his cold eyes burning into the side of his head.

The Bum patted the Boy softly on his shoulder. "In life one must be able to thoroughly exercise extreme patience. The last thing you ever want to do is make grave mistakes when it comes to life's circumstances. A hunter must be patient and lie in wait for his prey."The Bum laid the panther on his lap. "I know you have questions you feel you need answered and I want you to hold them until the end of the entire story if you can. I do believe if you are paying close attention to every facet of the details all you would want to ask will be answered throughout the contents of our travels through the life of Don Starchild."

The Boy's eyes fell to his lap. "Can I ask just one question?" he asked softly, his index finger pointed towards the heavens.

"I'll allow you three before the story is completed, but not the one concerning my name," the Bum said.

The Boy cleared his throat like he was about to make a speech before the masses. He sat upright on the bench. He felt as though a nest of butterflies was snugly in the pit of his stomach. "Do you know Don Starchild personally?"

The Bum kissed the panther on the crown of his head. "Yes," he replied quicker than the Boy initially expected. "But not many can truly say they know or knew Don Starchild. Let me tell you what happened after Don died." A smile formed at the corners of the Bum's mouth. "An intelligent man has the potential to do greater things in death than he could ever do in life. Life has the ability to rob a man of the substantial meaning of what immortality is to the very soul of a man."

The Boy reached into the bag and handed the Bum a sandwich. The Bum took a huge bite and swallowed without chewing. He took another and chewed slowly. It was like he could taste every individual particle of flavor on his taste buds.

The Bum was silent while he held the panther. His cold eyes were staring straight ahead as if he were preparing each segment of the story to be told with the equivalent amount of enthusiasm and hunger as he told the first story in order to impel the Boy to come back the next day.

A very refreshing breeze streamed through the park and ruffled a potato chip bag. Once the cool breeze passed like a drop of water in the hot Arabian desert, the heat burst into a series of movements on all sides of the park. The air became stifling, even in the area by the picnic tables which provided the most shade.

The Bum gulped down the last of his sandwich and dug into the bag for another. He bit into the sandwich in deep concentration and just stared straight ahead in a trance like state. The Boy watched him like a hawk and did not bother to ask him when he was going to start the story. A gut feeling told him something beyond spectacular was about to happen today.

A solid fifteen minutes went by before the Bum's lips curved into a knowing smile. His mind was luxuriating with the answers to the questions travelling through the Boy's head at the lightning speed of 1,120 feet per second.

The Bum lowered his eyes to the Boy. "Do you think Don is dead?" He rubbed the stomach of the female panther sitting on his lap. Her legs were spread apart and her yellow eyes were mere slits.

The Boy came to the edge of his seat and slowly extracted a sandwich from the bag. "Is this a trick question?" he asked.

The Bum released a hearty laugh. "How can a question be a trick to a man of extensive intelligence?" He tapped his feet on the ground. "It is either you know the answer or not. Any question to a wise man can never be tricky because he will only speak on what he knows and not what he believes to be the truth."

The Bum switched hands to rub the panther. "Now from what you have heard so far, do you think Don is dead?"

"I told you yesterday, I know he got on the passenger side for a reason, but you never said if he made it out of the car or not. When I asked you what happened to him, you told me to come back tomorrow to hear the rest of the story."

The Bum broke a negligible size of meat from in between his sandwich and fed half to both panthers. "It all depends on how you view life and death. There are many definitions of life and death. A man can be in a coma and be brain dead. A man can be in prison and be dead to society. A man can be dead and be very much revered in death far more than he was in life, just like the story of Jesus."

The Boy gritted his teeth together. "If you knew he died, then why did you tell me to come back tomorrow to hear the rest of the story?" The Boy's voice was starting to seethe with anger.

The Bum laid the sleeping panther back in the bag. He took the panther from the Boy and laid him in the bag also. The Bum's movements were slow and meticulous. He was in deep thought about what he was going to say next.

"It does not take much for a piece of a man to die while he appears to be very much alive." The Bum's eyes were slowly brimming with tears. "Don died the day his brother died and the day Nydia died and he went straight into the bottomless pit of hell."

The Bum's eyes were etched in sorrow and he sunk into a trance-like state. The Boy could see him closing his eyes and shaking his head from side to side as if he was shaking away a bad dream.

"So Don did die?" the Boy asked with urgency. He was sitting at the edge of the bench ready to get up and walk away once the Bum confirmed there was nothing left of the story of Don Starchild. Now he felt even more tricked than when the Bum tricked him with the coin. He had come back to hear the rest of the story and the thought there was no story to tell was causing his grief to grow like cancer in his mind.

The Bum removed his wool hat and stuck it into his pocket. His hair was white and full like lamb's wool. "Don Starchild died that day and I speak the truth to you."

The Boy was about to get up and leave when the Bum said, "but he came BACK FROM HELL."

Uninterrupted silence fell upon the entire park as though everyone heard what he said. The Boy slid back on the bench and a smile instantly formed on his full lips. He was now starting to come to terms with the true meaning of patience.

The Boy wanted to know everything there was to know about Don Starchild and how he came BACK FROM HELL!!!

CHAPTER ONE

Colossal balls of fire filled the sky surrounding Prince Street projects. The occasional detonation of cars disturbed the shocked officers from their thoughts. The roaring explosions were deafening to the ears of anyone standing close to the grand eruptions of fire and death.

The fire would cause the cars to burst into the air and fly in several directions. The officers gawked in disbelief at the sight of the twisted collision. Compassion dripped from their eyes for the slain officers engulfed in its inferno. Their faces were snarled in a state of agony of the thought it could've been them trapped in the chamber of death in front of them.

Detective Scott rolled onto his back and glanced up at the fumes from the deliquescing cars looming in the sky. Vapors suffused the once luxuriant blue sky like a dense black fog. The fog hung in the air like a black man from an Alabama tree.

Blaring sirens could be heard rushing towards the projects. The cars continued to explode and liquefy into the pavement. The colorful metal would softly bubble while it was still hot, but when it came in contact with air it would cause it to lie flat and slowly start to cool.

The thick smoke filled Scott's lungs and caused him to cough uncontrollably . He made an attempt to stand to his feet, but was knocked back down from the lack of air. All he could do was stare at the fire with his eyes notably bulging out of their sockets. His brows tightly knitted together as he tried to comprehend reason and logic to make sense of what had just happened.

The sight of the burning cars along with their occupants had Scott mesmerized and confused. Had he accelerated his speed instead of breaking, he would've been a participant of the nightmare before him. The thought of the flames stripping his flesh from his bones caused his heart to flutter in his congested chest.

News helicopters emerged from the crux of the black fog. Their rotating blades were fighting to remove the fog so their cameras will have a clear view of the news they were trying to report on the ground.

Although the helicopters were at a high altitude, the belly of the helicopters steamed from the torridness of the fire. Therefore, the pilot elevated the helicopters in the direction of the heavens, where everyone prayed the officers ascended for dying in the line of duty.

The fire trucks could be heard making their way through the Newark streets. The fire continued to burn and it didn't seem like it would let up without the help of water. The officers immediately went into action. They were knocking on doors for the Prince Street residents to evacuate their ghetto dwellings as a precaution while the fire continued to detonate and burn out of control. There were enough casualties from today's war and no need for anymore.

Scott noticed a shadow cast in front of him. He gazed up and saw James wiping away the residue of soot from his glasses. James wore a blank expression on his face. His guilt was well hidden considering he was a co-conspirator in today's atrocities. Don offered him a hundred thousand dollars and he quietly took it. He had two children he needed to put through college.

James extended his hand to help Scott to his feet. "I guess you called it." He handed Scott his handkerchief to wipe away the sod and sweat from his face. "Don sure made a mess of things."

Scott wiped his brow and the tears finally begun to fall once he was on his feet and able to take in the full view of the catastrophic sight of the mangled cars and the charred bodies of his friends.

"Who leaked out we were coming to the news?" Scott asked with a bitterness of the thought they lost their element of surprise.

James hunched his shoulders as if to say he didn't know. "I think that is the least of our worries at this point. This will place a huge damper on the Newark police department for the longest time."

Fire trucks finally made it to where they were gravely needed. They had to climb the sidewalks and travel through the narrow passages to get to the back of the projects where they extinguished the fire. The flames continued to ignite the gas tanks which released an earth shattering blast like a nuclear bomb had just been dropped.

Slowly the project occupants were escorted through the fleet of fire trucks. Women weren't fully dressed, and were in nightgowns. Children carried photo albums and toys like they would end up lost in the fire.

Everyone who took in the view of the fire gave a startled gasp at the sight of the burning cars and the men inside of them. This is what made today's events even more reprehensible to the ones shaking their heads with disbelief; a chase they were first watching on television ended at their doorstep.

Scott stumbled over the long water-hose as he desperately tried to back away from the fire that was starting to rage to new sections of dry ground. His lungs were singed and burned like he swallowed a box of halls cough drops. This came from inhaling the vapors of the fire for longer than he was supposed to.

Scott's lungs were the least of his worries. He suffered more from the sight of his fellow comrades consumed in the combustion of each explosion. His face was scarlet and swollen. A pained expression was securely etched in his features. His head constantly shook from side to side. He really needed to collect his sense of emotions. There was no need for him to keep fretting about today's events. What was done was done. Now was the time for healing to take place in order for everyone to move past today and strive to transcend far beyond this terrible moment in Newark's history.

Scott thought he saw something in his peripheral vision dart towards the back of the projects. His sanity forced him to shake away what he thought he saw.

For the first time today, Scott's face finally brightened at the sight of the raging fire. Scott's impression that Don Starchild was now drowning in the fire suddenly switched his emotions to a calm relief.

Scott flipped his wrist back to see the face of his watch and tried to narrow down the time to the exact second Don Starchild entered hell and would burn for all eternity.

OR WOULD HE?

CHAPTER TWO

A gusty wind slung its way through the frigid air and sent a minor chill to the bystanders at the memorial services of Don Starchild. His body wasn't there due to the fact the bones of everyone consumed within the fire had been intermingled into the concrete and bound into one heap of ash.

Carol Starchild later went and retrieved some of her son's ashes and placed seven handfuls inside a gold and black urn. The urn was placed inside of a coffin. She picked a location closer to the car her son was driving. All she needed was a symbol of his memory for the sake of closure for a terrible event.

The funeral dwellers were more than happy not to have to see the charred body of Don. They could imagine what he would've looked like from the sight they saw on television of him blowing up like he was in a car chase in a high speed action movie.

Today was a very solemn and sad day for all who loved Don and believed in everything he stood for. Friends from his youth had to show up and pay their respect. All of their eyes were bloodshot due to the fact that Don did ten years in prison, then came home and died less than three years after his release.

There were times when Carol Starchild would give an occasional glance up to the heavens with tear filled eyes. All she could do was ask God why didn't he keep Don in prison. She would rather have him in prison alive, instead of free and dead. A hurtful thought in hindsight, but one she could easily live with if it were a moments truth.

A stern wind swept through the green felt tent and caused the roses lying on top of Don's gold and ivory coffin to quiver. A choir stood around his coffin and sung the gospel song, "SOON AND VERY SOON WE ARE GOING TO SEE THE KING!"

The wailing of the guest could be heard echoing throughout the quiet cemetery like a wolf howling at the moon. The pall barriers were Dodirty and the rest of the men who fought to prevent the very sight before them today. There wasn't a dry eye anywhere in the place.

Jewel stared at the coffin with a dull empty ache gnawing at her soul. She held her newborn son Kasan on her lap. The entire time her heart was aching because she wasn't able to find the right words to steer Don away from the life he chose and the death it caused.

She now had a son to raise and didn't fully grasp how she was going to raise a MANCHILD in this PROMISE LAND alone. She would have to strive to teach him how to thrive within the confines of a world desperately wanting him to fail.

Where is the place words soulfully derive from, Jewel will need to determine where she would find the words to tell her first born son his father lived a short life, but died a brutal death. Also, how he came to bear the same name as his deceased uncle who died in the same year as his father. Her face contorted grotesquely as each fact slithered across her mind. This was like a ring of death. Now his father would have a tombstone next to his younger brother and all within a year of each other. Their deaths were so close and Kasan's grave was so fresh the earth had yet to settle.

A snarl of agony spread across Carol's face as she stared at the photo of her first born son at the foot of his grave. Her cries became heavy and nearly unbearable to the rest of the family and friends surrounding the grave. They knew her cries today weren't just for one son, but for two. Don, her first born and Kasan, her baby.

The sight of both graves in her view at once was too much for her to bear. She would double over in agony as she tried to gather herself. Carol had all three of her boys young and in fact, was still young herself. Never did she fathom in the inner cavity of her mind she would be alive to see any of her children die.

By having them young, she knew she would have spent a lot of time with them before she left this earth. Yet, she had buried two of them, the first and the last born.

Every childhood memory of Don swarmed into her mind all at once. The very vital circumstances of his birth and the means by which he came into this world.

A faint smile filled the corners of her mouth when she thought of how Don used to be scared of the dark and their little pet cat Bam Bam. In her eyes, Don could do no wrong. To Carol, he was just a child misunderstood by the world. She knew Don never allowed anyone to get to know him in every way. He had thoughts he shared with no one. This is what added to his infinite intelligence.

Frank buried his head into his girlfriend's shoulder. A spasm of nausea from his grief filled him as he replayed all important events leading up to this very day.

Frank clutched a fistful of his girlfriend's blouse from realizing he was just a hair's length away from death himself. The fact he was alive at this very moment secured him a front seat on a emotional roller coaster. He had to live with the unending thought of watching the death of his baby brother right before his very eyes.

Nevertheless, his mother would've lost all of her sons. His eyes scanned the high hats of the women sitting around his mother. Frank could only imagine what she had to be feeling. They were his brothers, but she had given birth to them. A chill shot through his spine. His girlfriend took it as a sign he was cold.

A surge of elation shot through his veins as he recalled a scene from the last moment of Sosa's life. He was grateful he was able to escape before Sosa was able to force him to suffer the identical fate as Kasan.

This would've prevented him from being able to inform Don of Sosa's transgressions against the family. Now he could live with the fact Sosa suffered ten times worse than his little brother. Sosa's death would never be able to equate to the lost of his two brothers. He still wanted them both back.

Now Don was dead and Frank had no one he could hold accountable for his death. It was now a major plight for him to now try to be every bit of the son his mother would need him to be, to endure the pain and suffering of this year's events.

This year was the blackest cloud over the Starchild family. There were many dark times, but death always found a way to become the leader of the darkest days of anyone's life. Frank just wondered what the future would hold for the rest of the family.

The gathering was starting to disperse due to the cold weather. A long black limousine was parked on the opposite side of the gathering. The glass was stained midnight black. The driver was about to get out of the car to open the door for his passenger to get out as he assumed he was going to the burial. The passenger declined with a sullen wave.

"I'll stay in the car and watch from here." The voice was a lifeless monotone. He didn't want to be disturbed until everyone had left.

Don eyed the faces of the crowd with mute appeal. They had known him to be dead for two weeks now. His name had been splashed on every television channel for the entire two weeks. Now he was hurt beyond belief by the pain he was causing to those who sincerely loved him. They were hurt because they presumed him to be dead, but he was very much alive. It was the dreams he once considered nightmares that had given him life saving knowledge to escape a sure death.

Why?

Why did the dreams start so long ago, but were vital to save his life thirteen years later? Through the dreams he was able to not only visually see this day, but feel it like it was as real as it was going to be. It gave him the proper information to change the inevitable. Don would've perished with the officers if he hadn't paid last minute attention to details of what his dreams has been striving to tell him for years.

If Don didn't climb over to the passenger's side and leap from the car seconds before impact, today's burial would've been as real as death could ever be to every life force on this earth.

The glass and doors of his car were bulletproof and he wouldn't have been able to kick them out. He had to altogether get out of the car.

Today, had to be the saddest day of his dead life. Don would've screamed for joy to just spring from the limousine and console each and everyone of the hearts crying for him, especially the woman he hurt the most.

Don still blamed himself for the death of Kasan. Had he killed Sosa that day, his brother would still be alive. No pain would have reached his mothers heart.

All he could do was imagine the pain she had to be feeling. He could see the wounded look in her eyes from afar. Since he was the oldest child, he knew more of the pain his mother went through first hand, the abuse and pain which nearly destroyed both of their lives.

This was a time long before his brothers were even born. The thought of knowing he added to her pain twice made him suffer the same fate and loss as she did. He could not only see her pain but he could feel it deep within the crevices of his soul.

The pain she was suffering was for all time. He figured he could stop the pain she was feeling of him dying by just leaping from the car and showing her he was very much alive.

For him to do so would give a clear sign to the world he is now walking in the shoes of fools and eating at the table of insane lunatics. If the world falsely presumed him to be dead, then it would be far better for it to remain as such. This wouldn't be the right time.

The Newark police would only need an inkling of information of him being alive after what everyone saw on prime time television and this would energetically have them hop on his trail like fire would to gasoline.

If he stayed dead, he wouldn't have to repeatedly look over his shoulder, nor have his face plastered on every television station. The world presumed him to be dead, then it would be best for him to allow them to remain in the dark as much as possible. They were still diligently searching for Cecil.

Don waited until the last of his family finally drifted away from his bogus grave before he edged his way over to the gravesite. He needed to have a close look for himself. He found it to be imperative for him to view the grave which would've imprisoned his corpse for all eternity.

The sight of his picture placed on top of the coffin was a visual contradiction of how he perceived it would feel to be dead. He didn't envision this is how his grave would look. He just found it abnormal to know he truly tricked the world into believing he was dead.

He removed all of the flowers from his coffin and laid them onto his brother's grave. He cleaned off the marble tombstone with his handkerchief. His gray eyes narrowed with disgust at the sight of his brothers grave. This was a sign of all his imperfections, of how he underestimated Sosa. Never did he think Sosa would involve his family in their dispute. Don was seconds away from killing Sosa's mother, or anyone of his immediate family members. The only reason he didn't was he didn't want to give him any new ideas and he killed Carol before Don could finish Sosa himself. Don's sanity would've been annihilated into oblivion. He would've been stuck in a padded room with an afro and smeared shit on the walls to kill time.

If he killed Sosa the day he robbed him, his brother would still be alive, Nydia would still be alive. In fact, he would still be alive. It was Sosa's death the police were coming after him for. If he didn't allow his emotions to get the best of him, Nydia wouldn't have been killed by the police.

Don hastily turned to face Nydia's grave. His gray eyes were filled with anguish at the sight of Nydia's coffin lying on top of the metal devices to lower it into the cold earth. He reached for the top half of the coffin. Initially, his breathing was shallow and his breath stuck in his throat. As he slowly raised the door of the coffin, it switched to a heavy panting like he was hyperventilating. He needed to look. He had to visibly look upon his second mistake which would haunt him for the rest of his life. The innocent were dying all because of him.

But he lived.

As the noon sun decreased its radiant rays of heat, the temperature plunged as if it was the middle of the night. Don raised the top half of the coffin and his knees buckled like they were zapped of all strength to stand. "I'm sorry," he cried. He touched his brother's tombstone and said in a faint whisper, "Both of ya'll please forgive me." His hands squeezed the dirt that would be used to cover her.

Don had to fight to get to his feet. He touched her soft hair. She looked like she was at peace, like the very first night they made love. Now, she looked like she was getting some of the best sleep she's had in years. This is how she looked the first night he watched her sleep. It was at that moment he knew he could fall in love with her and didn't want her to ever leave, now she was gone forever.

"I'm sorry baby," he whispered again. He stroked the softness of her wavy hair. He didn't want to destroy the mirage of her being asleep by touching her face. She was hard to his touch. He wanted his last memory of her to be when he felt the softness of her skin pressed against his very own in the heat of passion.

"It going to be hard to live without you," he cried.

Don heard the untimely news of her death while he was in a hospital in Elizabeth New Jersey getting his broken arm set into a cast. He watched as they carted her body out of the mansion and into a meat wagon.

The entire time Don had to use everything within his power to prevent him from responding to what he was seeing and hearing. He had to fight his emotions tooth and nail. He didn't want the nurses to become suspicious as to what emotional ties he had with the woman they were boastfully calling the sniper.

Nydia dead?

The thought of the first time he met her flashed before his eyes in High Definition. The first time he walked her into the mansion alive and now she was leaving dead. He wanted them to be able to create beautiful memories within its walls.

It was firmly planted within the goodhearted nature of Carol Starchild to take in Nydia's two children without any qualms. Don had left his mother enough money for the entire family to be taken care of for life.

The sun was relentlessly beginning to set behind the smoke filled clouds. The dusky sky was creating a night painting parallel to the day. The night stars were slowly starting to twinkle and fill the sky. A combination of lights would come together and provide a map of secrets of the galaxy. They were preparing to shine through the night with minimal rays of star light.

It was getting late. Don had a long drive ahead of him and he never got a chance to get a moment of rest. He needed to take one last drive through the city he loved and in which he learned so much about himself. This had to be his last day here. Under no circumstances whatsoever would he show his face here again. Doing so now was dangerous. His situation was still fresh in the minds of everyone.

He sauntered back to the limousine with a pensive look on his face and tears brimming in his eyes. The driver eyed him through the mirror. "Are you going to be okay buddy?" he asked. He fixed the front mirror so he could get a direct look at the quiet man in the back seat. "Was he a good friend of yours?"

Tears of pain were thrust into Don's throat. He was too choked up to even try to reply. He pressed the divider separating him from the driver. He spoke seconds before the window came all the way up.

"Take me down to Prince Street Projects." He was hoping to get one last look of Dodirty and the family before he left.

All he had built thus far would fall on the shoulders of his right hand man, whom he owed everyday of his life. If he wasn't so eager to pick up the next shipment and wasn't up early and watching the news, Don wouldn't have had time to make any plans for an escape.

Dodirty having the men on the roof for target practice on the oncoming police department was the life saving measure needed. Although they were stuck with the wrong thoughts of failing him, he just hoped they wouldn't suffer the guilt for long. He wished he could tell them they were the success he needed.

It was the brief moment the police were under extreme fire that gave him the much needed diversion to leap from the car on the passenger's side. This allowed the rest of the car to block him, since the police were not able to see him if he was on the other side.

The limousine was facing building 280. Dodirty and everyone hadn't gone home to change. They were all wearing designer suits and sitting around drinking in honor of their fallen friend.

Don noticed the changed look on Dodirty's face. He was the only one out of the group who had a personal connection with Don. The others had worked for him, but never saw, nor spoke with him. He had been a ghost some only saw for the first time when they thought his body was swept up in the ball of fire right before their very eyes.

Don watched as Dodirty and the group poured out a little liquor. He raised his glass in the back seat to make a toast with them. Although they were wishing he was Blessed In Peace, he was toasting for them to continually be able to live in peace and keep getting long money.

The driver was uneasy about being in the notorious Prince Street Projects. This was his first time ever in this place. He never had a reason to show up there. He was well aware this wasn't the place for any White man in his right state of mind to be parlaying.

The driver tapped the glass behind him. "You didn't pay for the insurance for the few hours you rented the car." He spoke with his head turned towards the tinted glass. "I think it would be best to leave before shit gets out of hand."

✳ ✳ ✳

Don went back to the limousine company and rented a small car. There was no way he would be able to fly with a duffel bag full of money and his two guns. He refused to ever be separated from his guns under any circumstance. They were now just as much apart of him as his lungs.

The drive to Miami wasn't as long as he initially expected. He drove non-stop. There was so much on his mind during his drive, it caused sleep to avoid him at all cost. All Don was striving to do was piece together the days of his future. Now he had a thorough understanding of exactly what Cecil was feeling at the time of his liberation. Now, Don didn't have the slightest idea of what to do at this point in his life.

He did not have an inkling of what tomorrow held for him. He just knew prison would never be a part of the equation under any circumstances whatsoever. It was the dreams which had first saved his life. Now he wondered what dreams would he have to aid him in escaping death in the future.

Don wondered if he would be able to escape the close call of death if it came again.

And it was coming.

CHAPTER THREE

Chico and his men were watching a picturesque view of the twenty-one gun salute the city of Newark was giving the murdered officers.

The announcing of every officer who fell casualty to Don's war caused Chico to shake his head in amazement. He could only imagine how many Don took with him. A story that took place all the way in Newark New Jersey had every channel in the nation frozen. Since it first happened, the story has been reported everyday.

Chico recalled one of the many conversations he and Don had by his pool. Now he had no choice but to believe his friends words were the truth when he said they would never take him alive. Today was a reminder of the absolute truth of the last of their conversation. Never did he ponder the fact that he would visually experience the prophetic revelation take place right before his eyes.

Chico watched the entire chase from the back seat of his limousine. Once he arrived at his dinner destination, he refused to get out of the car until he witnessed the conclusion of this matter regarding his friend.

Just to watch his friend die on national television was entirely too much for him to deal with at the time. Instead of joining the party, he went back home. Don's death was an honorable one in the eyes of a Gangster, but tragic in the hearts of those who loved him dearly.

Chico did love him. He loved Don the way a father loves his first born son.

Armondo shifted in his seat when he heard Don's name spoken from the chief of police's mouth. He didn't feel one way or another. If he had to display any emotion suited for this matter it would have to be one of extreme delight in knowing he would no longer have to see Don's face again. There was still bad blood between them, but Armondo not once leaked how he really felt about Don after they had their initial incident. He was portraying the image it was over, but hate continued to seethe in his heart.

Chico flopped down heavily in front of a pile of raw cocaine. He would sniff spoonful amounts in between words concerning his dear friend. Instead of the cocaine numbing his emotions, it made Chico feel even more sensitive. His emotions amplified his pain a hundred folds knowing he would never be able to see Don's face again.

The more coke he sniffed the more it was starting to feel like a cold fist was closing over his heart. His emotions were coming full circle and he didn't really want his men to see him any more distraught than he already was. It would be best for him to retire to the master bedroom for the evening where he could further indulge in his pain away from the presence of his men. He would have to get over this in preparation for the task he needed to take care of in the morning. Don was the only Black friend he had. His love for Don superseded any of the men in his organization.

The hallways of his mansion were long and extravagantly furnished with expensive art worth millions from all over the world. Chico had so much money and he just needed to waste it somewhere. It was all around his house.

Chico's pace through his mansion was slow. The problem with living in an opulent mansion was the long walks to different rooms and locations within the mansion. His mind was full of the memories of Don, when he heard a knock at the front door.

Usually, he would have Bonita answer the door, but since he was standing directly in front of it, he decided to answer it. Whoever was standing at his front door had to make it through the check point to get this far.

As soon as he opened the door, he fell to his knees and a shrieking scream escaped from his lungs. His men rushed from the other room like an army brigade. Each of them had his gun drawn and ready to fire.

Chico's eyes blinked with incredulity. Once they made an attempt to focus, they stared into a pair of alert gray eyes with fascinated horror. Chico's complexion went pale like he was standing in the presence of a ghost.

Don stood in the doorway tall and proud. He had a duffel bag draped over his good shoulder and the other was fixed in a cast. He wore a bandage over his right eye where his face hit the pavement.

Don noticed the shock on the faces of the men behind Chico. He lowered his gray eyes to the level of Chico's. "Chico, I need a place to stay."

CHAPTER FOUR

In one swift motion, Chico leaped from his knees onto his feet. A surge of elation coursed through his entire being once he wrapped his arms around Don's shoulders. He now believed for a surety Don wasn't a figment of his imagination; Don was living and breathing.

Everyone watching knew they had a valid proportion of divine love for each other. The situation Chico knew Don was involved with forced him to display the full range of his uncontrolled emotions.

This was Chico's very first time blatantly displaying his feelings for Don. Don wasn't the least surprised the effect his presence would have on anyone who presumed him to be dead. This would shock the most sane mind to see the man they all thought to be dead standing at Chico's door breathing the fresh Miami air.

Bonita strutted from the kitchen carrying a silver tray. She was rushing to see what all of the commotion was about. She paused in the foyer to set the tray down on a mahogany table. It was too late. She saw Don standing in the doorway with Chico's arms wrapped around him.

She clutched her chest like she was about to topple over from a heart-attack. "Oh Dios mio." (Oh My God) she exclaimed.

Chico rushed Don pass his men and into his study. They had a hard time coming to grips with seeing Don, although they were seeing him with their very own eyes. The only part to have them

24

baffled was how Chico was reacting to one of his customers who so happened to be Black at that.

Once Don entered the room and in the far corner of the study was a pile of cocaine gleaming on the floor. There was an even bigger pile sitting on top of Chico's desk.

Don knew Chico would sometimes indulge in the use of cocaine while he was entertaining friends, but he didn't see any friends. Don assumed the pile on the floor was the afterthought of his misfortune and Chico slung it across the room. Don was really starting to understand what everyone was going through in regards his repudiating death.

Chico took a huge sniff from the pile. The strength of the cocaine turned his nose beet red. He would gape at Don in stunned silence and look upon him with suspicious bewilderment.

Chico would occasionally shake his head from side to side with disbelief. "How in the fuck are you sitting in my house right now Don?" He dipped two fingers into a glass of Cognac and sniffed the liquid up into his nose to flush down the residue of cocaine. "I watched you blow up in the car with my own eyes."

Don moved over to the desk and scooped a handful of cocaine for himself similar to cleaning a pile of sugar from the table. Never did he engage in the use of drugs of any kind, but his nerves were all over the place. He just needed something to make him feel other than the way he was feeling.

No one could possibly grasp the technical experience of how he was truly feeling to be alive. Death had been seconds away from claiming the life force of his being. Don was just as amazed as anyone to be able to live and tell what happened.

The cocaine was a fast moving drug and would induce the user within a matter of seconds, but Don didn't feel any different. It did minimize the pain of his broken arm.

Don went to great lengths to fill Chico in on all of the details. As well as the reason why he was initially being sought after by the authorities in the first place.

"Was it Jewel they shot?" Chico asked. His eyes were now wide and alert from the cocaine.

Don sat the cocaine down. He had more than enough and knew he would never do it again. "It was another woman I had just gotten involved with named Nydia." The sound of her name echoed throughout his brain. Her name drowned his emotions into liquefied guilt.

A wounded look swept into Don's gray eyes. As Chico spoke, Don's face was etched with sorrow at the thought that he placed Nydia in the line of fire for the sake of getting away. She was a woman he believed he could have fallen madly in love with if he had the time to.

She was now gone.

Don was struck with a feeling of supreme wonder to what her life would've been like had he not been involved with her. She would have still been alive and being a mother to her children. It was these thoughts if he had just left her alone she would still be alive. These thoughts continually gnawed at the deeper regions of his soul.

The in depth thoughts of Nydia forced Don to become verbally subdued. Although Chico continued to bombard him with a barrage of questions, Don had nothing else to say. His mind has gone to a place far away from the thoughts of man. Nothing at this point in time could change the events of his past life and past losses.

Chico continued to fire off questions. He had to know every detail as to how Don escaped an exploding car. The part keeping Chico in doubt was the timing of when Don escaped from the car; how he was able to trick the undivided world into believing he was dead. Not only that, how he accomplished this feat on primetime television, as if he was an experienced magician.

It was fascinating that Don didn't have need for props or extra hands to pull off a trick of this magnitude. He tricked the world one by one and everyone was fooled into believing he was dead.

Don could understand why Chico would question him so extensively. Chico comfortably sat at the upper echelon's of the drug game. He didn't suffer the same trials and tribulations as a street hustler. His problem was how to hide the money he was making. Therefore, his joy came from hearing the gritty detailed stories of the streets which would read like an urban novel. If the story is properly told, it would place Chico directly into the theme of the story.

Finally, Chico observed the distant look in his friends eyes. He could only imagine the whirlwind of emotions Don must be experiencing at the time. The wounds were still fresh in his mind and heart. The room dropped into an abyss of silence once Chico ceased to ask anymore questions.

Bonita stood at the entrance of the door waiting for Chico to instruct her on anything needed to be done. "Show Don to his room upstairs and make sure he has something to eat."

Armondo paid close attention to Don as he strolled pass the entrance of the room. He had been struck with a feeling of uneasy puzzlement. While Chico was questioning Don, he was listening with an intense eagerness for the details of the great escape. After watching the chase himself, he would've bet his life he would never have to see the likes of Don again.

There wasn't a need for Don to follow behind Bonita. He knew the mansion better than any of Chico's other guest. All Don wanted to do was sleep. He drove all the way to Florida non-stop and his troubled mind had become extremely fatigued from what had taken place thus far.

It felt like days since he had any sound rest. His mind was racing and he hoped a deep sleep would relieve the tension and he would be able to function at a level higher than he was now.

Don laid down on the plush king size bed. His eyes were able to close as he marinated onto the satin sheets. His bandaged head was flush against the fluffy pillows.

Bonita kneeled down to remove Don's shoes. Don raised his head to peer up at her, as he slowly slipped his heel from her hands. "You don't have to do that," he said softly. "I only have one broken arm."

Don left Bonita no choice but to give him a warm smile. She should have known Don wouldn't allow her to serve him. Even though it was within the contractual agreement of her job description as a maid.

Don was the only man to have his own room in Chico's house.

The only Black man she has ever known to come directly to the house and deal with Chico. As far as Bonita was concerned, Don was everything other than what she had known a Black man to be.

Bonita saw to it that Don was settled and was about to leave the room. "Do you want anything to eat?" she asked in her heavy Colombian accent. Her eyes cast towards the floor and her olive skin glowed in his presence.

Don patted the bed beside him for Bonita to have a seat. He bit down on his lower lip as he carefully chose his words. "I just wanted you to know I do not kill for fun." He grimaced from the throbbing pain of his broken arm. "What happened was out of necessity and my will to be able to live the balance of my life as a free man." He shook his head greenly. "It would've killed me everyday to have to live the rest of my life in prison for serving real right justice."

He came up onto his good arm for support. "Those men killed my little brother and for the sake of my brother's honor, they had to suffer the penalties for hurting my mother's grieving heart."

The only thing Bonita could do was glance down into her folded hands on her lap. Her nerves caused her to fumble with the loose strings of her apron. She couldn't fathom why Don was explaining himself to her out of all the people in the house. Don was doing more talking to her than he did with Chico and she just didn't understand why.

She was just the maid, hired help and well aware the majority of the men who came to the house to visit Chico were killers. Murder was the profession many of the men were in. They had to kill to enforce their rule and ownership of territory.

Several times in the past, Bonita had to clean up a bucket worth of blood in the basement whenever a deal didn't go down the right way, or Chico lost his temper. Not once did Bonita feel the need to inquire where did all of this blood come from. She just pretended it was an everyday occurrence to mop up human blood in a residential area.

Don raised her head with the tips of his fingers until her soft brown eyes were leveled to his own. He spoke in his soft baritone voice. "I know you work for Chico, but as a woman, I have the utmost respect for you." He playfully clutched her chin. "You're beautiful just like your name." His gray eyes crinkled into mirthful crescents. "I have never viewed you as a servant, but a friend." He felt her dissolve at his touch. He stroked her smooth skin like a man admiring a royal treasure.

All Bonita could do was turn her head and kiss the palm of Don's hand. She bolted from the room and closed the door. She pressed her back against the door and took astronomical deep breaths to strive to calm the palpitating of her heart. Don's touch and soft words caused her to grow feverish with desire. She had to get away from him.

Bonita placed her back against the door and tightly closed her eyes. Instantly, she was starting to feel something for him. She nearly told him what she was feeling.

When she had heard Don was dead, she cried as if they shared a life of love together. Now she is beyond happy to know he is safe and on the other side of this door.

Don laid down with his eyes open and staring up at the ceiling with a blank expression on his face. He thought he would go to rest as soon as his head touched a soft place, but rest would evade him at all cost. There was too much on his mind for him to be able to relax and find peace. He lost too much in such a short period of time. There was no amount of money to replace the precious gems he had lost.

The walls within the room appeared to be breathing and closing in on him. He didn't need to be alone right now. He needed to avoid isolation with the hopes it will redirect his thoughts away from the pain attacking him on all sides of his conscious and subconscious mind. He desperately needed a distraction to allow him a moments breath away from the pain of the reality tearing at the core of his soul.

Sitting in this quiet room made his thoughts too loud for his sanity to bear. He agreed it would be better to take a drive around Miami to see the sights with the hopes of clearing his head.

As Don maneuvered towards Chico's room, he could hear faint, subtle, sounds of moaning escaping from inside the door. His mind went to the description of what the woman would look like apparently enjoying herself in Chico's bed. Ever since Don had known Chico he's had women of movie star caliber. He would fly them in from different parts of the world. This was done whenever he had the urge for their company.

Don hated to have to interrupt them, but he didn't have the slightest idea where Chico kept the keys to the cars. Don knocked on the door with his knuckles. "Chico I want to take a drive, but I don't know where the keys are."

Chico giggled on the other side of the door from whatever his companion was doing to him. "They're already in the cars, just pick whichever one you want and be safe out there. If you run into any problems make sure I am the first one you call."

Don strolled down the stairs with a emotionless smirk on his face. If he didn't need to call him the first time, what made him think he would need to call him now?

Don felt his two guns snuggle closer to his arm pits. He would regulate any situation on the spot. There would be no need for any telephone calls. Unless it was to the morgue to make the proper preparations for anyone trying to capture, or kill him. He was now aware Chico didn't have an idea of how his thoughts had shifted to always be the hunter and never the prey.

Don went down to the garage and eyed each of the cars. Every car was far too exotic and he didn't need anything to bring any unnecessary attention to himself. The last thing he wanted was to have the Dade county police department on his ass. He didn't have a problem with going through the ordeal again, but really didn't want to. He was ambiguous as to the results of the outcome.

He strutted back into the mansion and Bonita was sitting at the kitchen counter watching a Spanish soap opera on telemundo television. He cleared his throat to capture her attention. "Do you want to take a drive with me?" He ran his hand across the smooth surface of the counter top. "I don't really know my way around here and I really need to get out for awhile."

Bonita switched off the television. "Why not," she replied hopping off the stool. Her accent was heavy like she just arrived in this country a few days ago. She mainly used it as a throw off for some Americans to take her as slow and not as keen minded as she really was.

Don again surveyed the cars for the least conspicuous to a prominent eye. He turned to face Bonita. "Can we take your car?" Bonita threw him the keys. Don threw them back to her. "I think it would be better if you drive. My license expired the day I died."

✳ ✳ ✳

They drove around the inner city of Miami and the different sections predominately lived by the many ethnic groups. Don was able to jot down certain places to his memory and the directions of how to get there.

Bonita parked at a highly developed waterfront. It was nearing winter in Newark, but felt like mid summer in Miami. The water was calm. The only ripples came from the gentle breeze which would sporadically drift from the ocean onto the land.

Rows of palm trees were situated on both sides of the manicured lawn. The palm trees trailed around a paltry island professionally placed in the center of the glowing water. The sight alone manifested a calming effect on Bonita and Don. The sun was about to set. It was now lying lazily at the tip of the water like it was at the end of the earth and at any moment, it would topple over.

Don shifted his seat to lie all the way back and stretch his legs. He released a weary sigh in the process of drinking in the view of the glorious sight in front of him. The sun was proof of a higher power by its ability to give off light which brought forth life. Don was reveling in his gratitude to be able to live to see another day.

Bonita faced him. The last rays of the setting sun danced across her angelic features. "Are you sure you are going to be okay?" she asked. "The sound of your breathing makes you sound like you are still highly upset."

Don hit the switch to simultaneously lock all of the doors in the car. "I guess in time I will learn to be okay with the mistakes I've made in my life." He sucked in a huge amount of air. "Right now I am missing everything I love in this world."

The thought of Cecil caused Don's gray eyes to narrow with suspicion. His life was now in the identical faze as Cecil's life at the time he freed him from Trenton State prison, minus the death Don was lost. The major difference was they knew Cecil to be alive, but presumed Don Starchild to surely be dead.

Don had a thought if Cecil even heard the news he was dead on PrimeTime television. He thought of Cecil often when he sent him checks every month.

Bonita stared beyond the miniature island and through the heavenly sunset before her. She was looking at the way she came into this country from her native land of Colombia.

For Bonita, this was a land of promise. It really made her believe this to be the truth just by Don still being alive and knowing he should be dead had it not been for the dreams. Now she knew his life would never be the same again. This is what they both took upon themselves as the truth.

She wished the opportunity would come for her to be able to heal the wounds of Don's empty heart. Her feelings didn't manifest themselves out of obligation, but with an intense yearning deeply embedded in her heart for Don Starchild.

Chico made it clear she was to never fraternize with his guest for any reason. If she was caught, she would be terminated from her employment and possibly her life. This would not be for dealing with a guest, but the fact she knew too much.

Forgetting Chico's strict orders, Bonita leaned over and laid her head on his thumping chest. Immediately, she felt the warmth and compassion pulsating with each pronounced, rhythmic beating of his strong heart. She writhed with pleasure to just be alone and experiencing this moment in time together.

Don embraced her and ran his fingers through her long rust colored hair. He leaned further back into the seat and finally closed his eyes to listen to the beating of his very own heart thumping in his ears. It sounded like the soft beating of the drums he has been hearing whenever he dreamed.

Don pulled Bonita closer into him. For some reason, he didn't feel completely alone anymore. It now felt like he was holding onto an expression of his future. His understanding of his mistakes replayed in his mind with regards to Jewel and Nydia. If anything came of this brief encounter between he and Bonita, he had every intention of taking full advantage of it and for once he was going to fight to get it right.

CHAPTER FIVE

A busboy almost crashed into a waitress bringing food out of the swinging doors to an uncompromising customer. The five star restaurant was full to capacity with the immoderate rich and noticeably famous people of Miami Florida.

The only way to be able to pull up a chair in this place was by reservations only. This is only one of the elite restaurants Chico frequented whenever he had a taste for their famed Italian cuisine.

It's been a full year since Don joined the ranks of Chico's family. Don was hated by everyone and seemed to be loved only by Chico. He firmly accepted his joining the Dragon cartel wouldn't sit well with the other members just because of the undisputed fact he was a Black man.

This racial profiling went as far as them only speaking in Spanish in his presence just to keep Don from being able to intelligently follow their conversation. They would even try to confuse him by speaking overly poor English when speaking to him.

A Black man joining the strict ranks of a Colombian cartel was unheard of by any standards. The Columbians would seldom allow Blacks to purchase from them directly, if they were major in the distribution of cocaine. This was another level Don was able to accomplish with the greatest of ease. He was able to get cocaine dirt cheap and pure and his flip was far greater because he was plugged in to buy, but now he was on the front lines.

Columbians would never put an iota of trust in anyone not from their homeland. Nevertheless, the fact Don wasn't even of a Spanish nationality, they wanted to keep their ranks as pure as they wanted to keep their shipments of cocaine they sold throughout the world.

Don didn't care to start anywhere near the top. Chico would insist on putting Don directly under Armondo until Don learned the business at the level they operated on a daily basis. Armondo became vociferous in his burning dislike for Don. Don didn't care about the love of anyone, but he wanted to gain the men's respect and adhere to being a good soldier and take orders just like anyone else starting at the entry level of the family.

Although Don's maneuver was a contradiction to once being in charge of his own conglomerate, he could've just taken the money he had and just live a quiet life, but Don wanted to master the game. Burning ideas have found their way into the creative thoughts of his mind and he wanted to give birth to them in this lifetime.

He was okay with being knocked all the way down to a mere worker, but Don had to prove his worth. He knew it takes one to have been a good follower in order to be thoroughly respected as a good leader.

It was nights like this Don wished he could bring Bonita with him whenever he went to dinner. Don already had to sneak through life for whomever not to find out he was alive and he did prefer to move without anyone knowing who he really was, but if he had to be out and about, he wished he was with Bonita. She insisted they keep their relationship a secret.

Don hated this. She was slowly helping him heal from the loss he had experienced just a year ago. He was deeply in love with Bonita. She knew this and had something to tell him when the time was right.

The times he felt the most awkward was when Chico would introduce him to friends of the women he was with. Don would always decline some of the most attractive women on earth. Chico would joke as if the crash had messed up his plumbing. Don would laugh it off, because he couldn't tell Chico his loyalty was to Bonita and he refused to break it for any reason.

Chico wiped the corners of his mouth with his napkin. "Don you've been at my house for a year now, and I have yet to see you in the company of a woman."

Don felt the weight of Chico's words and instantly felt like he was under a microscope. All of the occupants at the table shifted their eyes towards him.

Don sipped from his glass of water. "I have other things to focus on at this time." He placed his glass down and smiled to make light of his words. "In our line of work a man must be able to focus with the least amount of distraction." His gray eyes became crystal clear. "Just because you don't see something Chico doesn't mean it doesn't exist. It just mean you haven't seen it." Don's mocking eyes stared at everyone.

Chico laughed. "Well don't forget your manhood exist."

Everyone at the table laughed loudly except for Don. Don believed they were laughing at him and not with him. Don considered none of them his friends to say the least. The only one he could trust was Chico. The only time any of the men would exemplify a drop of kindness towards Don was in the presence of their boss, otherwise, they ostracized Don any other time.

As the chattering of the crowd somewhat subsided, Chico dropped his napkin onto his plate and slid his chair closer towards Don. "Don I have a little problem I need for you to take care of for me, por favor." (Please) Chico ran his fingers through the hairs on his strong chin. "I seem to be having a bit of a problem with a Cuban that owes me four million dollars." He swished his wine around in his mouth like it was mouthwash. "I want for you to collect it for me."

This was Chico's first direct order to Don. Don shot Chico a quick look of suspicious bewilderment. His gray eyes became cold as he raked in the room. "Do you want him dead, or just the money?" Don asked. His question was without feeling and as cold as the food had become on his plate.

Chico's face was flushed with happiness. A gaunt smile licked his smooth lips. "If he doesn't have my money, then you know better than anybody else what to do."

Don leaned all the way back in his chair and surveyed the now sparse crowd in the restaurant. He wondered why Chico didn't ask Armondo to take care of this task. He knew nothing of this Cuban.

Don would normally get his orders from other men, Chico asked him this as if it was a personal favor he wanted Don to do for him.

In fact, Don was just here mainly for security purposes. The only money he ever handled was the money he brought with him. He didn't even ask Chico for payment for security. Don found it imperative to learn as much about the drug business on a much larger scale he, or any other Black man was accustomed to.

In the middle of his thoughts, Chico leaned into Don's ear. "If you get this job done, then I am going to have to move you up and there will be nothing anyone can say." He winked at Don and patted his hand. "Just take care of this for me. Take some men with you. Its time to place you at the table from which the family eats, but your offering has to come by the work you are willing to put in. This is your resume."

Don's expression was blank. The last thing he wanted to do was take anyone's position. He was already hated for being Black. Now if he completed this task, the ability to give orders would be bestowed upon him and he would get a cut of the shipments. This would cause even more dissension amongst Chico's men.

Surely, it would force them to formulate a plot for his demise. Don wouldn't even think about voicing this concern to Chico openly. He figured it would be better to chalk it up as paranoia.

Chico didn't get the chance to see how they treated Don when he wasn't around. When Chico was around, they would include Don in their jokes. Don was far smarter than he led them to believe. He was able to see through their mask of happy admiration and peer into the souls of envious men. A war had been waged between Don and them silently.

As everyone was making their way back to the tables, Don stood to his feet. "Chico, I enjoyed the dinner this evening, but I have to go."

Chico raised is hands in a what happened gesture. "But the night is still early. Plus, we haven't had desert and cigars to top the night off." Chico knew how Don enjoyed a Havanna cigar after a meal.

Don grinned in defiance in the direction of Armondo. If he were to be promoted to a higher position, it would have to be above Armondo in order to be safe for the other men to follow his orders and not do anything to him.

Don smooth out the wrinkles of his slacks. "I have an important matter to tend to. I'll see you once I get home."

Chico had a huge grin on his face. "Don't tell me you're slipping off to see a lady friend."

Don smiled like he had been caught. "I can never get anything past you Chico."

Chico handed Don a cigar to take with him. "Don't go to sleep, if you make it home before we do. We're going to watch the fight tonight."

Don nodded and left. He didn't mind being in the company of Chico, it was the others who made him feel only slightly uncomfortable. He didn't trust them and knew they would turn on him in a New York minute.

Don hoped Chico didn't take his aloofness as a sign he didn't enjoy their company together. He just didn't want the others to get too familiar with him. Also, he didn't want them to think he figured they were on good terms. Don would kill either one of them before anyone could verbally say die.

In Don's and Chico's quiet talks, he could tell Chico was gaining a lot of valuable information from him. Chico knew Don to be extremely intelligent and had the heart of a lion. The only thing Don lacked was the unchanging power and Colombian connections Chico had back at home.

Since Don was able to see the drug game being played on a wide scale, it had raised his expectations in the game a thousand degrees. He saw the bigger picture and it was far bigger than Chico was playing at the moment.

Don mapped out a plan to make more money than the Dragon cartel has ever seen, but he declined to make any suggestions to change the way they've been doing business long before he entered their line of work. He was merely contemplating a way to pass on his ideas to Chico, so he could think of them as his own. Don didn't want any credit.

Don entered the mansion through the back entrance. There were too many lights in the front of the mansion, and he wanted to talk with Bonita before he left. He wasn't sure he was going to make it back and their relationship had grown drastically in a year. She had taught Don more Spanish than Chico, or any of the others could imagine. He and Bonita could now speak an entire conversation in Spanish. Don understood every word Chico's men had said about him, they just didn't know he knew.

Bonita's room was closer to the kitchen and far away from the plush rooms of the mansion. When Don entered her room, her fawn colored eyes lit up at the sight of the man she loved.

Her hair was snatched back into a tight ponytail. Her olive skin looked like it had been kissed by the sun. Her legs had a smooth sheen and were clean shaven.

Don kissed her on the cheek and wrapped his arms around her petite waist. Her kisses became heavy as she kissed Don's mouth. The passion was starting to build up in her and she wanted him badly.

"Make love to me." Bonita breathed into his mouth in Spanish. "I need you," she said urgently.

Don had to push her away. "I can't right now. I have something very important to handle and you know you are too much of a freak to be okay with a quickie," he replied in Spanish.

Bonita figured there was no need in asking him, she would have to take matters into her own hands. The entire year they were together, they made love every day. This was the first time Don had declined to do so.

Bonita slid to the edge of the bed where Don was standing. She opened his pants and reached for his manhood the entire time peering deeply into his gray eyes.

Don stood still as she pulled his slacks down to his ankles. The look of pure lust in her eyes forced a steady flow of throbbing blood between his legs. All he intended to take care of would now have to wait. He needed to service this hot blooded Colombian.

Don gripped his pulsating love in his hand and rubbed the head slowly across her bottom lip. Bonita's smile became wide when she tasted the meager drops of his salty cum.

She wasted no time in taking every inch of him into her mouth. Don knew she was thirsty for him because she would choke on his love, but wouldn't alter her mouth stroke. She gorged on his muscle until the whites of her eyes turned red from her throat constricting as she took every inch of him .

Don couldn't take anymore of her mouth standing up. At certain points it felt like he was about to collapse onto the floor into a heap of flesh. He actually felt like a M & M and he was about to melt in her mouth.

He pushed her right shoulder to force her off of his manhood. Bonita fell backwards onto the bed and her mouth slid from the base of his manhood to its tip in one swift motion. She purposely allowed her lower teeth to gently scrape the head before it completely left her mouth.

Don got down on his knees and buried his face between her legs. His tongue initially circled her clit and ended with a suck as he rolled it between his full lips. He had two fingers embedded deep inside of her tickling her G spot. Don would repeat this method until Bonita body would tremble and rise off the bed as if he was performing an exorcism on her. Don allowed her to cum in his mouth three times before he made up his mind to thoroughly dust her off. Not only was he trying to push every ounce of lust out of her, he was also using this sex dance to remove the edge from his pending situation. Sex with the woman he loved always relaxed him. Don raised one of her legs into the fold of his arm. His arrow perfectly aimed to the middle of her target. This was the part Bonita enjoyed the most, when Don first entered the folds of her womanhood and he made her wetter that water. Don placed the tip of himself inside of her and stared into her eyes for the green light to thrash her. Bonita ran her tongue slowly across her lips and her eyes danced with anticipation. Don thrust himself deep inside of her. She gasped from the shock of feeling so much of the man she loved invade her inner lust as if it was an enemy attack. He dug deep each time he went inside of her. Bonita moaned with rendered hunger. As Don crashed every inch of himself inside of her, she would drive her hips up to meet his every stroke.

Don gritted his teeth and forcefully grabbed a fistful of hair and spun Bonita around on all fours. She landed in the middle of the bed. Don yanked her by her hair trying to bring her to the edge, while his feet were firmly planted on the floor. Bonita's olive skin was flushed. She glanced over her shoulder at Don with reverence as he used his knees to spread her knees apart. Don placed the tip of his lust at the entrance of heaven. Bonita writhed with pleasure as the after thought of pleasure entered her sexually conscious mind. Don slammed inside of her and gripped her hair like a cowboy would the reigns of a horse. The noise of their flesh slapping together interrupted the silence. As Don was slamming into Bonita with all his might she was crashing her hips into him. Don slapped her on her round ass as he felt the onslaught of his juices tingling at the tip of his head. This caused Bonita to pick up her pace to time her own orgasm with his. Don felt the release of his life force leave his body like the walls of a dam exploding from massive combustion of dynamite. Bonita could feel the hot sensations fill her womb. The hot liquid of desire fired off a chain reaction and brought her to the brink of shock as her body released every ounce of its energy. She collapsed onto her stomach and Don came crashing down right behind her, his manhood still snugly inside of her as they both took deep breaths to regain their composure. "You treat me with nothing but respect, Don," Bonita spoke in Spanish. "but when you are in bed, I feel like your whore."

Don smiled as he slowly removed himself from inside her. "This is the only way I know how to treat you." He started to get dressed. "This is the only way you want to be treated."

Bonita noticed how he was putting his clothes on. The sex made her forget he had something to do prior to their encounter. "Where are you going?" she asked pulling the covers over her body. "Don we never spend time together like we used to just lying in each other's arms."

Silence was his weapon for now.

Don went to the closet and got a box of ammunition for his guns. He eyed the bulletproof vest, but didn't want to take it with him. "That was when I was hurt and needed to heal and you were my nurse, but now I have a job to do."

"What do you have to do more important than me?" she asked and wished she could take her words back as soon as they left her mouth. She knew she was in violation.

Don gave her a warning look and continued to gather the things he was going to need for the night. He stopped at the door and gave her a long searching look. He wasn't sure if he was going to make it back safely and wondered how would she handle it if that were the case.

Bonita knew whatever Don had to do was for Chico and not once had she shown an undertone of concern, nor interest for the business, but the times have now changed. She had a man she loved with every fabric of her being involved in one of the most dangerous lifestyles to live. The fact he was a Black man didn't help matters either.

Bonita didn't know what he had to do and wished he would discuss it with her so she would know the measure of safety needed to make sure he would come back.

She just didn't want to see her man killed for any reason.

She knew death could come at any second and claim the life of Don Starchild.

Chapter Six

Don had to drive nine miles outside of Miami. The drive gave him a chance to absorb the predator within to better prepare himself for whatever laid in wait. He didn't know anything about this man named Pablo. Don felt a wave of acid well up in his belly as his intelligence started to make sense of this matter.

Chico asked for him to be the equalizer of a situation he had nothing to do with. Not only that, it was worth four million dollars. Now he knew for sure things weren't going to go so smoothly. If Pablo had any intentions to ever pay Chico the money, Chico would've given Don a second alternative if Pablo didn't pay.

Since Don was on this job alone and there were no other options, he was getting thirsty for the kill. This night would either place him in a grave where everyone already thought he was, or in a stratosphere of a pure gangster.

The opulent mansion was the size of one of Chico's and it was heavily guarded. There was a muscular man with a tight wavy cut parked at the front entrance of the door; A semi automatic gun in his hand and a radio attached to his hip with a wired ear piece going from his ear down his back. His eyes were hidden behind a pair of midnight shades.

Don figured he was merely one of the many men guarding the important occupants inside. He concluded it would be best to walk right up to the front door with the politeness of a Nun just to get a pulse beat on the good or bad blood between Chico and Pablo.

Don wore a form fitting wife beater as a clear sign he wasn't armed. His stride was completely relaxed and with each step he took, he scanned the parameters of the layout as if his gray eyes were night vision goggles and stored each segment into his computerized brain. What lights were on in what rooms of the mansion is what had to be burned into his memory. He had to burn this into his mind in case he made it inside of the mansion, he would know what rooms to pay attention to.

As he approached the guard, Don drunk in each and every aspect of him. He was striving to learn as much as he could about him at the onset. This was for the sake of gathering as much information as he could. He had to be able to make a quick assumption of the guard's character; making sure the guard wasn't touchy and quick to pull the trigger.

Once Don came into full view of the guard, the night became even more quiet. The guard examined Don's face owlishly for any clue as to why he was here.

The sound of crickets chirping in the nearby bushes disturbed the placid night. The guard automatically went on the defense immediately as Don walked within his view.

Don noticed how the guard switched his gun to his stronger hand, which was further away from Don in case Don made an attempt to disarm him.

A black cat ruffled a bush a few feet away from where they were standing. The guard didn't bother to look in the direction by turning his head, he shifted his eyes in the direction, but the glasses on his face hid his eyes. It looked like he never removed his stare from Don's face.

Don's face became flushed with happiness. "I . . . I . . . I . . . m . . . m . . . am here t.t.t.t speak wit . . . wit . . . wit. Pa . . . pa . . . pa . . ." Don stammered. He was solidifying the tolerance level the guard was willing to withstand.

The guard didn't wait for Don to finish what he had to say. He spoke in rapid Spanish into the thin mouthpiece positioned in front of his mouth. He removed the jack connected to the ear piece of the radio and handed the radio to Don.

Don placed the radio up to his ear and a voice barked. "What do you want?" The accent was heavy and the English was broken.

Don took a deep breath for the guard to know he was striving not to stutter. He cleared his throat and pressed the talk button. "I . . . I . . . I am here to pick up some money for Chico." Don said the last of it in one breath.

There was a moment of silence and then a strong voice roared back. "I don't owe that puta nathing! You here me? Nathing! Tell dem to no send a motherfuka to me house again for nathing." The voice said something Spanish to the guard for him to send Don away.

The guard flung his hand in the air at Don and said for him to move on. Don grinned at the guard and slightly bowed not out of respect, but to say let the games begin and the best man win.

Don's gray eyes were blazing murderously as he went back to the car. The first moment of his brutal attack continued to replay in his murderous thoughts over and over.

He went back to the car and went into the trunk. He meticulously strapped on his holsters for his two nine millimeters. He wrapped a belt full of clips around his waist. This was a self made device Don conjured up for a battle such as this.

Each clip of bullets were sticking straight out around his waist. This was so he could reload just by slamming the butt of his gun around his waist. The clips looked like metal spikes sticking out.

As he strolled through the quiet streets back towards the mansion, he attached the silencers to each of his guns. He was glad he followed his gut feeling. There was bad blood between them and it was now up to him to do the rest of the talking for Chico. This was going to show what he really was made of.

The night breeze drifted with a cooling force. Birds in the trees flapped their wings wildly as the black cat tried to make a sneak attack for the hunt. Don watched as the Black cat trotted across the street with its dinner clamped in its teeth. It reminded Don of a miniature Black Panther.

The closer Don got to the mansion, he begin to edge his way while going over the strategy he initially came up with once he studied the layout. He synchronized his breathing to the rhythmical beating of his heart. His feet were also moving on the same beat.

He heard the drums.

Don assumed this task as a way to show Chico what he was truly worth. If he so happened to succeed, then it would cause the others to recognize him as a man of qualified strength and loyalty to Chico. Don was placing his very own life on the crap table. He hoped he didn't crap out.

Don wasn't an extremely religious man, but he mumbled a prayer under his breath as he strolled through the night on his way to the feast. Don bit the tip of his tongue to physically taste the blood his soul was already drinking. He had a urgent thirst for more.

The beating of the drums became louder the closer he got to the mansion. A dangerous thought of human conviction crossed his mind. Why was he intoxicated with unfettered joy over the notion he was about to take the lives of anyone who got in his way?

What was he becoming?

Don's breathing instantly dropped decimals below its normal rate. His mouth closed tightly. Now he was breathing through his nostrils. His eyes peering in the direction he needed to go. Death's darkness was the beacon leading him right now.

He made sure not to take the same route he came. The guard was facing in that direction. Don had a better plan to assist him with the element of surprise. He would need this as a weapon in his arsenal, since he was alone and had to force his way into a fortress.

Don studied the back fence for any wires which might be connected to an alarm system in the house. There were none. This gave him a clear sign he could touch the fence and wouldn't have to worry about a ringing alarm.

Once he hoped over the fence, he stayed low to the ground and smelled deeply in the air. All he smelled were grapefruits and fresh

46

mangos, mixed with the smell of freshly cut grass. He was smelling for any clue of a dog. He should have checked this before he jumped over the fence.

His tread towards the mansion was slow and observant to the surroundings. His eyes scanned every inch of the perimeter of the yard. He noticed two dogs edging their way towards him with their teeth showing.

They were well trained dogs. Neither made a noise as they were preparing to attack. Don held one of his guns in his hand. Once they smelled Don and knew they were close enough, they took off running.

Don was able to fire one shot and hit one of the Dobermans. He fell to the ground, but the other one continued to race in his direction.

Don dropped his gun and caught the dog by the thick fur on the collar. The dog nipped at Don's face trying to bite him. Don brought both of his hands around the dogs neck and started to choke him until the dog went limp in his hands.

There was a scar at the throat of the dog. Now Don knew why they didn't bark. They were real attack dogs. Their throats were cut so they couldn't bark and this gave them the element of surprise over any intruder.

Don laid the dog down and struggled to relax his breathing. He came to the opposite side of the bushes and noticed the guard was still standing in front of the door.

He peeked through the open space of the bush. He was now standing right beside the guard. The only barrier between them were the bushes. The guard was staring straight ahead into the night. He would turn his head once he heard something go bump in the night. He wouldn't rely on the sound of the noise, but he had to also see what it was. If he didn't see anything, he would make his way in the direction for a complete confirmation of what it was.

Don visually measured the distance the guard was standing away from him. The guard didn't even know Don was standing right beside him. Don stuck his gun through the space in the bushes with such caution, the bushes didn't even move. He had to make his initial shot count and hit the guard dead on to make sure he wouldn't be able to fire a warning shot to alert the rest of the men there is a intruder on the premises.

The silencers on the barrel of the gun extended his gun further through the bushes. Don pressed the trigger and fired two shots into the guard's head. The hiss of the bullets escaping the barrel of the silencer was the only sounds to interrupt the quietness of the night. He had to make sure the shots landed at the side, so the guard wouldn't fall back and crash into the front door.

The guard started to fall in slow motion. Don lurched through the bushes as the guard was falling sideways into the bushes on the opposite side of where he was standing. The gun the guard was holding was still in his hand, Don rested his foot to the side of it before it was able to hit the ground. The gun could've gone off. Don wasn't leaving anything to chance and the gun went off. The guards finger were still on the trigger. A clear sign he didn't even know it was coming.

Don gently slipped the guard's finger off the trigger and strapped the gun onto his back. A puddle of blood was positioned steadily on top of the open wound of the guards head. The guard head moved once Don begun to search his pockets. The blood poured out of his head in enormous globs and trailed down the walk way until it reached the edge of the soil of the manicured lawn.

He searched the guards pockets until he found a ring of keys. Don used extreme caution to stick the round key into the alarm system hidden under the metal siding of the mansion. The red light of the alarm switched to green as a indication the alarm was now off.

Five keys into the search, Don found the key to open the front door. He cracked his knuckles as he turned the knob. Drops of sweat trickled down his arm pits. His senses were tingling not knowing what was on the other side of the door or what position the men were inside the mansion.

Don gazed in every direction of the front entrance of the mansion to make sure there weren't any cameras and he wasn't walking into a ambush.

He took a few deep breaths to calm himself for the confrontation soon to take place once it was learned an intruder was in the mansion. At this point, Don wouldn't turn around if he could. He liked to go against the odds and the odds were definitely stacked against him on this one.

Don thought about what he had just committed himself to a thousand times while his hand was turning the knob. This was it, the big show. This appeared to be a no win situation, but greatness only came to those who went against the odds. When failure was inevitable, his faith in himself and his two guns told him he could pull this off.

A car pranced down the street as Don stepped into the mansion. He quietly closed the door. A guard was standing at the top of the stairs, but was watching television in one of the rooms from where he was standing.

Seconds before the guard noticed him, Don placed both guns behind his back. "Pablo will speak with me now?" Don asked the man in perfect Spanish.

Don posed a question to the man to create an illusion of confusion. This was to buy him a few more seconds to fully drink in the layout of the mansion from the inside. He was taking a chance in asking a question, but he had to try every trick in the book. After all, only his life depended on it.

The guard's face was glazed in shock at the sight of Don. The guard wore a radio at his hip and knew the guard on the outside would've called him if he was going to allow anyone into the mansion. Something was wrong.

Don's eyes raked in the entire room in one glance. He counted each and every door as well as the architectural designs of the entire space before him.

He didn't give the guard a chance to reply. By the puzzled look on the guard's face, Don knew the guard wasn't falling for his ploy. The guard was trying to make sense of how to respond to the stranger in the mansion.

Don raised both guns and shot the guard dead in two shots. The guards finger froze on the trigger as a barrage of bullets escaped from the gun and into the high arched ceiling on his way down the spiral stairs.

What appeared to be an army swooped out of every door with their guns drawn and searching for the target. Don hurried and found refuge behind one of the sizeable, marble columns. He could hear his heart beating in his ears.

A nervous drop of sweat flowed in a gentle stream down the center of his scalp and down his forehead. It trailed all the way down the bridge of his nose and halted just at the tip.

Don curved his bottom lip upward to blow the sweat away from his nose. He sprung from behind the column shooting wildly at the guards at the top of the stairs. This was just to check their response time to his firing of bullets. The entire time they were shooting at him, he didn't shoot back.

Don was shooting at the same time he leaped into the air to switch locations to the next podium closer to the stairs and away from the mirrors decorating the spacious living room.

Two men at the top of the stairs screamed with pain as the bullets slammed into the softness of their bellies and exited out of their backs.

Don hit the release button of his gun with his thumbs and the clips fell onto the floor. He smashed the butt of his gun to his hips to reload. He closed his eyes to methodically mediate his next attack. Every bullet had to count at this point. The guards were assuming there was more than one shooting at them. Don would fire one gun in one direction and the other in another direction. Also, they didn't think any rational minded man would attempt this feat alone. Little did they know, the man shooting at them had thrown rationality out the window and was now relying on sheer courage to accomplish what he set his mind to.

The fact they thought Don wasn't alone on this hunt, it was forcing them to make major mistakes. All they had to do was rush after him all at once, instead of giving him a chance to force them into making mistakes. They were looking for more men and this caused them to overestimate the attack of a lone hunter.

The men were deliriously firing in his direction. Chips from the marble column flickered through the air, along with fragments of bullets.

The accumulation of marble fragments left heavy layers of dust and debris on Don's soft bottom shoes. He gritted his teeth wondering why he didn't put on a bulletproof vest, but calculated it was best he hadn't. He didn't intend to allow them to hit him with any bullets. Also, it was when he was vulnerable, he felt he was invincible. He was overlooking any conditions which would make him prone to defeat. It was when he had less, he had more. He knew the science for ensuring any victory is a mysterious secret.

A second thought filled the inner cortex of his mind. He couldn't allow them to hit him not even once. Not only would it make it nearly impossible for him to get out alive, but he couldn't allow one drop of his DNA to remain anywhere in this place. Any sign of his life force left behind would open up a full investigation of how would the DNA of a dead man arrive at a crime scene in Florida.

Don waited with patience for the firing to cease. He removed the gun from the guard outside from his back. He had to be frugal with his bullets. It would be a crying shame for him to run out of bullets in the middle of a war. Don had to make sure every shot fired would remove another gun from the radar.

Don brought the semi-automatic gun to the front of him and lunged from behind the podium and begin to fire profusely at the men standing at the top of the stairs. As the rapid gun fire came to a halt, three men were lying in a pool of blood dead. They didn't time the next flare of bullets and were out in the opening. Don cut them down before they could even fire.

Two men were hidden behind both corners in the upstairs hallway. Don knew he needed to bring this fiasco to a end before they got a chance to call for reinforcement, or the police were called from the resounding gunfire. It had to sound like it was Vietnam to the neighbors.

Don shot once standing up and then suddenly dropped down to one knee and killed two men. More shots rang through the air in his direction. The gun shots were coming so fast, it forced Don to slip behind a column to try and gain his composure. He continued to hear their shots and was now convinced they were scared and a bad shot. They would've never thought an attack would transpire directly inside of the mansion.

Don fired the automatic gun until the magazine was empty. He wiped the gun down with his shirt and tossed it to the side. He removed his two nines from his waist and spun around the column and aimed both guns towards the stairs. He charged in the direction of the stairs firing both guns at the same time. He was now placing his life in the hands of good luck.

His movements were like a stalking Black Panther on a night hunt. In his disorder of running in the direction of the greatest danger in the open, his mind was in perfected order. Don was so alert, he would shoot any man who moved out into the opening and attempted to raise their gun.

While Don was shooting his way up the stairs and onto the first landing, three more men unexpectedly burst through one of the doors. The bullets from his gun hit all three. They fell to the ground dead and landed on top of each other like weighty logs.

Don would aim and shoot and each bullet seemed to hit vital locations of his victims each time. Bodies filled the upper level of the mansion and some were piled in front of the doors they initially came out of.

Don was now five steps away from the upper landing. As he was about to reach the top of the stairs, the front door opened. He leaped in the air like a cat being thrown from a elevated platform. He twisted in mid-air and landed on his ass at the top of the stairs. He shot four of the men dead as soon as they came through the front door.

He flicked both of the release buttons with his thumbs to allow the empty clips to fall to the ground. He slammed the butt of his guns to his waist to reload.

Don edged his way to the main room of the mansion on the tips of his toes. This was the room the guards appeared to be defending with their lives. His gray eyes were intense. The blood thirst, still hadn't been fully quenched.

The atmosphere of the mansion suddenly became quiet. An un-expected stab of anxiety blasted him in his gut. It was the missing gun fire which made him nervous. He held both guns out to his side like he was being crucified. This was to cover any unknown danger to come out of nowhere.

He made sure to listen to the quietness with his entire body. His breathing became slow and shallow. He aimed at the open doors in front of which the dead bodies were piled. Don was anxiously waiting for a gun shot to fire from either one of the rooms unexpect-edly. The bodies strewn throughout the hallway was a lot, but he was ready, willing and able to continually contribute to its toll.

He kicked the door open and the room was sunk in darkness and appeared to be empty. His eyes scanned every square inch of the room with his gun pointed in every direction his eyes were looking. He was sure of the importance this room held to the men guarding it, but figured he should give it the equivalent amount of attention. He knew Pablo was here somewhere. He just spoke with him on the radio.

Don turned on the light switch with his elbow. It felt safe for him to keep both guns in his hand just in case he needed to drop more bodies to complete the task at hand. He had come too far to lose at this stage of the attack.

He closed the door to the room he was in. This would prevent any unnecessary surprises. Also, it would give him time to focus if anyone opened the door instead of it being wide open, thereby giv-ing the assailant a clear shot.

He went straight to the closed closets in the room. He found a man standing in the closet behind a rack of stiffly hanging coats and suit jackets shaking like a crap game.

Don gritted his teeth with controlled anger as he pulled Pablo from the closet by the back of his neck. Pablo was a pudgy, glutton of a man. There were huge patches of hair on parts of his body which made him appear half animal and half man. He seemed to be about fifty and had five to six strands of hair lying across the bald spot at the top of his head as if they could cover it.

A blonde haired woman moved in the bed in front of Don. Don examined Pablo's face owlishly before throwing him to the floor. He wasted no time in firing at the silicone breasted woman in the bed. He was taking no prisoners. The sheet she held in front of her body instantly turned crimson.

Don yanked Pablo from the floor by his arm like he was a rag doll. He slapped him with the neck of his gun. "I told you I came for Chico's money," he said in perfect Spanish. "Now where is it?"

Pablo gulped furiously for air and pointed in the direction of the adjoining room, the master-bedroom. "De utter room."

Don kicked him square in his naked ass with the fine point of his shoe. "Well get your fat ass in there and get it." He kicked him once more. "Putting me through all of this bullshit."

Pablo led Don to the other room. A pool table sat in the center of the room which was the recreation room. He hit a button in one of the corner pockets of the pool table and the green felt cushion at the top of the table slid to one side. A safe the same length of the table was embedded inside.

Pablo swallowed the lump in his throat as he thumbed the combination on the safe. His hands weren't moving as fast as his thoughts. The part to baffle him the most was how one man was able to penetrate his well guarded fortress like it was cheap wallpaper.

Pablo's knees buckled as he stepped away from the safe and fell onto the plush carpet. This was to give Don a clear sight of all the money Pablo kept in the mansion. The safe was full to capacity. Don knew the most honorable thing to do was take what was owed and leave the rest. Considering he almost lost his life, he was taking it all and some.

Don's hands trailed over the large sums of money inside the safe. He eyed Pablo with a calmness. "Do you have any suitcases?"

"In the closet," Pablo replied. His voice didn't carry the same vigor as it did when he barked at Don on the radio.

Don waited for Pablo to get up. When he didn't, he slapped him with his gun. "What do you expect for me to get them myself.?"

Pablo pulled down a rack of suitcases from the top of the walkin closet. Don had one of his guns in his waist. He didn't have to order Pablo to fill them with money, he was now moving on automatic pilot. He didn't want to get hit with the gun anymore. There were already two knots on his head and the center of his ass was screaming with pain from the kicks it endured.

It took six substantial suitcases to empty out the safe. The suitcases were full of hundred dollar bills. Pablo's face was long and twisted in anguish. He couldn't believe this was happening to him of all people.

Don woke him out of his dazed expression by smacking him with the gun twice in the face. "Where are the drugs?"

"What? What?" Pablo said twice. The assault had him virtually discombobulated. He didn't know what to expect from the lone assailant standing before him. Pablo was even more surprised by the Black man's ability to speak fluent Spanish with a Colombian dialect. "No drugs here," he replied while wiping the dripping blood from his nose.

"Where do you keep it and how much do you have?"

Pablo elaborately swung his hand around the spacious room. "To fill this room. I'll give it all to you. Just don't kill me." He spoke in Spanish for the first time.

Don peered down at Pablo like one would a pair of manure stained boots. "We can use the truck you got out back."

Don had Pablo drive to Sarasota Florida to a deserted location. They made the trek in complete silence. Pablo praying his nightmare was finally about to come to an end. Tonight's events were weighing heavily on his nerves.

Don made Pablo load every box of cocaine onto the flat bed truck. Pablo was in such bad shape, he was completely out of breath by the time he placed the last of the boxes onto the truck.

Pablo stared into the recess of darkness surrounding the rest of the warehouse. "That's all of it." He wiped the sweat from his beefy cheeks. "You have more than I owed Chico."

Don had a wicked grin on his face. "I guess this is the end of the road for us."

Pablo's eyes widened with alarm. "I thought you said you weren't going to kill me. I gave you everything I have." His voice trembled in desperation.

Don shook his head from side to side with disgust. "I think money has made you a terribly foolish man Pablo. What would I look like leaving an enemy behind to haunt the family after taking all you have." He smiled as the thought of Sosa flashed in his mind. "I've been there, done that and already got the ticket for it."

Don begun to scrape his foot across the ground to clean off the heavy build up of dirt on the bottom of his shoe. "Those who seek to achieve power in this way of life should never show mercy to an enemy. I've done this once before and paid the price of thoroughly learning this lesson by the loss of my little brother. Therefore, reconciliation is altogether out of the question at this phase of both of our lives."

Don pulled the neck of his gun back and aimed it at Pablo's head. "Only one side can win and it must win totally." He pulled the trigger and shot Pablo in the center of his head. Pablo fell backwards and the last drop of air to escape his lungs were the only sound to be heard in the night, hissing like a punctured tire.

Don climbed onto the truck and sped down the dirt road to the main highway. He totally crushed the enemy of Chico and made sure to take from him everything except his language. Now Chico would be able to supply the demand in Pablo's territory and would never have to worry about him coming back for revenge.

Don knew he had no other choice but to kill Pablo. The lesson of losing his little brother had been firmly planted in his head and he vowed to never make that mistake again. He knew a man would be slow to repay a favor, but quick to repay a hurt. Death was the only tool to finalize any future threats. By all means, he intended to kill anyone who got in his way.

Anyone.

CHAPTER SEVEN

Chico and his men were sitting in his study drinking the best of wines and watching the fight when Don casually strolled into the study with the greatest of ease.

He carried the bags of money on a luggage carrier. Initially, he was going to bring all he could carry, but he wanted the prize to be shown all at once. This would heighten the immediate effect that he was able to accomplish the task, but when they hear about all he killed to do so, it would show the sourly murderous man he could be at the drop of a dime.

Don laid the hard-bitten cases down one by one next to Chico. Everyone in the room was silent and watched him with intense stares. He even went out for ice cream after he put Pablo exactly were he needed to be. It was a celebration for being the coldest man alive.

Chico glanced over at Don and eyed the splattered blood on his cream colored silk shirt. Chico shuffled out of his chair and turned towards Don. "What happened?" he asked with his eyes wide and alert. His voice rose an octave above normal. "Did you cut yourself or something?" He scanned Don's entire body checking for any open wounds.

Don kneeled down to flip open one of the cases. The money poured out like a pot of boiling water. "It's the blood of your enemy." All of the suitcases were now lined up. "Here's the money he owed you and some. I have an entire shipment out in the truck." Don smiled. "I took the truck to get weighed and it came up to five tons."

Chico's mind thoroughly struggled to formulate the thoughts into the English language. When he finally was able to say something, his voice quivered. "Don you went and killed Pablo and took everything he had?" His eyes scrutinized Don's cold gray eyes and over each of the suitcases spilling over with money and added. "By yourself?"

Don walked over to the well stocked bar and fixed himself a stiff drink of Vodka. The only substance to dilute his drink was the square ice cubes. He glanced over at Chico while his hands breezed over the money and smiled inwardly.

Don sniffed the expensive vodka in his glass like a true connoisseur. He tossed a mouthful into his mouth and sneered violently at the searing sensation running down his throat.

He had no such intentions of giving Chico the full details of this heist. He preferred for Chico to hear of this great feat through other sources. The news will more than likely cover the scene and better speak of the gory details Don left behind.

He was a humble man and wouldn't tell the story in a grandiosity manner to glorify himself in the least. He didn't feel the need to verbally communicate how he was able to capitalize off of the mistakes of his enemies poor defense.

Don could only imagine what the crime scene would look like to the first person to stumble upon this grizzly discovery, of the bullet riddled bodies sprawled throughout the house and also, the body of Pablo far away from the war zone at his own mansion. It would appear as if an army ran through the place, because of the many men killed. Only Chico and the men in the room today would know Don did this alone, at the spur of the moment. There wasn't even a tangible amount of time to formulate a plausible plan. Therefore, by keeping the plan to himself and allowing all matters to remain a mystery, it would allow the others to speculate what happened. This would exaggerate his abilities and make his task seem effortless, especially when he didn't even have a scratch on him.

Chico shook his head from side to side in a rare state of confusion. "Don I didn't tell you to do this by yourself." Chico blew out a stream of hot air. "I was going to send help with you."

"Then you should have told all of us at the same time," Don said. He studied each of the men in the room and gave them a once over. "All they would've tried to do was kill me once my back was turned, and just pretend I was a casualty of war." Don laughed shortly. "I wouldn't carry a bucket of piss through the hot Arabian desert with anyone of them to save my life."

"Don you don't have any trust for my men?" Chico swept his hand across the room at his men. "They've been with me for years and they know how I fell about you." Chico studied each of their faces for reassurance. "Tell him."

Each of them agreed loudly, but none looking at Don. They only looked at Chico while Don studied all of their faces and knew they would turn on him at the drop of a dime. Only an absolute fool will trust any man who hates him because of his birthright, that was a choice he had no control over, but was now hated for something he had nothing to do with. He would kill everyone in this room except for Chico.

Chico was the only one he thought of going to once he made it over the hurdle of death. This was the only man he could trust not born from the same African origin as himself.

Don's gray eyes stared at them like a hawk would his prey, or an Angel in the highest altitude within the upper firmaments of heaven watching the human race on earth.

"Their loyalty is to you and to you alone." Don smiled softly. "In their eyes, I am disposable like a tampon dripping with blood from a syphilis infected pussy." He swallowed down his drink in one gulp. "My chances of making it out of there alive was far better alone." He pointed a stern finger at all of them. "How can I watch Pablo's men and the ones I came with?"

Armondo and Colon both eyed Don out of the corner of their eyes. His words were the absolute truth. They have stupidly underestimated his abilities. They were aware of the cops he killed and how he was now presumed to be dead. They figured it was just mere luck and not a stroke of killer genius.

This night had proved them to be totally wrong about this Black man now a part of a Colombian cartel. Tonight outright validated him as a cold blooded killer. Don finalized a matter of ill feelings between two families in one night, a task Armondo couldn't accomplish in two years. Don didn't want to tell them what he was going to do, it was about showing what he was about to do. He used faith as the head chemist to overly convince himself he was making it out alive.

Against all odds.

Chico playfully tapped Don on the cheek with the back of his knuckles. He wore the biggest smile on his face he's had for the entire night. "You're one crazy boy. I knew it when I first met you." He grabbed Don around his neck. "I am glad you are on my side." He dug into his pocket and handed Don a five dollar bill. "Let me pay you for the sandwich you brought me last week. I don't want you to take me out for a sandwich." Chico released a wheezy chuckle.

Don smiled for the first time during their conversation. He was still reveling at the shocked look on the faces of the men. "I present myself as a sane man, but in all reality Chico," he glanced over at Armondo, his hands balled into a fist. "I'm nothing but a sick motherfuckin lunatic. My power comes from just being able to fully let go when the time calls for me to summon the madness and the thirst for blood and retain my madness only in civilized conditions."

Don took a few steps closer to the money and Chico. "For a man to have to contend with failure, which is a straight trickster I might add. It is bolstered with an ironic enthusiasm and can be very cunning. Failure takes great delight in tripping a man up when the success he has yearned for is nearly within his reach." Don ran his hands across the money. He didn't want one penny of it. This was his moment. "To conquer is nothing when a man is on the quest to leave behind a legacy. He must also be able to prosper for his willingness to kill a thousand men, just to send a message to one."

Chico sipped his drink and spit it halfway across the room. He began to cough loudly and with a force, it caused a wine glass on the table to topple over. It was a rough cough Don had heard before and warned Chico to get it checked out.

Don rushed into the kitchen to get him a glass of water. Chico desperately tried to take a few sips, but couldn't get a hold on the cough rumbling in his chest. A strong cough would come through and vibrate throughout the entire room. A mouthful of blood seeped past his lips and onto his white terry cloth robe.

Chico waved Don away with a dismissive wave. "I'll be all right. It's just a little chest cold."

"This is more than that. You need to see a doctor. I'm taking you to the hospital." Don waved for Armondo to come over. "Help me get him into the car."

Armondo didn't show any signs of reluctance to the way Don barked an order at him. He's known of his cough for years, and knew if Chico just so happen to die, he would take over the family and Don would be the first problem he squashed.

Chico coughed profusely all the way to the hospital until he passed out in the back seat. More blood spewed from his mouth. Bonita cradled him in her arms for the entire ride. Not only was she striving to comfort him, but she was making sure he didn't suffocate on his own blood as they sped their way down the highway towards the hospital.

Don hated the smell of hospitals. Its sterile environment made him feel like a trapdoor opened in the floor of his stomach. He could imagine the microscopic germs floating around in a fine mist the naked eye could hardly detect. But this was a place for the sick to get healed.

The nurses rushed Chico into a room to check his vital signs before a doctor came in to see him. Bonita explained to the nurses the symptoms Chico has had for years. While cleaning the bathroom, she had discovered blood mixed with phlegm and knew only he had coughed it up.

Armondo seemed frustrated because the doctors were taking too long. He paced back and forth and made repeated trips to the bathroom. Don watched him and the others closely. He was trying to read into their actions to determine how they really felt about Chico's unexpected condition. He was too sick to run the family at this point. Don was striving to detect their subtle signs of greed and lust for Chico's seat of power. He was especially paying close attention to Armondo.

By the time the doctors came back, Armondo had left to handle a deal worth five million dollars with some guys from California. The doctor who came into the room was medium height, with horned rimmed glasses sitting at the top of a pampered nose. He figured it would be best to keep Chico overnight to further run test on him. He whispered to Bonita he didn't think it looked too good for Chico, but in the medical field there was always miracles to go against his knowledge of medicine.

Don sat down at the foot of Chico's bed. "I told you to leave that coke alone."

Chico forced a smile. "I don't think it is the coke. Believe it or not, but the coke helps with the cough."

Don studied Chico's face and the color was drained from his cheeks. His complexion was now pale and the vigor he had at dinner had evaporated.

Chico pushed himself up to his elbows. "I need to talk to you about something of importance Don." Bonita was about to leave the room. "Bonita you can stay. I know all about you and Don sneaking around. He is loyal to you and you both have my blessings."

Bonita came and stood next to Don and firmly took his hand into hers. "We didn't plan to fall in love Chico. It just happened."

Don grinned at Chico who seemed to never miss a beat. "So what's up?"

Chico words came slow and for the first time he spoke in Spanish. "You're a very thorough man Mr. Starchild. The only Black man I would ever trust with my life. A proven asset to this family." Bonita was listening closely to the words coming out of Chico's mouth. This was her first time being allowed to hear a conversation of great importance.

Chico continued. "I now know what I've always known and you're willing to place yourself in the line of fire for me without a second thought. I am thankful you do not try and take advantage of our friendship to get a free pass. You've been that way since I've known you as a child."

Don placed a hand on Chico's arm. He could see the emotions of his words starting to come to the surface. This was unnatural for Chico. He's always kept his feelings hidden. Don knew whatever Chico had to say must really mean something to him.

"If anything fucked up happens to me Don," Chico began, "I want for you to take over my family." Don was about to interrupt. Chico held up his hand to prevent him from doing so. "I know this may come as a shock and it is unheard of for an American Black to run a Colombian family, but you're going to make your own way and prove everyone wrong. You've always been honest with me and not for the sake of what I could do for you, but because you were my friend." Chico took a deep breath to fight back the building tears. "I think of you as a son Don."

"Chico stop speaking like this is the end of your journey. You are going to be all right," Don said.

"Only for the moment," Chico replied as he flopped back onto his pillows. "I'm thinking about the future, and you are the best man for my spot. Tonight has proven that."

Don placed a cold wash cloth on Chico's forehead at the first sight of sweat. "Live for now and we will cross that bridge when we get there. Now get you some rest. I'll be right outside if you need me."

It appeared their conversation had Chico totally fatigued and exhausted. Don placed one of the fluffy pillows under his head. Chico closed his eyes as soon as his head hit the pillow. There was no need for anymore protest. He was experiencing the most excruciating pain he was allowing anyone else to know.

Don and Bonita were sitting and talking in Spanish. She was trying to talk Don out of leaping into the trenches of the obligations Chico was trying to place upon him. She didn't want him to have anything to do with the business if Chico were to pass away. She only wanted to move far away and live a life without violence and drugs.

Don listened intently to her protest, but really didn't care to respond. He was thinking over every alternative if the crown jewels were to fall into his lap and he was named the King.

Blood would definitely flow through the earth like the Nile river. It was the only way. Death to his enemies was the only tool by which to remove all threats and options from his enemies grasp. It was by blood the sins of man can be cleansed. Don believed this, but he knew their cleansing would stain his soul.

He really didn't care.

Chapter Eight

The next morning, Don was on his way back from the cafeteria with breakfast for Bonita. He didn't have a appetite. His mind was stuck on the idea of taking over the family if anything happened to Chico. All Don was doing was struggling with the opposition of what he would do. He really needed to bring order to his chaotic thoughts.

Voices could be heard coming from Chico's room through the thick oak door. He slowly opened the door so as not to interrupt the conversation. Bonita and the doctor were standing near the spacious window, while Chico laid in the bed staring up at the ceiling perturbed by the information he heard.

Chico had a stricken look on his face. Like the sound of the doctors words weren't penetrating his conscious thoughts. Don quietly sat the tray down by the bedside, he noticed how Chico's bottom lip began to curl. Something the doctor had said made Chico highly upset.

Chico coughed loudly before he leaned up on his elbows. "Don I'm not going to make it," he said softly. "They said I have lung Cancer."

Don spun around on his heels towards the doctor. "That's not a problem right? You can cure this thing with chemotherapy?"

The doctor shook his head numbly. "I'm sorry, but he's too far gone in the process. The Cancer has spread to both lungs. Of course we will try, but why suffer against the expected any way?"

"What about money?" Don asked, his voice rising an octave. "Find a lung donor and put him at the top of the list. Like I said, money ain't a thing."

The doctor gritted his teeth. "That still could take up to five years, and I don't think he even has that much time. All we can do is prepare him and walk him through the process with the minimal amount of pain as possible."

Chico clutched the blanket and took exceptionally deep breaths. His words were caught in his throat. Never did he imagine he would die from a sickness. He even fucked with condoms. He reckoned since he lived by the sword, he would also die by the sword, an assassination to say the least. It really didn't bother Chico if he died a brutal death. It was all a part of the life he lived.

Also, he didn't know the date and time it would happen. The thought to know he was dying beforehand nearly brought him to the brink of insanity. To know he was finally near the end of his life cycle was entirely too much for a sane mind to handle.

Chico calculated he had enough money to buy a thousand lungs, but it still wouldn't save him. He could go to Colombia and have a live man give him both lungs just to know he will be able to properly feed his family.

Now, the one thing Don always told him, the one thing we cannot buy is time. There comes a point in our lives we need more of it, but it runs out on its own. There is nothing in life to replenish the prepaid account of time once it runs empty. Chico finally understood the old adage; What does it profit a man to gain the whole world and lose his soul.

Armondo stepped into the room. Immediately, he observed Chico's eyes were haunted by an inner pain, a pain he hasn't felt since his father died while he was just twenty years old.

The room was smothered in tension. Everyone had a questioning look on their faces as to what to say to console Chico. It was almost like they were trying to figure out the $64,000 question of why is the sky blue.

Chico ordered everyone out of the room except for Don and

Armondo. His face still pinched with sorrow, but his mind was now concerned about the family. Slowly, Chico began to relax since he no longer pondered on his death, but the family business.

He faced Armondo slow and easy. "Armondo," he said in Spanish. "you and I have grown up together and I do love you like a brother." He cleared the residue of blood from his throat. "The doctor said I only have a year to live if I'm lucky." Chico wiped the forming tears from his eyes. "When it's my time, I want Don to run the family and for you to give him the same loyalty you've given me for all of the years of our growing up."

Armondo suddenly stepped back as if Chico's words had pulled the floor from under his feet. He exchanged a questioning glance at Don, but since Chico spoke in Spanish, he figured Don didn't hear what Chico just said. Don stood expressionless, but with a crafty smile on his face.

He gave Chico a slow, appraising glance. "What!" he exclaimed with a vicious tone. "You're going to let this pussy nigger run our family?" he spoke in rapid Spanish, but pointed at Don.

Don swiftly removed his gun from its holster and calmly walked over to the other side of the bed towards Armondo. At the speed of light, Don cracked him across the bridge of his nose with the butt of his gun. As Armondo crashed to the floor in uninterrupted agony, blood poured from his nose like Niagara Falls.

Don placed his right foot on Armondo's chest to prevent him from getting up. He snatched the neck of his gun back and aimed it at Armondo's head. A crazed look was on Don's face.

Don's mouth contorted grotesquely. "I swear by the God I know, I will blow your fucking brains out right here and right now." Don spat down at him, it landed inches away from his head. "I dare you to say it again." His gray eyes shone with controlled rage. "Say it again!"

Chico leaned back on his fluffy white pillows with an anticipated look on his face. On the early news, Chico watched the massacre at Pablo's mansion. The news reporter said it was as tragic as a war in a third world country. Chico knew Don wouldn't need to think twice about putting a bullet into Armondo's head.

Any sane man with a nip of intelligence could perceive Don was a sophisticated psychopath. He had the stomach for anything. He could snatch a man's eye out of its socket and watch it dangle out of his head by its stringy optic nerves and suddenly have a dire taste for a plate of spaghetti and meatballs soon after.

At this point in his life, he had no problem with killing in the least. In fact, he now consumed an appetite for it. Death was used to enforce the rules of the game. Anyone not willing to honor the rules must die as far as he was concerned. There was no middle ground.

Armondo finally glanced at Chico with a surrendering look of appeal in his eyes for Chico to calm this Black Panther pouncing on his chest.

Chico quickly turned his head and peered out of the spacious window at the well lined palm trees across the street. The image of the first time he met Don flashed before his eyes. He hurt Armondo and had the power to kill him if need be, but gave in to him. It was like deja vu, but this time they were in the future. Chico knew now, Don would surely kill him and think nothing about it.

He had to allow Don to firmly establish his respect. Chico knew respect amongst the men in his craft had to be thoroughly legislated by total violence. Don could only liberate this respect from all of the men by starting with Armondo first. This display would properly inform them Don would even kill them if they stepped out of line for the smallest of reasons.

For the first time since he was rushed into the hospital, Chico's eyes glinted with pleasure and he felt a sunny feeling deep within the inner folds of his soul. Who would've thought the day he met Don when he was a boy and now he is a man and he is everything of a man Chico never was within himself. This is why he loved Don. Don would be able to easily do all the things he never could fathom within the confines of his own mind.

After watching the news this morning, Chico finally understood Don. He used murder and intelligence as another form of politics. If a man didn't respect Don while he was alive, Don believed the silence by his death would compel the respect he outright demanded.

Chico hoped Don wouldn't kill Armondo for something so small, but he knew men to die for less. Don manifested his ingenuity on many occasions. Chico perceived it to be genius.

"You broke my fucking nose you . . . " Armondo cut his ill words in mid-air as the blood seeped from between his fingers. This moment reminded him of their first encounter also. Don was a boy than, but had him in the same predicament again.

Don stood directly over Armondo. "I am now in control of your life and death. Blaspheme against this God and see how fast your soul will go into the bottomless pit of hell." He spoke in eloquent Spanish.

Bonita heard the commotion from outside of the room. She rushed inside and observed Armondo holding his throbbing nose as spews of thick red blood rushed from between his fingers. She also noticed Don's gray eyes blazing murderously and his gun drawn.

Chico coughed up a mouthful of blood into a piece of tissue. "This isn't about friendship. It is always what is best for the family."

Armondo spoke through the bundle of tissue in his hand covering his nose. "But Chico we've been together too long for you to pass me. I already know the business inside out." His words came out nasal.

Chico's bullish eyes became stern and focused. "You only know what I taught you about this business, which is not enough. Although Don hasn't handled the quantity I have, he is much more thorough in killing and intelligence. There are no explanations and excuses with him. He gives nothing but results." He sucked in a mouthful of air. "There is a line that has to be crossed for real power and control over the life we live. Nobody has complete control over this life. There is no order. Lines need to be crossed and I haven't a thread of heart to cross it. Not once have you ever mentioned it throughout our entire time in this life. Don mentioned it on his visit back to me, but I don't know how. Don wouldn't give too much of anything a second thought because the first is usually the right path for him to take and he will take it. It's in his eyes."

Don cocked his head to one side trying to make sense of what

Chico was openly saying to him. What did he have the heart to do? What he did last night? Don sensed there was more to the story. He wondered what did Chico see in him at the moment. Yes, Don wanted supreme power, but he hated it had to come at the loss of a dear friend.

Now Don know what Chico meant when he said one day he will be a King. This was the time Chico taught him the many ways to cut heroin. Don was about to sit on the throne and there was nothing Armondo could do or say about it.

Chico coughed so forcefully, the metal frames of the bed shook like there was an 9.9 earthquake. Don rushed to grab the emergency button for the nurse to come. He hit the red button with such force, it clicked once and permanently jammed into the hand held device.

Somehow, the doctor found out Chico was a major drug lord and the frantic noises of battle he was hearing, would come off as all to natural for a Colombian kingpin. He didn't want to barge in a room and see anything, which would prevent him from being able to live and see another day.

"I need a shot," Chico said as he continued to repeatedly cough. "I'm in terrible fucking pain."

The doctor twisted the valve to turn the air up besides Chico's bed. "I can't keep giving you high does of morphine. After awhile it would become obsolete to your pain."

"Send me home," Chico demanded turning over in the bed. He had access to more morphine than the hospital could get their hands on at one time. He had barrels of it.

✻ ✻ ✻

In a matter of hours, Chico had checked out of the hospital and made sure a barrel of morphine was going to beat him there. He preferred to spend his last days of life at home around more comfortable surroundings. It was beneath his standards to have to beg for anything to give him relief; especially when he had access to enough morphine to supply every cancer patient in the hospital. Now he could comprehend the mentality of an addict.

Don drove him home and refused to ride in any car with Armondo. Bonita immediately tucked Chico into bed as soon as they got home. When they were about to leave the room, Chico called out to him. "Call for another maid and find me a good nurse." He smiled before he turned over. "Bonita is your woman and should not work for me any longer."

"I'll take care of that," Don said.

"Before I am all morphined out of my mind and forget, make flight reservations to Colombia. I have to introduce you to the man I work for; the head of the family."

"I thought you were the head," Don said.

"My father gave it to him. He has the coca fields and makes sure the cocaine is processed and shipments are sent. I am the head for America and for selling it. He has to want you to be the head over here, if not, then there is nothing I can do." Chico closed his eyes. "Don I believe in you. If I didn't believe in you, I wouldn't go this far."

Don closed the door to the enormous master-bedroom as Chico's last words were completely spoken. The enticing thoughts of power excited him enormously. He found his soul swept up in a whirlwind of euphoric feelings. He was now starting to taste the power waiting for him.

Never in a million years did he expect to ever hold Chico's spot in the family. It was a thought he not once considered. He believed he would have his own as a branch of the bigger family. He was buying it with the shipment and money he took from Pablo.

Slowly, Don was starting to adopt the fact this had the potential to happen. The other half of the decision now was left up to the man in Colombia Chico spoke about. This was the first time Don questioned whether he would ever sit on the throne. There seemed to be too many stumbling blocks trying to get in his way.

He strolled through the mansion but wasn't going in the direction of his room. He was headed through the kitchen to Bonita's room. There was no need to wait for everyone to retire, their relationship was already out of the bag. She had worked since she was a child in the sugar cane fields. Never had she visualize never having to work a day in her life again.

Don was sitting at the end of the bed removing his clothes. Bonita came up behind him and wrapped her arms around his still, well sculpted shoulders. "I have more good news for you Papi."

Don kissed her forearms. "What could be any better than power and money?"

"How about a baby girl?"

Don arched his back to crack his muscles. "How do you know it is going to be a girl?"

"My family is full of girls. Men only marry into my family."

Don slipped under the blankets with Bonita snuggled up against him. He ran his palm across her stomach with the anticipated thought of a life force inside of her which belonged to him.

This thought forced him to think about his two sons and wonder what kind of life they were living without him. He knew nothing bad was happening, but he didn't know how they were thinking about life. He couldn't speak with them. He wish he could find a way to let them know he loved them both, without letting them know he was still alive.

It was the silence of death killing him softly.

A huge grin came to his face at the thought of his friend Dodirty and all he had done for him to get away. Dodirty was the kind of friend he could count on as well as Cecil.

Dodirty would still come to Miami and pick up from Chico. Don made it so Chico contacted him and let him know he was Don's main connect and it was okay for him to come down and pick up what he needed. The only caution Don had was for Chico not to inform Dodirty he was alive under any circumstances.

Don laid his head on Bonita's stomach, while he massaged her lower belly, gently stroking the life forming in her womb. His eyes began to close and he heard the drums beating loudly in his ears. The chants in a strange language marinated with the wonderful sounds of the drums. He saw himself surrounded by the sky and nothing holding him up in the air. He saw himself falling at a high speed and there was nothing there to catch him.

Don broke into a sweat. It felt like a cold fist had engulfed his soul. His skin was clammy and wet. He sucked in air as if it was being sucked out of his lungs while he was plummeting through the clouds at the pace which prevented him from being able to breathe correctly.

He heard the drums!

He heard the chanting.

He saw the eyes of a beast.

He saw his death!

CHAPTER NINE

The streets of Newark were desperately fighting to get back to normalcy. In a very extreme manner, Don thoroughly left a filthy taste in the mouths of the Newark police department. The mayor of Newark verbally committed to establishing the campaign to crack down on all known drug dealers in the city of Newark. He vowed to tear down every housing project in the city and rebuild something to better aid the police in getting in and out of areas of Newark.

He didn't know how a devious devil like Don Starchild was able to operate in the city undetected, as well as escape the detection of the Newark Intelligence Task Force.

He spoke these words openly on all news stations and verbally reprimanded the Narcotics Division and related how he intended to make crucial revisions to the department. He announced a man of this magnitude will never rise in this city again to ever disgrace this city history the way Don did.

Dodirty watched the Mayor's speech on a colossal size television. He would curse the Mayor's speech every time he had a ill word to say about his friend. He knew there was no way they were going to stop anything for him. He had the best coke in the city.

Sure, he hasn't been able to fully operate in the city like when he and Don were a year ago. There were only minor restrictions to the way he needed to conform the troops, but he was operating out of state with immunity. Millions of dollars were still being made daily.

In his quiet times, he would have a Cuban cigar and a glass of Chardonnay, two of Don's favorite things, and watch the tape of his friend's last day. A bizarre feeling would overcome him every time he watched it. He would study it acutely for the moment of impact when his friend left this earth, in the eyes of many.

Dodirty threw on a pair of designer slacks and dress shirt. He was on his way to visit Don's son Kasan. He felt sorry for both of Don's sons more than anything. Anthony had a step-father helping his mother raise him, Kasan had no one. Therefore, Dodirty was taking it upon himself to fill the empty void in his life as a surrogate father. This was his way of thanking his friend for showing him the biggest picture in life.

Dodirty made it to Virginia in three hours in his new Black Porshe. Once he turned onto the road, he saw Kasan in the middle of the street playing tag football with some of the neighborhood kids who lived in the condominium.

"Hey, little man," Dodirty said to a sweating Kasan. He seemed to be growing every time he came down to see him. "Where's your mama?"

Kasan wiped his gritty hands on his shirt. He was the splitting image of Don. He was smaller than the other kids he played with, but highly intelligent. He inherited it from his father.

For his age, he was a smart child. Dodirty found at times when he spoke with Kasan, it was like speaking to a young Don. Even his pronunciation was like his fathers and Don had been dead before Kasan could even talk. The only feature to differ from his father was his eyes, Kasan's was light brown.

"She's in the house," Kasan replied and took off running.

Jewel was lying on the couch watching the daytime soaps. Life hasn't been the same since Don left this earth. She didn't have the same spunk she once had before Don's demise. She stayed in the house and didn't give another man a chance to heal her wounded heart, nor try and help her forget. She was madly in love with Don, but while he was alive, would never admit this to him openly. She wanted him out of the life which killed him. She needed to move on with her life, but didn't know how.

Jewel sat up on the couch when Dodirty came through the door. "When did you get here?"

Dodirty kissed her on the cheek. "I just pulled up."

Jewel ran her fingers through her hair. It was in complete disarray. "You should've called before you came Dodirty." She sat up on the couch. "I would've at least fixed myself up."

Dodirty eyed her and smiled inwardly at her remark. It seemed to be her favorite line. Every time he would walk through the door and find her lying on the couch, she would say these exact words and make the same gesture. This made Dodirty wonder if she was still in control of all her mental faculties. He didn't spend much time around her to know if she was slipping or not. The death of Don had done something to her. In fact, it had done something to everyone who knew and loved him.

Kasan charged into the house screaming and crying. As soon as he burst through the door, he ran into Jewel's arms. "What's the matter?" Jewel asked urgently.

Kasan was trying to fight back the rest of the tears waiting to fall from his light brown eyes. He just needed a moment to speak. His mouth would open, but nothing would come out. He gritted his teeth to force the words out. "Tony Boy hit me." His cries became even louder.

Dodirty went to the balcony to see who his Godson was speaking about. A snotty nose kid was standing on the sidewalk throwing the ball he bought for Kasan on his birthday. He was bigger than Kasan, but to Dodirty it meant nothing.

"Go out there and kick his ass!." Dodirty said ruthlessly.

Jewel brought Kasan closer to her chest and kissed him on his forehead. By no means did she want her son out in the streets fighting. She believed it was the only way to shield him from the violence which claimed his father's life.

"Go in the room and take off your clothes and get in the tub," Jewel ordered.

As Kasan stalked in the direction of the bathroom like a kicked dog, Dodirty grabbed him firmly by his arm and carried him outside. He stood him in front of the kid they called Tony Boy.

"Now hit him back," Dodirty ordered Kasan.

Kasan stood in front of the boy with his arms folded and tears streaming down his cheeks. Tony Boy was taunting him by continuing to throw the ball up in the air. Jewel was standing on the balcony yelling for Dodirty to bring Kasan back into the house.

A spasm of irritation crossed Dodirty's face. "If you don't hit him back, I'm going to take you in the house and whip your ass real good, better than he would. Now hit him back."

Kasan navigated up to Tony Boy and tapped him lightly on the arm. Tony Boy swung back a haymaker punch that knocked Kasan to the ground. Kasan found his way back to his feet holding his stomach. He mustered up enough strength to run into his mother's arms. Dodirty stalked angrily after him.

He snatched Kasan from out of the safety of his mother's arms and led him into one of the bedrooms. He removed his belt and started whipping him. Although he wasn't hitting Kasan hard, he was screaming like Dodirty was trying to murder him.

This was merely a tactic to alert his mother. Dodirty was only giving Kasan the same treatment his mother had given him when he didn't want to fight. It had made a difference in his life, and he was hoping it would make one in his Godson life.

Kasan screamed at the top of his lungs like Dodirty was killing him. Dodirty was only tapping him with the flimsy belt. Kasan wasn't use to getting hit of any kind. His mother spoiled him. He was the only child.

Jewel caught the back swing of Dodirty's hand and snatched the belt from him. "Are you crazy?" she screamed. "Don't whip my son because he don't want to fight."

Dodirty didn't want to see Kasan allowing a bully to push him around like he didn't count. "That boy can't let anybody hit him and he doesn't fight back. You know his daddy would never stand by and allow him to be a punk like that. I'm only doing what Don would do."

Dodirty bit the tip of his tongue as the last sentence escaped out of his mouth. The last name he wish he hadn't mentioned was Don's name. He knew Don's name would ignite a level of anger in Jewel which had the potential to prove fatal.

Jewel's eyes instantly filled with tears. Dodirty struck a major nerve in her. In her eyes, Don abandoned the both of them, for a life of crime which led to his death.

"He doesn't have a father," her voice dripped with menace. "His father is dead and the dead doesn't direct the living from no fuckin grave. I don't care who he left in charge."

Dodirty leaned against the threshold of the door. The last thing he wanted to do was drive all the way down here to open old wounds and make them fresh again. Sometimes it was hard for even him to accept the fact Don was dead. He now made the mistake of using the name which would cause Jewel to sink deeper into her world of depression.

Dodirty glanced at Kasan who was still crying and holding onto his mother's leg. "Why don't you let me take him for the summer? I'll have him back by September when school starts for him." He took a step closer towards Jewel. "You need some time to yourself to work through your own problems. He needs to be around a man to teach him how to be one."

Jewel sniffed back tears. She realized she needed some time to focus on herself for a change. She had to move on from the bad memories twirling around in her head. She couldn't continue to live the way she was living and do her son any good stuck in this state of mind.

She eyed Kasan. "Do you want to go with your uncle?"

Kasan hurriedly shook his head no to dispel any signs he would even consider going with Dodirty. He held onto his mother even tighter to further emphasize his point.

Dodirty rushed up into the closet and pulled down two of the biggest suitcases. "Like your daddy used to tell me, this isn't a democracy," he said to Kasan. "So your vote means nothing at this point." This caused Kasan to cry even louder, while Dodirty filled the empty suitcases with his clothes.

Dodirty snapped the last suitcase shut. "Go get into the car and carry one of your bags down."

Kasan already figured it was a lost cause to continue on with the tantrums of protest. For some odd reason, this man he hardly knew was able to dictate what his mother should and shouldn't do with regards to him. Now he wished he had hit Tony Boy back. He didn't want to be away from his mother for any period of time.

The three years he lived with his mother seemed more like a lifetime. He never had anyone else take care of him and really didn't feel the need for a father figure. He was just fine with his mother.

Kasan never received a whipping. He liked the fact he was the only child and had his mother all to himself. He didn't have a problem with how his mother treated him. He was okay with it. Many times he got his way with his mother. Jewel was convinced she wasn't helping her son by being lenient with him.

Jewel watched as Dodirty pulled out of the parking lot with her son. She didn't have any qualms over Dodirty taking him for the summer. She knew how he stood for his father on the day of his death.

Don was staring down the throat of the death penalty. If he was lucky, he would've gotten life in prison and Dodirty wouldn't let Don down in life or in death. She just yearned for the days when she would perhaps be able to forget the life and love she shared with a man she found hard to forget.

Jewel needed her heart to be able to move on from this pain nipping at her heels daily. She had to find a way to stop thinking about the love of a man who had left this earth to never return again, a man she would only be able to see in her dreams.

So she thought.

CHAPTER TEN

Dodirty took Kasan to see Carol Starchild. Since Kasan was all the way up north, Carol didn't get a chance to see him as often as she would like. She had moved into Don's mansion days after his death. After a few months of living there, she still couldn't open the hidden safe. Her recollection of the procedures of how to get it to open baffled her.

Out of nowhere, a Spanish speaking man wearing diamonds came to open the safe. Chico made sure to smile at her broadly before he left. This was to give her comfort everything was okay. He came in like he didn't speak any English, or Carol would sternly inquire how did he know to come and open the safe. He came days before the mansion was about to go into foreclosure. She never saw Chico again.

Enough money was in the safe for her to take care of herself and her grandchildren for the rest of her life. She would also be able to pay for each of them to go to the best colleges. She was beyond surprised to visually see how much money Don made from selling drugs.

By no means did she condone his illegal activities. It was the thought of his actions which counted the most. He was thinking of his family even if death was to overcome him. He just died before he was able to properly divide it up.

Dodirty beeped his horn as his Porshe edged up to the opulent mansion. When Kasan's grandmother came through the doors of the mansion, he leaped from the car and into her arms. In his young mind, if anyone could save him from Dodirty, he presumed it would be his grandmother.

"There goes my Grand-baby," Carol said kneeling down for Kasan to run into her open arms.

Carol appeared to have aged twenty years since the death of her two sons. Dodirty couldn't fathom how it felt for a woman to carry a child under her heart for nine months and have to bury the child before his time. It had to be a hurting thing for any mother, but it was happening all over America.

"Can I stay with you Grandma?" Kasan whined as he asked. His lips curled like he was about to start crying again. He forgot his tears didn't faze his Grandmother either.

Carol gave Dodirty a suspicious look. "What's my Grand- baby doing all the way up here? Where's Jewel?" She looked behind him to see if Jewel was in the car.

Dodirty ran his palm across Kasan's head. "Jewel said I can keep him for the whole summer."

Carol blinked with surprise. "For the whole summer Do?" She would always shorten his name.

Dodirty nodded. "We both agreed he needed a man in his life."

Carol pointed a stern finger at him. "You better take care of my Grandson and don't have him out in the streets all hours of the night."

"I got him Ms. Starchild. I'm putting him in karate school some-time next week to teach him how to really throw down."

Kasan cut his eye at him. This was the first time he ever heard anything about a fighting school and for some reason it caught his interest.

They stayed for an hour more as it was getting late. When Dodirty informed Kasan they were leaving, Kasan's eyes were haunted with an inner pain. All it took was for Dodirty to give him a 'you better not look.' It forced him to quickly switch up the tears to sway his Grandmother.

He was really starting to accept it was a lost cause and no need in wasting anymore tears for nothing. He had to go with this man and there was nothing he could do.

✳ ✳ ✳

As they rode the elevator up to Dodirty's place, Kasan remained silent the entire time and was looking miserable. Dodirty gazed down at him. "Don't worry about anything. You will respect me for this when you get older."

Kasan strolled into the condo and immediately went to the photos aligned along the entire wall. He saw the photos of his father. Dodirty had pictures of Don and him displayed throughout the entire house. It was the only thing to capture Kasan's undivided attention. The sight of his father removed all fear of being away from his mother. At a young age, his mind was obsessed with knowing all he could about his father.

"You knew my father?" Kasan asked. His thin eyebrows rose waiting for Dodirty to answer.

Dodirty nodded proudly. He could sense this was something consequential for Kasan. "We were like this." He crossed his fingers around each other. "I was with him until the end."

"You saw him die?"

Dodirty considered it inappropriate to discuss the death of Don with his three year old son, although he wondered if Jewel had been able to answer the questions he knew Kasan had. Did she really give him all of the details so Kasan could fully understand what happened to his father?

"I was there," Dodirty replied to lighten the mood. "How about if we go and get a bowl of ice cream." He hoped this would distract his questions.

Kasan didn't respond. This was his first time seeing the set of photos he was now studying with intensity. At home, he could spend hours gazing at pictures his mother kept around the house. She's even given him one when Don was holding him when he first came home from the hospital. Don had a huge smile on his face.

The death of his father was the first lesson learned no one could live forever. Even he had to one day die. This knowledge at a young age had the capacity to persuade him to view death on a whole other plateau. This was the major reason he was scared to fight. Somehow he knew it greatly increased his chances of meeting death.

Kasan quietly followed Dodirty into the kitchen, but the entire time, holding onto the mental image of his father's pictures. "Tell me what you know about my daddy." Kasan spoke in a child-like voice, but with the sureness and confidence of an adult male.

Dodirty carried their bowls of ice cream into the well decorated living-room. He tossed a tape into the VCR. He and Kasan sat side by side each other with their bowls on the table.

Dodirty rewound the tape to the beginning of the chase of his father. He preferred for Kasan to watch it all for himself and view it in the exact motion picture effect everyone else spoke about the day after the war.

Some may view it as being harsh and insensitive to show such a crime to a child. Not any child, but the child of Don Starchild. Dodirty figured this was a reality Kasan would soon have to face. He couldn't help it if the boy was curious.

This would be the day Kasan would come to terms with the life and death of his father. He was sitting with the man who could tell more than anybody besides his father himself. Kasan had never witnessed his father in photos with other men. In fact, Don was against taking photos with just anyone. If a man was in the photo with him, he could say he knew Don. Don didn't want that.

Dodirty's main reason for allowing Kasan to watch the tape for himself was because he didn't have the words in his limited vocabulary to make Kasan understand. Kasan didn't have to have faith his father was dead, he had to believe it. He didn't have to know his father was dead, he had to see it. This was the first step in being a man. Accepting the cruelest realities life had to offer.

When the tape was completed Dodirty had dusted off the last scoop of ice cream in his bowl while Kasan had a bowl of liquid. His eyes were stuck on watching the chase. He didn't even blink. This wasn't a cartoon, but the reality of his father's last day.

"I'm about to hop in the shower," Dodirty said. "Once I am done you will take a bath."

Kasan picked up the remote control. "Can you show me how to work this and get it to go back to the beginning?"

Dodirty showed him how to operate the remote control. Kasan rewound it back and forth. He was scrutinizing each frame like a forensic scientist. In the recess of his little mind, he was paying close attention to every detail and formulating his own conclusion. He didn't know why, but there was something compelling him to look deeper into the last day of his father's life.

Kasan was placing himself inside the car with his father. He was on the passenger side. He used one of the photos from Dodirty's wall for his father's image in the car. He was trying to grasp what his father felt for his last moments of life.

Dodirty came out of the shower and realized it was getting late. Kasan was in the middle of the tape and his finger was firmly fixed on the rewind button. He didn't appear to be the least bit sleepy. He was happily trapped in the realm of doubt and confusion. Kasan needed answers and they would only come from the tape he was watching.

While Dodirty was tucking him into bed, Kasan was asking him a million questions. Dodirty answered all of the questions as honestly as he could. The last thing he would ever do is lie to Don's son about anything.

If Kasan had enough intelligence to ask, then he found it befitting to give him the truth. It was important to properly make Kasan not only understand how Don lived, but also, how he was willing to die for the life he lived.

Dodirty was about to leave the room when Kasan called out to him. "How do they know my daddy was in the car that caught on fire." He sat up in the bed. "They thought the person shooting out the window was my father, but it was a lady."

Dodirty twisted on his heels and gave Kasan a weary half smile. It was a shocking question to come from a child his age. How was he able to analyze the situation and find fault in what adults had already accepted as real? This was a question he never considered asking. Now Dodirty found himself trapped in doubts of what he believed to be the truth. It made him wonder how did Kasan formulate the idea death was a circumstance a man had the ability to escape?

Kasan kicked his legs over the side of the bed. Dodirty stole a quick glance at him as he was reaching for the light switch. It would be far easier to try and convince him Santa Clause, or the tooth fairy was real. He shook his head in doubt and thought out why he found it to be difficult to convince Kasan his father actually died that day.

Dodirty turned off the lights in the room and said. "They saw him when he shot out of the garage."

Kasan was sitting up in his bed. His silhouette outlined in the dark room. "They only saw the car leave the house, but they couldn't see him. My mommy said they couldn't find his body in the car." He cleared his throat. "Uncle Dodirty do you think my father is still alive?"

Dodirty leaned against the wall with a tight knot in the middle of his stomach. It pained him to see and hear how Kasan wouldn't accept his father's death so easily. His young, alert mind was grasping for any scenario to deem Don to be alive.

Dodirty didn't have the slightest clue how to reply to the question posed to him by a three year old. He was more afraid of destroying any sense of hope Kasan was holding onto, but at the same time, he didn't think it was suitable to allow him to continue to believe a lie.

Dodirty departed from Kasan's room with a despairing look on his face. He didn't even try and answer. In time, he would try to find the words to explain to his nephew for him to better understand. As for now, he considered his age was the major reason to determine it was impossible for him to understand the absolute truth right now.

Kasan's words were causing him to doubt his own theories. Why was he allowing a three year old who wasn't even there to cause him to reconsider what he saw with his very own eyes?

Dodirty needed to shake the doubt boggling his brain and was starting to give him a migraine headache. For a few seconds, he thought he was slipping into a state of insanity. He had a front row seat to Don's last moment on earth. He saw when the cars crashed into each other and blew up. Had his friend been alive, he would've been the first one Don would've contacted to tell him he was alive and well.

By no means could Don make it out of that inferno. There was no way out. It all happened too fast. It was like Don wanted to die before he was sent back to prison. He could've given up, but he rammed his car into the police cars in front of him.

Out of nowhere, the thought about Chico calling him out of the blue months after Don was dead, shot through his mind. When Chico sent for him, Dodirty wondered how did he know his number. Chico reached him on a private line only Don and he would talk on.

These were the questions Kasan's doubt of his father's death was causing him to ponder, how things didn't add up. Not once did Don ever mention the connect. Dodirty hadn't met Chico until after Don died.

Dodirty now found himself troubled by the questions of a three year old. Finally, he allowed his mind to go blank and was slowly drifting off to sleep. He felt Kasan jump into his bed.

"Why didn't you answer my question?" Kasan asked. "Do you think my father is still alive?"

Dodirty rolled over with a dazed sleepy look in his eyes. "Take your ass back to bed. We can talk about this in the morning."

Kasan didn't budged. He stood as still as a statue in Central Park. His eyes were firmly fixed upon Dodirty's eyes. His defiance forced Dodirty to leap from his bed and snatch his belt from the door. He refused to tolerate Kasan's disobedience for his authority as his uncle. The respect had to start today.

Kasan raised his head to level his eyes to Dodirty's. As Dodirty raised the belt strap high in the air, Kasan took a step forward. "You can hit me, but you're still going to have to answer my question."

Dodirty blew out a stream of air and tossed the flimsy belt on the chair in the far corner of the room. "Naw, your daddy ain't dead. He lives in you."

Kasan hitched up his pajamas with a triumphant grin on his face. This was the first time anyone referred to him as his father. He truly was proud.

Dodirty noticed Kasan's smile had the ability to light up the entire room. He had a smile just like his father. Dodirty could see his friends face in his son.

Kasan strolled back to bed as if a sense of justification came from Dodirty's reply to his question. Not once did he ponder on the mentioned technicality of Dodirty's statement. Nor did he fully understand its meaning in totality, but for his name to be uttered in the same breath as his father could only mean something good.

Dodirty struggled to go back to sleep. He sat in the kitchen sipping on a cup of steaming coffee. The strong aroma was clearing away any chances of sleep. He was wide awake and in deep thought over Kasan's questions.

It wasn't just Kasan's looks which convinced him he had Don's son in his house, but his fearlessness and intelligence. These were qualities he didn't find in grown men. Kasan exemplified it without strain, or stress, a 360-degree turn from when they were in Virginia.

Dodirty went to his room and was just sitting in the dark. There was so much he had to do. He had every intention to spread out and make as much money he possibly could. His intentions were to make enough money to give to both of Don's sons so they would never have to assume the life which took their father away from this world.

Dodirty was thankful Chico continued to deal with him. Don must've spoke highly of him to Chico for him to embrace him the way he has. He was able to make triple the amount he paid and that was on the wholesale. Business was still good, but he wanted for it to be better.

A thin light entered the room from the night light in the hallway for Kasan to find his way to the bathroom. Dodirty laid perfectly still in his bed.

Dodirty gripped the handle of the gun he kept in the crease of the box spring and mattress. His gun was the only woman he allowed in his bed. It was the one thing he could trust outside of Don to protect him and now the life of his son.

Kasan pushed the door open all the way. "Are you sleeping yet uncle Dodirty?" He asked from the door.

Dodirty was seconds away from scolding him to go back to bed, but well aware of how Kasan was feeling about Dodirty being the only one to not only know his father well, but was giving him the truth of his father's life and death. He was searching for answers.

"What do you want now Kasan?"

Kasan climbed into the bed and sat on his heels and peered down at Dodirty. "Can you teach me how to be like my father?" He lowered his head. "Since you know him, you know how he was."

Dodirty closed his eyes to prevent the forming tears in his eyes from falling and making a fool out of him. "It would be my honor."

Kasan slid under the heavy quilt and went right into a deep sleep. Dodirty watched his angelic face from the glare of the night light in the hallway. He was going to have a talk with Jewel about keeping Kasan for good. He believed he owed Don that much.

Plus, he recognized great potential in Kasan. Kasan needed someone to show him the ways of a man and not just any man. The man responsible for his life on this earth.

He wanted to be like Don Starchild.

Chapter Eleven

The doctor severely warned Chico to wait until winter to make the trip to Colombia. The choked air of the tropical climate wouldn't help with his breathing. He was relying upon oxygen tanks to aid in perpetuating the flow of air in and out of his lungs. The lack of hydrogen in the air lowers the levels of oxygen. This is how all hot climates are. The sun burns hotter in those darker regions of the earth.

It appeared everyday his condition would take a turn for the worst. His once smooth skin was now harshly damaged with pock marks from the constant use of needles to inject morphine and sometimes heroin. He needed this on a daily basis to contend with the prospect of slowly losing his breath of life.

His lungs were functioning poorly, but it was imperative for him to take this trip. Chico believed the air in his body was now like a overturned time glass and the sand slowly slipping to the other side was his breath of life.

If he didn't recommend Don for his position out of his own mouth, the position would automatically be given to Armondo. This is the last thing Chico wanted to happen.

This was very important to him. He made up his mind long ago. Don Starchild was the man to lead his family. This would be history in the land of cocaine.

Although Chico was slowly dying, he still thought of his enemies waiting like vultures for him to be officially announced dead. They would try to pounce on his territory and take all he had. It was for this reason alone, he wanted to make sure they would be thoroughly destroyed, just as Don did to Pablo in one night. Chico certainly knew Armondo could never do this in a million years.

Don was entirely cut from a different fabric then any man he has ever known. Chico knew Don's name would ring as soon as he is placed on the throne. He would expand the kingdom to supersede any dynasty of the drug game.

Chico also wanted revenge. He wanted his enemies to be as dead as he would soon be. It exhilarated him knowing they would soon retire to their very own graves soon after he would, if not sooner. Don knew how to make this death dream a potent reality.

Don was the only man qualified to do his bidding under the Dragon Cartel. It was the demise of Pablo, which showed Don could accomplish this task by any means necessary.

Thus far, Don was controlling a good part of the everyday operations of the family. Not once did he try to advocate for new laws into its already functioning curriculum. He made sure to pay close attention to how Chico ran things and the customers and every known drug trafficker in America. He made mental notes of the things he had every intention of revising with the use of intelligence and bloodshed.

Even Chico knew Don would eventually do it his own way. Don was showing the greatest respect and allowing him to maintain the crux of his power until he finally passed on the ring of power to him. It was the highest regard Don could openly display for his friend.

As they rode the plane to Colombia, Don made sure to sit next to Chico. By the derisive smile daily on Armondo's face, Don knew he was going to argue his point to the other half of the power.

Don believed stepping on Colombian soil was putting himself not only at great risk, but a particular disadvantage. He would've felt comfortable for the meeting to take place on American soil.

By all means, he was outnumbered in a land not his own. Not even America was his home, but it would be far safer than here.

The color of his skin was another mitigating factor unjustly planted against him.

Don knew the business like the back of his hand. If anything, he should be rewarded with the connection to the motherland of cocaine and be fronted one thousand kilo's of cocaine and heroin, to build a family of his own.

On the other hand, he knew too much and he really was never to rise above the level of a customer. This would give the other side more than enough reason to prevent him from ever stepping on American soil again. It would mean a bullet in his head and there was nothing Chico could do about it. He was too weak to even breath on his own. His days were numbered.

The thoughts of danger lurking in the shadows forced him to keep his thoughts all to himself. No one could tell in his demeanor he was the least bit fazed by what could happen. Never would he show any signs of weakness under these circumstances. His only presentation at this point was of strength and confidence. There was no need for him to internally debate over the things he had no real control over. The only thing he had unlimited control over was himself and the sure death of anyone who threatens his life.

He didn't want to block his mind with doubts to interfere with him making the most rational decisions he would need to make at a second's notice. He would have to make decisions he would have to live or die with for the rest of his life. His main objective at this point was to make it back home alive. Any seemly unfortunate situation making him feel uncomfortable, he had every intention of dealing with it accordingly.

"We're here." Don said as the private jet slowly circled the runway of the airport's landing strip.

The plane landed in Colombia and a fleet of long, black limousines were waiting in front of the airport's terminal. It was hot in the States, but this heat was blistering compared to anywhere else in the world.

Don removed his parachute and left it on the plane. He didn't need it unless he was up in the air. He rushed out of his suit jacket which felt like a mink coat. He slackened the knot in his tie to release the heat from around his neck and opened the first three buttons on his shirt.

"Why don't you still have your parachute on?" Chico joked from behind the mask. This caused the other men to laugh also, but none had the nerve to ask Don the questions Chico would say openly.

Don grinned a grin of confidence. "Because I am not up in the air."

"Don't tell me you're scared of flying Don?"

Don wheeled Chico to the awaiting car. "Fear keeps a man alive when he listens to it. It alerts his senses to his surroundings for the sake of protecting himself against unknown circumstances." Don glanced over at Armondo, "and so-called unknown dangers."

His gray eyes became intense and focused. He placed Chico into the car and tucked his wheelchair into the trunk. "I just don't allow my enemy to control my fear. I don't allow it to handicap me and turn me into a yellow back coward. It affects me differently Chico. It allows for me to prepare for the unknown dangers."

Don grinned at Chico when he knew he was soaking up the things he was saying. "I will kill a thousand men in order to place fear into one. I place all my fears into my enemies. Therefore, my victories aren't always gained by the numbers I kill, but by the numbers I frighten."

Chico released a wheezy laugh from behind the mask. "I'm so glad I've never met you as my enemy, but as my friend." He cleared the heavy build up of mucus from his throat and spit it into a napkin. "Would you have pulled the trigger the day of the festival?" The memory always haunted Chico to this very day.

Don glanced out of the window and then back at Chico. He knew this question meant something to him. It was the only time Don showed any signs of aggression towards his safety.

"No," Don replied with a warm smile. "I wouldn't have pulled the trigger. I could never hurt you, Chico."

Chico knew Don was lying, because of the statement he had just made. Don did the exact thing to him when he was merely a child.

He had frightened Chico. This was another reason he wanted Don to take his place. Don was prepared to go down the darkest road.

"So why do you wear the parachute?" Chico asked.

Don continued to stare out of the window at the sight of everyone in the other cars who were in their homeland. He was the only one in the car not born here. This was his first time here. He saw male and female peasants walking with sacks of coca leaves on their backs, along dirt roads. Never could he see such a sight in America.

"I had a dream I fell out of a plane," Don said softly. He knew no one would understand his dreams. He didn't even understand them.

"A dream?" Chico asked surprised. "You see you didn't fall out of the plane. You are just paranoid."

Don laughed to make light of his dreams. "I've learned it is far better to prepare for war in the time of peace. I had a dream I fell out of a plane and I don't know if I was going to, or coming back from Colombia." Don felt the blood in his body elevating his pulse and caused it to roar in his ears. It was the thought he had to fly back home which troubled him.

"I fell Chico. I was either coming from Colombia, or going to Colombia." He grabbed Chico by his wrist to further emphasize his point. "I just don't know if I died or not."

CHAPTER TWELVE

Colombia was in the North West of South America; a land of mountains and tropical lowlands. It has vast uninhabited areas. The varying terrain has been partially responsible for regional tensions. An estimated 25,000 were killed as the volcano Nevado Del Ruiz, 135 miles NW of Bogota the capital, erupted sending raging waters and a sea of mud through surrounding valleys and obliterating entire villages.

The Andes, with peaks of nearly 19,000 ft. (5,795 m), cover the NW third of the country and provide coal, platinum, and petroleum. Coffee from the mountains accounts for about 50% of the export sales. Between the mountains and the equatorial lowlands, grassy plains provide good beef-cattle lands. Sugar- cane, cotton, tobacco, bananas and coca grow well in Colombia.

Some 60% of Colombians are mixed White and Indian blood, and many of these mestizos take active part in public life. Another 20% of the population is of European descent, while Indians, Blacks, and Mulattoes make up the remaining 20%. In the 20th century, people have moved to the cities, and about 70% of the population live in urban areas. Spanish is the official language, and Roman Catholicism is the country's religion. About 12% of the people are illiterate.

The constitution calls for a president, who cannot succeed himself, a senate, and a chamber of representatives. The liberal and conservative parties are the most powerful.

The conservatives won the election, but the liberals returned. They were faced with increasing terrorism and drug related murders by the country's powerful drug gangs, which supply some 90% of the world's cocaine.

Drug trafficking has infiltrated Colombian politics to the extent that drug cartels often pressure or threaten political power and control, as has been evidenced by numerous assassinations of government figures and journalist. The assassination of a presidential candidate in August prompted a sweeping crack- down on cartel activity.

Colombia renewed its policy of extraditing criminals to the United States, and in response the drug cartels declared "total war" on the Colombian government. The crackdown has led to widespread violence and numerous threats to the government figures which resulted in several resignations of officials in high positions.

Don had an eerie feeling about being here in this nearly lawless place. If death intended to be the end result of the trip, he had his guns to make sure he had a fighting chance.

It didn't take a rocket scientist to know Armondo would try for revenge the second he could get the other half of the family to side with him. Chico would be solely too weak to prevent anything from happening. Don was starting to wish he was anywhere in the world right now but here. He came here because Chico wanted him to be, not because he weighed it was in his best interest. As he added and subtracted, this entire situation didn't tally in his favor.

The cars were initially spotless when they first left the airport, but were now covered in thick dust from the unpaved streets. Don observed the field workers in the field with straw hats tending to bushels of coca leaves. There were more coca fields than anything else. He wondered how much were the field workers paid for their long hours tending to the fields, compared to the profits of the end results of their labor?

"So this is where it all starts?" Don asked Chico.

Chico slid the oxygen mask to one side of his face so he could speak. "These are our fields. We have a big factory for mass production to process the leaves into liquid and then powder."

Don felt a rush of heat to his face. "So the hardest part is exporting it to different countries?"

"That's where the competition comes in. Whichever family is able to successfully get the largest shipment through any of the borders, can control the price. There are times when we are the only ones with product. I have routes I have flown for years to get in."

Don nodded. "Its not about one way."

"I have routes nobody used. I have been the only one to fly them. That is why the price of cocaine goes up and down like the stock market on Wall Street." Chico made a strong attempt to laugh at his own joke, but erupted into a spasm of coughs.

Don quickly placed the oxygen mask over his mouth. "Save your strength, I'll find out everything I need to know about this place sooner or later."

After a three hours drive through the hills and desolate mountain areas, they finally turned off to another dirt road which led to a castle the size of a New York city block.

Horses and many other tamed animals roamed freely on the innumerable acres of land. The mansion was built like a Gothic castle of ancient times. The polygonal towers were bounded by straight lines, bay windows, balconies and richly decorated woodwork. The building materials used were modernized, but completed the image.

A central air system the size of a huge generator was responsible for keeping the entire castle as cool as the North Pole.

A slim man with a hawk nose and beady black eyes came to great them. He was small in stature, but carried himself with an extreme air of supreme power. He bent down to glance searchingly into each car as it went past him. There were guards posted all around him and throughout the acres of land.

He snatched open the door of the car Don and Chico were riding in. He fell inside of the car and into Chico's lap. "Mi hermano! Mi hermano!" My brother he continued to exclaim over and over.

Don's eyes widened and he gave a startled gasp. This was Chico's brother. He slowly began to somewhat relax. Chico never told him the other half of the family was his oldest brother. Don wondered if this would mean things would be all right after all. Although now he felt he had a greater chance, he still made sure he had a bullet in each chamber of his guns. He refused to allow his feelings and emotions to overcome his reason and logic. Don was far from anybody's fool.

Chico held his hand out to his brother to help him out of the car. His brother was overly devastated by the sight of his sickly brother.

"I told you I would make it Fuentes." Chico's words were faint and now close to a whisper.

Fuentes embraced everyone as they exited the other cars and came up to greet him, except for Don. He made a head motion towards Chico.

"Who is this?" He spoke in Spanish and the tone of his voice was very business-like. A sneaky grin found its way to the corners of Armondo's mouth. He was positive Fuentes already developed a mistrust for Don. Don was the darkest man standing amongst the Colombians.

Chico never mentioned Don to his brother, nor did he suitably prepare him for the pivotal reason of why he was here. Also, as to why Don accompanied him on this trip. He knew Fuentes had the potential to be excessively arrogant. It would be for the best to execute this argument face to face. Fuentes lived like an honorable king in this poor country. This is what caused him to be very insensitive to the feelings of others around him.

Chico was gasping for air, so one of the other bodyguards named Hector replied for him in Spanish.

Fuentes gave Don a once over and turned towards Chico. "Is this a nigger?" he asked pointing past Don.

Don was standing on the side of Chico's chair. The expression on his face was blank as if he didn't have a clue of what was said about him in a foreign tongue.

Don stared adoringly at Fuentes before he took a step towards him with his hand extended and said in perfect Spanish. "My name is Don Starchild, and you're Jose Fuentes?" Don recalled Chico used his name in one of their past conversations.

Fuentes glanced down at Chico in astonishment. He was beyond surprised to hear a Black man from America speak with such a swift Colombian dialect.

As he was turning his head towards Don to acknowledge him, Don hit him with a sturdy gut shot, knocking every drop of air out of his lungs. The brawny blow accelerated Fuentes's heartbeat and through necessity he crumbled to the ground gasping for the much needed air, while his body locked into a fetal position.

Don took a few steps and was now standing directly over Fuentes. Out of nowhere, Armondo had the audacity to snatch his gun from his waist. His teeth gritted and his face lit with bitter triumph.

This was his chance.

In one swift motion, Don spun around and dropped to one knee and drew his gun. He shot Armondo one time in the neck to quickly disable any chances for surviving. He snatched his other gun out of the holster and shot him in the heart and than the center of his forehead. This was to remove any subconscious thought for him to be able to pull the trigger. His last shot caused Armondo's head to split apart from his eyebrows on up. The other bodyguards went for their guns.

Don extended both arms with his guns pointed down the line of men. "Here we go." Don's voice was thick with insinuation. "Now what's it going to be." His gray eyes was filled with every bit of murder. He ground his words between clenched teeth. "Anyone of you pull your guns in defense of this piece of shit better not miss, or you will all be in hell ten seconds before your body hits the motherfuckin ground. Now play the game spic niggas!"

Don regarded each of the men with cold speculation. This was to give them a clear view of hell in his eyes. His breathing was shallow and his eyes scanned over each of them for the slightest movement. He was prepared to fire upon them at will. Don was ready to kill.

Chico studied Don from the seat of his wheelchair. It surprised him to see Don buried deep within the confines of his gangster element.

Fuentes men ran from the fields, Don snatched open his shirt and displayed the clips around his waist for easy access and said to

Chico. "It is whatever the fuck it is! Kill or be killed. I'm ready. Bring it!" He spoke in Spanish and his voice was as cold as death.

Don hurriedly moved away from Chico and stood out in the opening alone, but as if he had an army of a thousand men standing with him. His confidence was extreme. "Here I go. Act like you want to do something and see what I'm going to do." Don studied each of the men to mentally disarm them with his confidence.

Chico raised his hand for his men to relax. He had no control over Fuentes' men. Don noticed how quick they were to take Armondo's side. He wasn't going to wait to see if Armondo was going to shoot or not. He acted like he was and for that reason, Don killed him.

Don wasn't taking any chances with the only life God gave him. He would rather be judged by twelve, than to be carried by six. It was always kill first and ask questions last.

Fuentes finally got a gush of air into his lungs. He waved his men away still holding his stomach. He slowly rose upright. He still felt the full effects of Don's punch, but grateful not to have felt the full effects of his bullets.

"So you speak our language?" Fuentes asked in Spanish.

Fuentes now wore a tight smile on his face. He could have had his men fire on Don with the hopes he wouldn't be able to stand up to the many bullets fired his way, but his eyes were filled with a profound respect for this Black man before him. Don stood up to every gun like a stone cold general leading an army of men into war.

There was no fear, but Chico knew better. This was the discussion he and Don had at the airport. Don placed his fear into each of the men. The death of Armondo meant he was serious about killing. He wasn't going to tell them he would kill, he had to show them, for them to fully understand he meant business. No one wanted to touch their guns. It would introduce them to an immediate confrontation, which had full potential to lead to death.

"Very well," Don replied when each of the men hands went to their sides. His guns were still in his hands and ready to fire. "So you will have to find another language to call me outside of my name, and if I so happen to discover its meaning, then we shall relive this moment a thousand times." He spoke in perfect Spanish the way Bonita taught him.

Chico's raspy chuckle was muffled by the oxygen mask. He told Don to just be himself and Don was taking his advice. He hated to see Armondo lying on the ground dead, but he warned them both to never act like they were about to do harm to anyone in the family after the day in the hospital room. It was their rule of thumb. Armondo was going to use the fact Don hit Fuentes to justify his reason for killing Don. Don just beat him to the punch.

Fuentes ambled over to where Armondo was lying. The blood gushing out of his neck was making bubbling sounds. The blood coming out of his head was spewing onto the ground with chunks of gray matter.

Fuentes had known Armondo's family since they were children and it pained him to see him lying on the ground dead. He glanced over at Don who still held each of the men in his stare. He was waiting for this matter to reach its conclusion before he would consider putting his guns away. As for now, he was on point.

Fuentes bent down to take a better look at Armondo. He swatted away the flies rushing through the air at the first scent of blood and sadly shook his head. The feeling of Armondo being dead had long passed. For all he knew, it could've been him on the ground dead. He believed the Black man Chico unexpectedly brought with him was professionally capable of killing without second thought.

"Take him to the fields and bury him," Fuentes ordered his men.

As they carried Armondo's body out to the fields, they occasionally glanced over their shoulders at the Black man still holding his guns in his hands and were thankful they weren't asked to try and kill him. There was something evil about the man. It was his eyes which really made them think he was a man possessed by evil spirits. There was a prophecy of a man like him. He had gray eyes.

Don heard the drums in his ears go silent. He placed both of his guns into his holster. Don glanced down at the sight of Armondo's blood.

"I thirst," he said smiling.

CHAPTER THIRTEEN

Everyone trailed behind Fuentes as he went into the castle. The men who came with Chico and Don were deeply surprised at how their trip took a turn for the worst with the potential to be far more deadly in the next few seconds of their confrontation with Don.

Fuentes made sure to pay close attention. As they all walked into the castle, he would peer at Don from out of the corner of his eye. The way he shot and killed Armondo and thoroughly held his ground against the other guns made him wonder if his brother brought a deranged lunatic along for the ride.

Fuentes didn't sense a dram of fear from the man walking on the side of him pushing Chico. This has never happened to him in his lifetime. The only killing to ever happen on his land was when he gave the order. This was the second sign of disrespect from the man. Fuentes couldn't believe Don hit him.

Don's punch brought him to reality of the days when he was poor and didn't have money, or power. He made a mental note to be more mindful of the things he said and did. He didn't think Don spoke Spanish. For all he knew, the bullet Armondo took could've easily had his blood on it.

Don gasped at the sight of the inside of the castle. An elephantine fish tank full of baby sharks trailed one side of the entire room. There was a wired cage on top of the tank full of live rats. Don reached into the cage and removed a rat by its tail and held it over the aqua colored tank. The rat struggled as if it knew its fate and had no intention of going peacefully.

He dropped the rat into the center of the tank. The sharks circled around the struggling rat knowing it had nowhere to go, because it was out of it's element. Once the rat finally stopped kicking its legs and accepted its fate, the sharks attacked its flesh from every side and tore the rat into pieces. They maneuvered in for a group attack as if they were hunters in the Atlantic Ocean.

Don learned a very particular lesson from his observation of nature's hunters and knew he had to always be the hunter and never the prey. A hunter will never lay the same trap for the wolf as he would for the fox. He never sets bait where his prey will never take it. He must know his prey thoroughly. Its habits and hideaways and this is how he must set his hunt for his prey according to its greatest weakness.

Fuentes watched as Don fondly fed the sharks, and became excited by their vicious attack on the rat. His gray eyes widened when the blood filled the water like a puff of smoke. Fuentes never had the stomach to watch them devour their live food. He felt his cheeks suddenly bloat as if he was about to throw up by watching Don exhaustively enjoy himself.

Fuentes liked the way shark meat tasted on his plate with beans and rice. He would raise them in the small tanks until they outgrew them. He would then place them in the manmade lake he had out back to grow to their full potential. Many times he would feed his sharks human meat as a treat.

"Don," Fuentes called to get Don's attention.

Don faced him with a blissful smile still planted on his face. "I like the sharks, Fuentes," Don said in Spanish. He sat down next to Chico and bit Chico on his shoulder. "That is how you eat your enemy. The rat knew it was gravely defeated as soon as it hit the water. It was in fear of drowning, but the sharks took care of that moments before it drowned by killing it."

Don hit his chest proudly. "An enemy must confess defeat from the bottom of their heart, not with words, but always with their lives." He pointed two fingers towards his eyes. "Your victory can only come from when you see this defeat in their eyes and know what is in their heart and soul." He glanced over at Fuentes with a stern look. "I'm going to get me a tank to further my study of them. The only way to become a sufficient hunter is to study the tactics of all hunters," he said to Chico.

Chico patted Don's hand. "First things first."

Fuentes cleared his throat to get Don's attention. "Don did you know who I was when you hit me?" He wanted to make sure Don didn't hit him out of impulse. This was to know if he would ever respect his position of authority."

Don flashed a grin of superiority and spoke in Spanish. "I knew exactly who you were and are. Does that give you the right to ever disrespect me as a man and call me by a name forced upon my people. My people have been defending themselves against the meaning of that word for centuries and have died as the word being the last word they heard before death claimed them. I am willing to carry on the tradition and also die if need be."

Don warmed his smile. "Your wrongs have been altogether forgiven, but if you continue in your contempt and disrespect of Don Starchild as a man, most importantly a Black man, then we shall relive this moment a thousand times until we get it right." He winked at Fuentes with a broad smile. "Entiendo?" (Understand)

Fuentes smiled at Don's choice of words. "If I turn my head and look away while you speak, I would swear I was speaking with a born and bred Colombian. Your Spanish is equal to mine, if not better."

Don placed his arm around Chico's frail shoulders. "Your brother taught me everything I know."

Chico slipped his mask to one side of his mouth. "He's only flattering me Jose. He's made millions of dollars on his own and learned how to speak the language with the help of his fiancee." He coughed into his fist. "I've known him since he was a child." Chico placed the mask over his mouth and closed his eyes and began to breath deeply. "I want for Don to take my place and run the family in the states."

Fuentes eyes filled with dark portents. "No disrespect to you Don, but we've never allowed any man who wasn't of Colombian blood to head our family in any shape, form, or fashion. It has nothing to do with you being Black, because we have Blacks who live here."

"Save the lies, Fuentes," Don said quickly. "It has everything to do with Black. I know Columbians can be as racist as an American White. We can barely buy directly from you, but Chico and I are friends and he asked this of me." Don tapped Chico on the chin. "I don't know what he sees in me, but I agreed since he's done so much for me. I didn't want to let him down and this is why I flew all the way over here with a parachute on my back."

Chico sat upright in his chair. He removed the newspaper clippings of the police killed in the city of Newark New Jersey, as well as the murderous clippings from the Miami Herald of the men Don destroyed at Pablo's mansion.

Fuentes eyed each of the clippings skeptically. "He did all of this by himself and is standing here without a scar?" Fuentes brows shot up with surprise.

Fuentes continued to read the clippings in their entirety like a archaeologist examining an archive which led to an ancient city in the Andes, occasionally, glancing up into Don's quiet gray eyes in total disbelief of what he was reading.

The man responsible for all he was reading was sitting in front of him as calm as ever. It was easy to just kill a man, but from the clippings, Don went against the odds. Not once, but twice and probably many times yet to be reported.

Fuentes handed the clippings back to Chico and said to Don. "They believe you're dead?" He took a deep breath with his forehead crinkled in thought. He removed a cigar from a gold plated box on his coffee table. He handed a cigar to Don, but he preferred his Cuban.

Chico suddenly began to excessively cough as if the cigars from both men were effecting his breathing. He continued to repeatedly cough even though Don turned the air up, it still didn't help.

Don snatched Chico up into his arms. "He needs to lie down for awhile."

Fuentes poured drinks for them both. Don laid Chico to bed and quickly returned. Since they were now alone, Fuentes wanted to see if Don was also a thinker and not just a doer. The politics of the family not only relied on ones ability to kill, but in making the money which was the essential fuel which has driven the family for years.

Fuentes re-lit his cigar. The two aromas from each cigar twirled around the room and created a sweet fragrance of its own.

"What would you change about the business of the family if you were to be appointed to my little brothers position?"

Don stared at Fuentes for a long moment in thought. "Every thing." He finally said, "I believe the methods now used are completely outdated and should be yesterday's trash. We should be striving for it all."

Fuentes swayed his hands in the air as a gesture. "Meaning?"

Don scooted to the edge of his seat. "There are a lot of people you allow to get in the way. They continue to fumble and make the most important aspects of the business harder for everyone involved; especially with the major air, water and ground routes to smuggle in the drugs. They're getting busted with a measly five and six hundred kilo's of cocaine and heroin. Now customs learn of these routes and watch them for any signs of activity. I will cultivate new, air, water and land routes to get the larger shipments through unmolested and use the ones they know as dummies."

"How would you be able to put something of that magnitude together?"

Don pulled on the cigar and watched as the tip lit up. He blew out a flux of thick white smoke. "I have my ways," he replied sharply, crossing his legs.

Fuentes shook his head greenly. "There would be no cooperation amongst the other families. It sounds impossible."

"Nothing is impossible no matter how improbable it may seem." Don tapped the ash into the oversized crystal ashtray. "Colombia is responsible for ninety percent of the cocaine in the world. No other country makes this stuff, which means Colombia wholesales the ten percent to the Mexican cartels to make money on the routes they know. I would make sure the Dragon cartel is at least accountable for no less than eighty-five percent of the demand around the world. So what if a few make it past us, we will corner the game to the point we wouldn't even miss it."

Fuentes crossed his legs in doubt. "They would never go for it. It would start a war right here in Colombia and the States."

Don waved his finger to say no. "Naturally, but once the ground work is laid in America first, it will be the war to end all wars and give the Dragon cartel a chance to completely monopolize the entire drug trade as we know it."

Fuentes chuckled. "Do you really believe in your mind you can pull something off that big?"

"Lessons not learned through bloodshed and violence are easily forgotten Fuentes." Don's gray eyes became cold. "The law which needs to be laid down is murder." He dropped some more ash into the ashtray. "The one who wins is not necessarily the strongest, but the one who strikes first and can maneuver the prey into a element different to what they are use to. Anyone we think might oppose this new structure must be eliminated." Don sat his cigar down. "Its not personal. Murder is the universal language throughout this entire earth. We just have to be extremely brutal in order to be successful."

"What about my friends?"

"What about them?" Don laughed shortly. "If they are your friends then you really need to get rid of them. There is no such thing as friendship in our line of work. If you believe so, then you would be better off turning them into your enemies. They would prove to be more reliable and even more trustworthy, and work ten times harder as your enemy to try and win your loyalty and trust. Word is bond."

Fuentes squinted his eyes. "Now I see what Chico is talking about with regards to you and how you do things. How do you think you can accomplish something like this? I just can't see it happening."

Don strolled over to the tank and removed another trembling rat from the wire cage and dropped it into the water. He watched as the sharks repeated the identical ritual as before.

"We apply the laws of nature to our politics and we hunt our prey that is in the way of what we are striving for."

The sharks tore into the rat and devoured every morsel of flesh before Don walked away and went back to his seat with a murdering gleam in his eyes. This evil look was starting to excite Fuentes. Although he didn't have a clue of exactly what Don was referring to, he doubted it would even be possible. He was just enjoying their conversation. It was original.

"So we hunt?" Fuentes repeated jokingly.

Don nodded his head yes and stared into Fuentes eyes. "Before we become the prey of another man's hunt. We can never underestimate our enemy and think we are the first to come up with this idea. We have to be the first to do it."

Don slid all the way back in the plush chair. "I don't have an ounce of loyalty with the ones you've climbed trees with for bananas in the years of your youth. I only pledge my allegiance to the Dragon cartel." Don sauntered over to Fuentes and took his hand and kissed his ring and silently farted.

"What's that smell?" Fuentes asked with his nose wrinkled.

"I don't know," Don said smiling.

CHAPTER FOURTEEN

Don remained in Colombia until Chico finally took his last breath. There was no major need to bring him all the way back to the states, just to ship his body back once he died.

Don now wore the ring Fuentes had given him. This was a sign of his leadership of the family. Chico removed his ring seconds before he had taken his last breath and gave it to Don. This was a gesture of friendship and for Don to carry on his memory.

Don immediately noticed the difference in the demeanor of the men who had come along with him. They spoke to him with a high degree of respect and verbally displayed their loyalty to the one wearing the ring.

Instead of Don flying back to Miami with the rest of the men, he chartered a flight to Barbados. There was no time like right now to pay a visit to his friend. It has been a long time since he last spoke with Cecil.

Even when the world presumed Don to be dead, he made sure to religiously mail Cecil's monthly check like he promised. This was for him to be able to live on and stay under the radar.

The island was as beautiful and majestic as Don had long ago anticipated. Cecil was able to stay under detection because he could easily pass for an islander. His rich black skin was darker than most of the people who lived on the island all of their lives.

Cecil wore a bright yellow hard hat, a pair of jeans and work-boots.

A form fitted, tank top clung to his muscles as they rippled through his black skin.

Cecil was so busy giving orders to the construction workers he hired to help make additions to his house, he didn't see Don making his way in his direction.

Don politely took a hard hat from one of the workers closes to him. He strolled over to Cecil and stood behind him like a shadow. Cecil didn't notice Don standing behind him until he heard the familiar voice he thought he would never hear again.

"I see you found your niche over here."

Cecil slowly turned around to the sound behind him. A surge of elation shot through his entire body all at once. As his raven black eyes focused on his friend, he could do nothing but fall to his knees in shock and disbelief.

Cecil's smile broadened and for once the sadness that once plagued him was replaced with hope. It was so powerful, it burst through his body like a bullet ricocheting inside of a metal room.

It took faith for him to believe his lying eyes. It was hard, but he was starting to accept his friend as being dead. In matter of seconds, he wondered if the man standing in front of him was merely a ghost, or a figment of his sick imagination.

A huge satellite dish occupied the front yard and was able to pick up every channel in the world. Although he didn't watch the live chase, he caught the repeat of it and it hurt as if it was actually happening live. Like everyone else in the world, he thought his friend was dead and gone. Guilt captured his conscience every month his monthly check still landed in his PO Box.

Cecil leaped to his feet and gave his friend a vigorous hug. He picked Don up off his feet like he weighed next to nothing. Cecil hasn't been this happy since . . .

Never.

There was nothing on this earth to equal seeing his friend was alive and kicking. Don had once again beaten the powers that be at their own game. Don did it when he freed Cecil and again when the world thought he was dead.

Slowly, Cecil began to come to grips with his friend actually standing before him. He owed Don not only his freedom but his life. The question he asked himself in the first few minutes of him coming to grips with Don standing before him, was why was he here?

"I thought you were dead," Cecil said wiping the tears from his eyes. "I watched it on TV and it looked like you died."

"I was dead to you until today," Don replied with a playful humor. "I was resurrected to come and see how my brother was getting by out here in paradise." Don took a look inside of Cecil's well furnished home. "I see you're living like a King over here like I said you would when I sent you."

Cecil's smile broadened. "Your money and my entrepreneurial investments made all of this happen for the kid."

Don's eyes scanned the house. "Where's the lady of the house and the babies?"

"There is none," he answered removing his hard hat from his head and wiping the beads of sweat from his brow with his forearm. "I didn't want to make a life over here. After I saw you were dead, I was planning on coming back to the States."

"For what?"

Cecil shrugged his shoulders nonchalantly. "I still feel like I'm in prison, but I have just a few extra privileges to do just a little more. I'm tired of running and hiding." Cecil held out his hands in front of him. "According to these." He rubbed his fingertips together. "I'm not who I am. I just have the same face. I want to come home."

Don nodded accepting how his friend was feeling. He too was on the run, but didn't leave the country to hide. The reason he picked the island was because they spoke English. It was to make it easy for Cecil. He wouldn't want to be far away from the land he knew best. It would be hard to adjust.

"That's why I am here," Don said with a smile as he was slowly letting the cat out of the bag. "I have claimed a bigger plan then you could ever imagine." Don thoroughly informed him of all the details of what had just taken place in Colombia and the major connections he now had at his disposal.

Cecil's raven colored eyes sparkled. "That's a big responsibility."

Don thumbed the tip of his nose and wiped the tiny particles of dust from his slacks. "This is about to be the pinnacle of what every street hustler craves for in the game. I wanted this the day I sold my first joint for two dollars. This is it."

"I guess Dodirty is going bananas at how far in the game ya'll done made it to."

"He doesn't know." Don glanced away at the tropical setting of the backdrop of the rest of the house. There were wild fruits hanging from the trees just waiting to be picked. He faced Cecil. "You're the only one who knows anything about me being alive. I haven't been to Newark since all of this shit happened."

Cecil cleared his throat and mildly nodded his head. "Looks like we're in the same boat at this point, huh?"

"This is why I need you to come back with me." Don placed both hands firmly on Cecil's shoulders. "I need someone I can really trust. I'm the only nigga on my own team and the rest are Colombians. In case they turn on me, I would like to have a extra set of eyes and ears to watch my back."

Cecil wiped his grungy hands on his pants and held his hand out to Don. "You know you can count me in. I already owe you more than I can ever pay you right now." His brows came together and for the first time he regarded his friend with suspicion. "What's up with the strange accent?"

Don released a raspy chuckle. "I tend to speak more Spanish than English nowadays. I can't help it when I roll my R's when I speak English."

"I guess it would be wise for me to learn it too?"

"Knowledge is always wise to have as a weapon in your arsenal. Ignorance is not a defense in life." Don grinned. "Get yourself a Spanish woman and she'll teach you everything you need to know."

Cecil smiled spastically. "When do you want me to pack?"

Don rubbed his hands together in thought. "I am planning a party for my election to the highest office of the Dragon cartel. It would only be right to have you there." He smiled at the excitement in Cecil's eyes. "Do you still know how to shoot a gun?"

Cecil rushed into the house and came back with a rifle and a pair of high tech, night vision goggles. "It's pitch black around here at night and these will help you see in the night like it is daytime. I like to practice shooting at night."

Don examined the goggles. "Do you have another pair of these?"

"Brand new in the house."

"I think these would go well with the outfits I have for us to wear."

Don had sent a open invitation to all of the major traffickers to a party he was having tomorrow night. It was all in the name of Chico's death. This was to inform the other families he was now running the Dragon cartel.

Hector took Armondo's place and was adamantly against a meeting of such. He warned Don several times it wouldn't be a good idea. The other traffickers intentions would be to try and get rid of the Dragon cartel.

Hector told him it wouldn't be wise to even be in the same building with these men. Death could come to Don from any direction and every man in the room would be considered the number one suspect. Each of them would have a reason to want Don dead and out of the way; just as they wanted Chico, but he had certain alliances which prevented his demise. All bets were now off and the Dragon cartel stood alone now that Chico was dead.

Not once did Don show any concerns for Hector's reservations about the party and the invitations he sent out to the awaiting vultures. As long as he kept his eyes on everything and everybody, he would be safe. He now had Cecil to watch his back which counted for a lot. Don recalled the days when they were down in Trenton and had done battle with a group of prisoners. Don and Cecil didn't even have weapons, but since Don wanted to continue to fight, Cecil stayed by his side.

Don only needed one he could trust and he had that in Cecil. He understood the genuine concerns of Hector. Don was inviting the vultures into his midst. In the jungle vultures have it the easiest. The hard work of the hunt of others becomes their nourishment. Hector knew they were plotting for the free meal. Don wasn't worried the least bit and everyone wanted to know why.

Don found no need to explain the vision he had for the family. There was no need to appease the doubt and misunderstandings stuck within the confines of their limited intelligence. He didn't need everyone to know what he knew. These methods were the strategic ways of a leader paying close attention to those looking for the free lunch. He would make sure it was laced with violent poison.

They wanted the throne Don was sitting on and he wasn't impressed by the seat he was sitting on. It was of no use if he didn't have the respect and power to go along with it. His intention was one of power and how to outright dominate every inch of the spectrum of those competing against him.

Unlike his past mistakes in dealing with Sosa, he intended to deal with them in a manner of utter deception to win them over. This is what is meant by keeping your enemies close. He had a banquet prepared in their honor.

Death would be his final agreement with any of his enemies who had an inkling he would allow them to take anything that didn't belong to them.

Death would be the only reward for any who try.

Chapter Fifteen

The grandiosity of the ballroom superseded any in the country. The design was comparable to a classical hacienda. Luxuriant chandeliers were properly spaced throughout the oval ballroom. Corinthian wood-columned portico, along with foliate carved doors were at the entrance. Imported cedar from Lebanon had been thoroughly polished and trailed throughout the entire ballroom. It was named 'Una Muerta Bonita.' (A Beautiful Death)

As each of the men entered the ballroom, they were searched and politely asked to surrender their weapons. This was supposed to be a peaceful gathering for each of the men to reach a final agreement on how business was to be done from here on out. Every man complied out of his own interest.

Hector wore a flowered shirt and slacks. His thin frame was far from intimidating to the men as they sauntered through the door. Don made him the supervisor of this event since he knew the majority of the men by face.

Hector would check their names off the list Don gave him. The entire time he would give a sidelong glance at each of the men as they entered the main entrance of the building. To him this was a bad idea, an unheard of gesture.

Hector was wondering why was Don doing everything Chico would never do. Some of the men making their way into the ballroom had not only been Chico's lifetime enemies, but were his greatest competition. He was convinced Don didn't have an ideas of what he was up against. If he showed any sign of weakness, it could cause a cataclysm of problems for the rest of the family with the final conclusion being total annihilation of the Dragon cartel in America.

Don made sure to secure another room down the hall from the main ballroom. Inside of the other room were four major drug lords. Don separated them from the group as they were coming through the front entrance.

All of the men attending today's event were chauffeured in by a fleet of limousines courtesy of Don. This method was to prevent a heavy build up of cars in front of the building. This meeting was by invitation only, and none of the men knew the real gist of why they were here.

An extravagant table of Spanish food was being offered to the guest. The bar was stocked with all sorts of wines and champagnes. The mood was being set to relax the guest.

A song by Celia Cruz was blaring from the four speakers in each of the corners of the ballroom. A group of men were dancing Salsa as if they had a lovely Spanish woman in their arms, twirling around the dance floor with their eyes closed.

The music and the sweet aroma of the food calmed any of the men who was initially wary of the invitation sent to them. They heard of Chico's death and believed this day was more of a celebration than . . .

The lights in the ballroom were dimmed. Don stood in the corner next to the stage and observed each man as he came into the room and mingled amongst the other guest. These men had known each other for years. Don kept a list of his own to make sure everyone showed. Once the last man came through the door, Don drew a line through his name and climbed the back stairs to the DJ booth. Now he would be able to watch the guest through the two way mirror overlooking the floor. Cecil was safely tucked away behind the dark maroon curtains on the stage.

Hector glanced up at the DJ's booth and raised the phone in the air for Don to pick up. "That's everybody," he said as he ran a line through the name of the last man to enter the ballroom.

"Make sure you are not on the floor in the next few seconds."

"Why is that?" Hector asked. He gave the phone a slow and appraising glance.

"Don't ask questions just follow my orders," Don replied sharply and added, "Make sure the front door is bolted from the outside. We don't want these cockroaches scattering everywhere."

There were a total of three hundred and fifty men on the floor. Not counting the four men in the other room. Some of the men on the floor were whispering amongst themselves. This wasn't a regular procedure for all of them to come together in such large numbers. It took no time for one to question this event and he spread the word around to the others.

As the party went on, some were starting to think this was some kind of ingenious scheme by the feds to gather them together and lock them all up at once. These were major players in the drug trade. Not only in America, but all over the world. Don was able to gather them all together.

Don waited until each of the men had their meal and were now smoking cigars. He leaped down the stairs and onto the stage. He slowly stepped through the curtains in a pair of black, designer slacks and black shirt. He lightly tapped the microphone to make sure it was working. The sound reverberated through the speakers and this caused the entire room to face the stage and sink into silence.

Don's gray eyes peered out into the crowd at the faces of the men who came. He knew a few of them from dealing with Chico, but they were all strangers to him.

"I am happy you came," Don said slowly. "I am pretty sure you would like to know why you were brought here today." He was speaking in Spanish to make sure all of the men knew what he was saying. His eyes continued to search the crowd and he saw a few faces he once shared drinks and laughs with along with Chico.

There were a few murmurs throughout the crowd. Don continued. "I am here to announce today my appointment as the head of the Dragon family." He raised his hand in the air for all of the men to see. The only members of the Dragon family there was Hector.

Don continued. "Since I am now in charge there is going to be some revisions to the way business is done from here on out. There are too many different families at war with each other. Now we must bring it all to a close because it is bad for business."

"So what do you think you are going to do about it?" Someone yelled from the middle of the crowd. "We don't even know you."

A half hearted grin formed on Don's lips as he stared in the direction the comment came from. "This is why we are here today to bring peace to every fraction of the business. Things have to be more disciplined for us to reap the full benefits of our labor." He placed the microphone in his hand and began to pace the stage. "Today my friends is the last day of your uncivilized means and methods of doing business."

"Do you think we are going to take orders from a nigger?" Someone said in English from the crowd. "Who died and made you boss?"

Don smiled along with the rest of the crowd at the comment. He placed his palm against his cheek. "Chico De La Fuentes died and made me boss."

Someone else was about to make another snide remark, but Don held up his hand for them to hold their thoughts. He slipped behind the curtain and Cecil handed him a sizable machine gun used for warfare. The gun was firmly stationed on a stance. Cecil held a long coil of ammunition, while Don held the gun in his hands.

Don and Cecil removed two pair of night vision goggles from a briefcase and put them on. Don nodded towards Hector at the far end of the stage. Hector slammed down all of the switches connected to the breaker box and the entire auditorium plunged into a state of triple darkness.

Once the curtains opened, Don aimed the gun in the direction of the men on the floor. He applied a minimal amount of pressure to the hairline trigger and a barrage of bullets began to fire rapidly into the crowd.

The entire group bolted towards the entrance they initially came in, but the door was locked shut and there was no chance they were going to make it outside. There was no way out. The only way out for them at this point was death.

They strolled into the ballroom with extreme confidence, but were now screaming like a battered wife being beaten by her insane husband.

Don was firing in the crowd relentlessly. His main objective was to make sure every man in the room was dead. The only ones to remain alive in this room called Una Muerta Bonita were to be Cecil, Hector and himself. This was the only way he knew to get rid of Chico's enemies and pave his way to the top. It was treachery to the fullest, but all was fair in love and war.

Through the night vision goggles, Don saw a group of men curled up in the far corner of the ballroom. They were merely trying to hold out until their eyes adequately adjusted to the darkness. The only light to interrupt the darkness was the sparks from the gun as it continuously spit death. They couldn't make out who was shooting. All they had to defend themselves were their bare hands, and wished they would've seen through the ploy of giving up their weapons at the door. They were defenseless, and if they didn't do something fast, they were going to end up dead like the bodies they were tripping over in their hasty retreat to safety.

Deep within the confines of the darkness, Cecil distinguished four men slinking their way in the direction of the stage. First, he had to make sure the bullets in the gun Don was holding was leveled and wouldn't jam in the gun, before he removed a Desert Eagle from his waistband and fired on the men.

Cecil wasn't sure if they were really dead, or just playing dead. He jumped from the stage and shot each of the men in the head and walked around the room kicking bodies to see who was still alive, so he would put them out of their misery. It was the least he could do.

By the time the lights were turned on, the walls and the cedar floors were drenched in flesh and blood. Although Don had orchestrated this massacre, it took a lot for him to remain in control of the feelings overwhelming him at the sight of what he had done. He secured a major victory for the family today, but stained his soul in the process.

The sight of three hundred and fifty disfigured bodies sprawled throughout the ballroom dead nearly devastated his humanity. He could feel his sanity slowly trickling from his conscience into the river of blood at his feet.

Don's gray eyes stared around the room and all he could smell was blood and bowels of the dead men. He knew what had to be done today, but seeing it before his eyes drove his face deep into the reality of the matter. He found himself caught in a waking nightmare and he was the monster in his very own dream.

This all reminded him of the Nazis extermination of the Jews per orders of Hitler. They were killed in excessive numbers in order for one man to exalt himself above a race of people.

Don was starting to believe he had fallen victim to the madness which claimed the sanity of one man and he caused it to spread to a race of Germans. What he did here today wasn't common thought for the human mind.

Don had known some of the men lying dead on the floor, but it really didn't matter much to him anymore. If he was able to turn back the hands of time from the moment they all walked through the door, he would do it all over again. The only time he felt sorry was when he thought about the past and wished he had told Chico about this day and they could've done it sooner.

His nostrils contracted reflexively at the sight of all the dead men before him, their bodies contorted into grotesque positions as they were riddled with bullets. Blood was pouring out of their heads along with chunks of brain matter.

Don closed his eyes fighting to remove this sight of the dead bodies from his memory, but he still saw them. Finally a smile danced across his full lips. His face brightened and the thought of today's victory intoxicated his spirit.

It was at this very moment, Don truly understood the price every great man had to pay for the ultimate power. Although he won, his soul was stained. It was all for the price of power.

Don removed his handkerchief from his breast pocket and silently wept.

Chapter Sixteen

"Wrap the bodies in plastic and take them to the crematory in South Beach. I've already arranged for the bodies to be taken care of," Don said wiping tears from his eyes.

Cecil and Hector and four other men began to do as Don ordered. The entire time Hector was shaking his head numbly while he wrapped each of the bodies in plastic.

Never would he have thought it would come to this. Now he thoroughly understood what Don meant by saying this was the beginning of the end of all wars.

He now pondered what Don was going to do with the four men waiting in the other room. They were the more esteemed smugglers and he wondered if he intended to make them suffer the same fate. Just the lost of them alone would put a huge dent in the drug trade, which had the potential to calculate into billions of dollars.

From what had taken place to bring Don to Miami; what happened at Pablo's mansion and now this, Hector now understood what it was Chico saw in this Black man. In less than twenty-four hours, Don made a way for the Dragon cartel to totally dominate the drug trade undisturbed.

The room was now blanketed with a stench of urine and feces from the dead bodies. Two of the men had weak stomachs from the sight before their eyes and threw up everything in their stomachs.

The walls and floor were so drenched in blood, a death fragrance wavered over the dead bodies. The air conditioner helped to propel the sickly aroma throughout the room and into the air ducts and out into the Miami air.

Cecil also shook his head in a state of confusion. When the lights were off the blood appeared to be a translucent syrup spraying in the air. Now the lights were on, the grimy reality of what had taken place wasn't hidden by the night vision goggles. It showed the absolute mental sickness of his friend. Death filled his nostrils like a thick film of mucus.

Don made sure he was the one to strike first. Any enemy of Chico's was a enemy of his, and he refused to allow the lesson burned into his soul to this very day to be forgotten. Only a fool made the same mistake twice and expected different results. Sosa taught him a lesson he would never forget.

This day would signify how brutally deceptive and uncompromising he could be. Everyone thought there was going to be a peace talk, but Don came to steal their lives from them like a thief in the night.

While the men worked to prepare the bodies, Salsa music played as a tribute to their deaths. They never had a chance. In war, he didn't care if he had to kill a thousand men just to send a message to one. Death was the only way to secure a safe victory from any enemy who had the potential to threaten his seat of power. This was a lesson he had to learn the hard way. The sight of his brother lying peacefully in the casket flashed before his eyes. It took his death to teach him the art of all wars. He refused to ever allow an ember of fire to smolder from his enemy. He wouldn't even allow a spark to survive, so a fire could never manifest itself within the ashes of defeat.

Don splashed a handful of water on his face before making his way down the long hallway leading to the room where the four men were being held.

The walk was to calm himself and not force the men to sink into fear and close their minds to reason. He could imagine how on edge they would be after hearing the grand gunfire taking place just a few feet away from them. The room they were in wasn't soundproof and they heard each and every bullet as it left the deadly machine gun.

They couldn't up and leave. Don had two men posted in front of the door. He wasn't going to allow them to leave before he got the chance to proposition them into the deal of a lifetime.

Don sauntered into the quiet room and sat down at the head of the rectangular, mahogany table. His calm demeanor gave him a chance to study their features for clues of what their thoughts were in regards to what they heard. They were all using their imagination to make sense of what had just happened. Each man was searching Don's eyes and attitude to determine to what fate they would succumb.

Don had become a master of manipulation. He didn't have the look of a mass murderer. Nor did his appearance give away the fact he had just killed three hundred and fifty men minutes ago. He appeared to have just come in from a pleasant stroll in a glorious garden and not from the valley of death.

There were two Colombians sitting on the right side of Don. They were Eduardo Cortez and Alejandro Sanchez; a Mexican was on the opposite side of the table named Felipe Valdez and one Cuban, Diego Ortiz.

All four of these men had a earning power of three hundred million dollars a year, which was far more than the hundred million Chico was able to bring in. In this one room there were over one billion dollars sitting at the table. By Don removing the others from the drug trade in the other room, he stood to make one billion all by himself.

Don continued to smile warmly at each of the men. This was his main weapon to put them at ease. "How are you doing today?" Don asked in Spanish. Everyone was surprised to hear how well he knew the language.

Each man's eyes darted back and forth at one another. They knew their gut feeling was telling them they would be next to fall to the same fate as the others in the other room. All they could do was wait until the young man sitting in front of them was ready to snuff out their lives like a wet cloth would do to the flame of a candle.

Eduardo felt the small hairs stand up on the back of his neck.

He cleared his throat. "Why are we here?" he asked nervously. His stomach was doing somersaults and he was mentally kicking himself in the ass for willingly walking into what he considered a trap of this magnitude, a deadly trap at that.

Don dried his hands on a towel. "We're here to talk business."

Alejandro's breath quickened as he scooted to the edge of his seat. "Business is already good for me." He felt the sensation of a spider crawling down his back. "What is there to talk about?"

Don held up a finger. "I am so glad you asked. Sure business is good, but now it can be even better. Every man in this room will be able to first control a region of America." Don eyed each of the men as the words left his mouth. "We are not speaking about a territory, but states. Each man will be responsible for every bottle of cocaine and every bag of heroin sold in the wilderness of North America and soon we will cover the entire world and have continents to ourselves."

Felipe was a dark skin Mexican. He was several shades darker than Don, about the same complexion as Cecil. He filled his glass with water from a pitcher in the middle of the table. He scratched his head before he drank. "I don't feel good about this." He examined Don's face owlishly. "Tell me exactly what happened in the other room?"

Don tightened his lips together and drummed his fingers on the well shellacked mahogany table to a Miles Davis symphony playing in his head. "What happened was me getting rid of any and everything that had the potential of standing in our way," he smiled warmly at them. "At this very moment, the only one to stop us is us."

Diego blinked with surprise. He was the oldest of everyone in the room by twenty years. He's been in the business while each of the men were still suckling at their mothers breast.

Diego's face was full of wrinkles and a head full of gray hair. "You killed every man that came with us that quickly?"

Don lowered his head as if the scene of the bodies replaying in his mind was haunting him. He gave Deigo a sad and despairing look. "Yes I did," he said just above a whisper. "Only a handful were my enemies and half was everyone elses in total."

"What about the rest?" Diego inquired with his gray eyebrows narrowing. "Why did you kill them?"

Don hunched his shoulders and curled his lower lip. "The others were simply in the way of progress of this monumental moment in history my friends. I did us all a big favor free of charge."

"We don't do business like that," Eduardo said. His voice nervously rising an octave as he voiced his thoughts. "We have ties that go all the way back to Colombia."

Don's gray eyes were haunted by a inner pain. "Chico also suffered from the same grand illusions of loyalty to vultures." Don's brows came together in thought. "This is why Chico chose me for his seat. I know there are many dimensions to warfare. In the name of my brother, I can only believe in complete annihilation of all who oppose the plan being laid before you gentleman today."

Don stood to his feet and walked around to the other side of the table. "You are not the reason for what has happened here today. No blood stains your hands, or souls. I did this!" For the first time the hate danced across his face. "And if the God I serve seeks repercussions for what has happened here today, then only my soul alone shall dwell in the fire of hell for all eternity."

Don's gray eyes glinted with excitement. "As a man, I always do what I feel is right for me. As a friend and confidant, I can only suggest what would be right for you."

Felipe gave Don a half smile. Don figured he had already won him over. Felipe was short and stocky. He was rich and wanted everyone to know it. He made sure to dress the part of a rich man. He wore expensive suits and gold chains. "What do you want from us?"

Don raised his hands in a surrendering gesture. "Your friendship first and I would like to assist each and everyone of you in making more money than we could ever imagine." He grinned down the table at each of them. "I think today has proven how serious I am about this and my capabilities to get the ball rolling."

Eduardo was about to run his fingers through his hair, but remembered it was thick with gel. He wore it slick back like the Fonze from Happy Days. "I still don't understand what you need from us.

You could kill us like everyone else and have it all for yourself." He eyed each of the men in the room who was in the same position as he was before Don. "If we don't agree then what?"

Diego nodded in agreement with Eduardo. "Yeah, aren't you going to kill us?"

Don sat down and closed his eyes as if he was in deep meditative thought. He could've just killed them, but he had his reason for them to still be alive. They were important to pulling off a take over this complex.

The two Colombians were alive for their control of the fields in Colombia. This would help produce mass quantities of cocaine to supply the demand. Felipe would now be in charge of all the Mexican cartels and the mass production of heroin. Diego would be of use when Don needed to negotiate with Cuban officials to store large quantities of drugs on the island to prepare for it to be shipped to America and other locations in the West Indies.

They were still alive because they each knew what had to be done in order to make as much money as possible. They lived because of their knowledge of how things functioned. Now they stood alone in competition. All they could do now was make money with the greatest of ease.

Don leaned in with both elbows on the table. "It's not about how much money I can make. We all have more than we can spend in our lifetime. If this life we live isn't in order, we all stand to lose everything we worked for over a situation which could be prevented."

Don faced Eduardo. "To answer your question my friend. Yes it would seem easy to just kill you, but I know I can learn something from every man in this room and that is why you are here. You're legends in every right and I only wish to be thoroughly connected to strength and intelligence. Killing you would be a sin, a stain I wouldn't want my soul to bare."

Don paid attention as the stress lines slowly disappeared from each of the men's faces. He was using flattery to win them over, giving them the title of master and he the willing student. They would only relax if he made them feel comfortable and superior as if he needed them.

Instead of giving them insecurity, he was disarming them with glory. Discreet flattery is much more powerful than blowing their brains out. The absolute truth of why Don was allowing them to live was being bodyguarded by lies.

By making them appear to be more intelligent then him and acting naive made it seem like he really needed their expertise. The entire time, using his pretended weakness of lack of intelligence to disguise his strengths to secretly control them. They were mistaking his false sincerity for honesty. This tactic forced them off balance, so there was no way for them to prepare a defense against him.

Alejandro was the first to smile at Don's plan. He calculated what had taken place in the other room and realized there was a huge market just waiting to be filled. This young Black man had made it all possible.

"So how can we bring all of this together?" Alejandro asked.

Don leaned all the way back in his chair. "I will be solely responsible for all shipments into America. All you will have to do is distribute your product to your said region." Don caressed his bald head and rested his hand on his chin. "There is no more competition at this point they are all dead." A diplomatic grin formed at his mouth. "No more wars and we all know you can't make money in war."

Diego squinted his eyes out of confusion. "How will you be able to get tons of cocaine and heroin into the country without any of our help?" He cleared his throat. "I ask because, this is a great obstacle for all of us. We lose far more shipments than we're able to get in."

Don drummed his fingers on the table. "This is why I am offering everyone a profitable solution to this problem and my solution will be highly beneficial to all sitting at this round-table." Don made a joke to try and lighten what had happened in the other room. He was implying they were the knights of the round-table.

He stood to his feet and towered over the men still sitting down. "I will make sure not one shipment of ours will get lost. We will give them something to make the news of a big bust, but the major shipments for profit will always make it through. I am changing the routes and the shipments they will catch will be from the routes they already know."

"You don't need our help?" Alejandro asked.

Don mildly shook his head no.

Felipe blinked repeatedly. "How will you do this by yourself?"

"With the cooperation of some friends in powerful positions inside and outside of this country," Don replied.

"Who?" Eduardo asked quickly. "Who's going to help you?"

Don's smile became even more polite. He magically removed a coin from behind Eduardo's ear. "A magician never reveals how he does his tricks. It would spoil the illusion and the audience would become dissatisfied and feel cheated by knowing the trick, and want a full refund." He placed his hand sternly on Eduardo's shoulder. "I think it would be best if some of the things I am capable of are left in the dark." He blew on his hand and the coin disappeared.

All four of the men marveled at the Black man who came from out of nowhere to run the Dragon cartel, eloquently speaking their language and performing magic and murder right before their very eyes.

Felipe chimed in. "Okay, I'm not worried about that." He scooted to the edge of his chair. "I do want to know how much is all of this elite service going to cost us?"

Don heard his question, but had every intention to be slow with his answer. He poured himself a glass of cold water from the clear pitcher in the middle of the table. He downed the glass of water like it was filled with Vodka.

He removed a fresh Cuban cigar from his breast pocket. A huge grin danced across Diego's face once he saw the seal of the cigar and Don offered him one. Diego rubbed the cigar across his mustache and kissed it once he smelled the aroma of his homeland. As a boy he worked in the same cigar house as the one he was now holding.

Don lit both cigars and drew in the smoke along with his thoughts. Diego inhaled the cigar with his eyes closed relishing in its taste. Both men blew out a misty fragrance of smoke. The smoke leaped from the cigar in a thin stream and was sucked into the air duct in the center of the room.

Don finally broke the silence and replied. "Half."

Felipe shook his head in disagreement. "That's too much."

Every man in the room agreed with Felipe. Half sounded like a lot and Don knew it was. He was merely trying to buy enough time when he and Fuentes were able to establish a thorough production team in Colombia. Once this was firmly established, they would have to buy from Don in order to sell anywhere in the world. He had to be able to supply the demand. Until then, he was going to be able to get free cocaine and all he had to do was transport the product into the country.

Don laid his cigar in a seaweed green ashtray. He licked his full lips to taste the residue of his cigar. "If you lose more shipments than you bring in, I will make sure with my system you will get every shipment, why would half seem like a lot?"

Don slid a pen and pad across the table. "Each of you bring in four tons a year which totals sixteen tons a year. Out of your own mouth, you said you always lose half." He drew a line on the paper. "I will take the half you lose for my services and deliver two tons right to your front door. You won't be losing."

"This will give you eight tons of cocaine. We're not even talking about the heroin," Felipe said. "What about that?"

"The eight tons will go to me instead of customs." Don replied as calm as ever. "The deal on the heroin will stand the same as everything else." He pulled on his cigar to bring its embers back to life. The red fire glowed at its end. "In fact, you brought in four tons when there was tremendous competition. We don't have the problem anymore, so you will have to double what you brought in before and it will now be thirty-two tons and I will take sixteen."

Don figured there was nothing else to say on the matter. He had given them his proposal and figured there was nothing else to negotiate at this point. He refused to compromise after he had just killed over three hundred and fifty men.

Don's gray eyes bore into Felipe, but he was speaking to each of the four men. "I will give you time to talk things over amongst yourselves. I have some other business to attend to." Don stood to his feet.

Deigo's eyes squinted as Don stood. "Are there others you are making this deal with?"

Don nodded yes as he closed the door to the office and strolled over to the next room. He had needle size microphones and cameras embedded into the walls of the room. He wanted to be able to see and hear what they had to say while he was out the room.

Cecil was sitting at the controls watching Don as he was having the meeting with four of the biggest men in the drug trade. Although he didn't understand a word they were saying, he was just making sure no harm came to his friend. Surprised by how fluent Don was in the language.

Don came into the room and sat quietly next to Cecil. He slipped on the headphones and closely listened to their conversations and said something to Cecil prior to his re-entry into the room. He had already known who was in agreement with the plan. He spoke with Hector while he guarded the door and stepped into the room as if he hadn't heard one word of their conversation while he was out the room.

"Do we have a deal?" he asked as he was sitting down.

Diego nodded and shook Don's hand. "I'm in."

Eduardo did the same and so did Alejandro. Felipe's was slow. His face paled as the room became silent while waiting for his response.

"What about you Felipe?" Don asked softly. All eyes in the room stared at him with intensity. The others wanted to witness if his disagreement would mean final death. They didn't agree out of fear, but believed it was a sound plan and the best deal for them to move way more product than before without competition and their enemies were now dead.

Don not only ensured they wouldn't die at the hands of their enemy, but they would also make more money than they ever have at one time. They would now be a part of a movement which would control the drug trade of cocaine throughout the world.

Felipe studied each of the men in the room skeptically, especially

Don. He didn't like the way he did business. Sure it was a good deal, but he feared the man sitting at the head of the table and in control of the entire operation. It was his fear of being in the midst of this Black demon on future occasions that was gnawing at his conscience. He didn't know when a time like today would repeat itself and he would end up dead like the other men in the next room. Also, he's been in business too long to submit under the rules and regulations of a Black man who was young enough to be his son.

The only noise to cut the silence of the room was the gush of air coming from the central air system.

Felipe cleared his throat as if he had every intention of making an important speech. "Its not good for me," he replied slowly. "I'd rather do business the old fashioned way. After seeing what I've seen and knowing what I know, I find it hard to trust someone like you."

Don placed a firm hand on Felipe's shoulder and smiled at him like a son would his father for teaching him how to ride a bike.

"You have every right to follow your heart," Don said. "But please do not question my loyalty and my integrity if we were to ever become the best of friends. I am not driven by money to cross the ones thoroughly a part of my family." He eyed each of the men. "Today, we have become family," he faced Felipe. "No harm will come to you. One of my men will take you wherever you need to go."

Felipe stood up and faced Don. He swallowed dryly while his knees quaked. Don peered back at him with a warm smile. "So I won't lose my life because I don't want anything to do with this?"

Don extended his hand and shook his head no. "Every man has the right to determine whatever direction he would want for his life and business to go," Don smiled warmly at him. "For you not to trust me, why would you say no if you believed your life to be in danger?"

Felipe was about to reply. Don held his hand up. "The deal will always be open to you if you ever change your mind." He handed Felipe a Cuban cigar to take along with him as well as his card. "Call me if you ever change your mind."

Felipe swallowed down his water to aid his cotton mouth. He gave a startled gasp as he headed for the door to leave. He couldn't believe he was walking out with his life after the massacre he knew had taken place prior to speaking with the man he considered was the devil here on earth.

Felipe continued to try and make some kind of sense out of what had just happened. Today would be a moment in history many would wonder about for years to come. He had never heard of Don Starchild, but on their first meeting, he witnessed him kill a room full of men and acted as if what he had done was normal to a sane mind.

He meant what he had to find the nerve to say to Don's face. He didn't trust him to say the least. He figured Don was a cold blooded killer and he couldn't trust him for a second. He still couldn't fathom how Don was able to commit a magnitude of murders and appear as if he had just Christened his first born son. It was Don's calmness after the murders that was bothering him.

Don patiently waited until Felipe left the room. "Is there anybody else who wants out?" He held each of the men within his stare.

All three of the men shot glances at each other to see who would leave next. They couldn't understand how Felipe would just walk away from the best deal they've ever had laid before them since they were involved in the business of drugs.

For some odd reason, they knew the man calling the shots was dangerous, but they were beyond convinced they could trust him. They wondered if Felipe would try to cut his stake in the drug trade without them.

All three of the men shook their heads no.

Don clapped his hands like he was trying to catch thunder. "Well let's sit down and get our politics in order. Is anybody hungry?" he asked.

The men began to ask for special dishes they saw on their way into the place which now earned its name as Una Muerta Bonita.

Diego noticed Don didn't order anything. "Aren't you going to eat?" he asked.

Don thought about the massacre in the other room. "I've already eaten," he replied with a sly grin.

CHAPTER SEVENTEEN

Felipe inched his way past the sealed ballroom doors and into the paltry vestibule leading to the outside of the building. A thousand nightmarish thoughts raced through his head. Nauseating spurts of fear coursed through his body, clouding his sense of direction of how to get out of the building.

As if he was stuck in a heinous horror movie, he heard a cart squeaking from the weight of the dead bodies as someone was wheeling them out of the ballroom to a refrigerated truck stationed at the back of the building.

The sky was the color of a week old bruise, as the sun attempted to cast miniature rays of light from behind the milky clouds, before it made its way to the other side of the equator.

A long black limousine pulled up and Felipe rushed inside at a speed which even astounded him. He had to get away from this evil place in case the devil changed his mind. He could feel his heart beating thunderously against his rib cage.

In the back of the limousine was a wooden rack with bottles of brandy and Vodka. Felipe tossed two cubes of ice into a glass and filled it with vodka. He hoped this remedy would calm his tattered nerves. Not only was he surprise he made it this far, but the fact he was still breathing was a miracle in itself.

He guzzled down his drink and could feel its burning sensation fill his empty belly. A euphoric feeling swarmed over his entire being as he finished the first glass and prepared another.

He glanced out of the back window to see the distance the limousine had put between him and the ballroom of death. He sighed with relief once the car turned the corner taking him back to his car. Now he knew he would live.

After watching him leave unharmed, Felipe wondered why the other three men didn't come with him. He sunk down into the plush seat and was trying to figure out how he was going to kill the man who allowed him to escape. It was the only way he would be able to get money.

Also, he knew if their paths crossed again, he may not be provided with the same opportunity he had been afforded here today. Somebody had to die out of the two. Since it wasn't his turn while he was at the ballroom, along with the other men, then it would have to be the Black devil.

Felipe had every intention to capitalize from the massacre on this day. He didn't have a idea of the exact number dead, but it had to be enough to widely open the market for a major supplier to fill. Mentally, he patted himself on the back for his courageousness to refuse the offer when his back was against the wall.

The limousine sped in and out of traffic with the expertise of an experienced driver. The further he got away from the auditorium the more relieved he became. He couldn't wait to tell the tale of exactly what had happened on this day. A day he will never forget for as long as he lived.

Felipe had met the man who was about to steal the cocaine business from every major supplier involved in dealing drugs on a wide scale. For some, today was their first and last day of meeting him.

There was something about Don which caused Felipe to fear him and respect him at the same time. He didn't just respect him for keeping his word and not taking his life, but the way he was able to lead every man to slaughter and they didn't have the slightest idea of what they were getting themselves into.

The driver was separated by a tinted divider. The window finally came down once the limousine came to a complete halt.

"This is where I'm going to have to let you out," the driver said in English.

Felipe studied the location and saw an empty lot of hay colored weeds encased inside of a short metal fence. On the opposite side of the street was a funeral parlor. Felipe didn't know it because the awning had been pulled back to cover up the name.

His neck twisted as he stole a glance from each of the windows. "This isn't where my car is. Take me to the airport." He removed the cap from the vodka about to make himself another drink.

The driver's window came all the way down to the base of the divider. Cecil's raven colored eyes focused on Felipe. He aimed a 45 automatic at him attached to a silencer.

Cecil began to unload the entire clip into Felipe's face and chest. Felipe's body jerked like he was having an epileptic seizure. Cecil continued to riddle Felipe's body with bullets until he slumped in the seat dead. Blood and white cotton padding from the seat's upholstery filled the back-seat.

No man was allowed to live if Don didn't want them to. The only reason he didn't kill Felipe right then and there was he wanted to see what the other men would do once they watched him leave the meeting with his life.

Once they believed they could leave if they wanted to, but they didn't, Don knew they were all the way in, because they saw the vision of success right before their eyes.

Night had chased away the day in a matter of seconds. Stars twinkled as if they were standing for role call by transmitting messages of light through the universe in Morse code.

Cecil threw a worn towel over Felipe's head and carried his lifeless body into the crematory to be cremated along with the other dead men.

Hector was pulling in with the truck full of dead bodies as Cecil was leaving the crematory. Cecil saluted him as he passed the truck and said in Spanish. "All in a days work."

CHAPTER EIGHTEEN

FIFTEEN YEARS LATER:

A drug epidemic had thoroughly engulfed the country and hovered over inner cities like a plague. This pandemic was faithfully spreading into all suburban communities throughout the country. America finally admitted there was a drug problem when drug tentacles escaped inner city ghettos and were now reaching the likes of little White boys and little White girls.

Although the customs department boasted on television of the prodigious shipments they were intercepting, there seemed to be more drugs pouring into the country in the last fifteen years, than there ever was.

Dealers on the street had access to pure cocaine. There never was a drought. The discovered shipments by customs always came from tips. Certain times there would be a tip about a shipment on the ground, next in the air, next on a boat. Their bust didn't even put a dent in the drug trade. It was thriving more than ever.

A new campaign was in the process of being introduced to the public. There would now be a civil war between the law and the lawless in the homeland, and it was a war on drugs.

The president of the United States allocated billions of dollars to Special division teams. Diligent task forces were formed to attack the problems in inner cities, but to no avail did it prevent the steady flow of narcotics in the country.

Homeland security went after cartels living in the country, but they weren't the main suppliers and had nothing to do with smuggling the drugs into the country. The major players hid behind the cartels used to sell the drugs. The leaders of the cartels didn't even know who they worked for.

From prestigious politicians to bank executives, everyone had their hands in the pot reaping the benefits for aiding the newly enriched millionaires around the world.

In New Jersey and New York, Dodirty was the main source for the majority of the drugs in the state. He began to spread to other states as his army grew, but many would come far and wide to purchase from him. His connection was able to supply him with more drugs than he could sell in just one state. He had to spread.

If he purchased five hundred kilos, his connect would front him another five hundred. He wished Don was alive to see how much money he was making. For him, it wasn't about the money anymore. His thrills came from the gripping power he had over the darkside of the city, which was now circulating to major businesses to aid him in laundering millions.

Dodirty finally came to understand what Don was always trying to tell him. How power came with a double edge sword. His money had brought him to the attention of the local Mafioso. They now wanted a piece of Dodirty's empire, but Dodirty was unswayable to their threats. He told them on many occasions the only thing he had for them was bullets and blood. He paid punk dues to no one. He figured he took all of the risk, therefore the only one deserving of the rewards.

Dodirty led a army which consisted of nearly five hundred men and was growing as he conquered another state. Once his connect informed him he was too far out of his territory and to leave it alone. Dodirty never asked any questions. He just moved on. His only concerns were for Kasan. It would kill him if anything every happened to Kasan over one of his street beefs.

Dodirty's reflections came from the grave circumstances of Kasan's uncle, which led to Don's death. This is why Dodirty was extra careful. He didn't want any repercussions brought on by his illegal status to befall Don's son.

Kasan zipped his smoked black BMW in a vacant spot like a professional. Dodirty gave it to him as a gift for his eighteenth birthday. He wanted Kasan to have the best, but at times was starting to think the car was too flashy for a eighteen year old child. Carol said he spoils him.

Kasan could now pass for the identical twin of his father, minus the gray eyes. His body was defined from his daily practice of martial arts. He could break a stack of bricks with any part of his body and could shoot a gun with accurate precision of a true marksman.

Although Kasan had become a walking weapon, he was one of the most charming and humble young man anyone would ever meet. His relaxed demeanor gave him the ability to put anyone at ease.

Dodirty desperately wanted Kasan to live any other life other than the one he and Don lived. It appeared as if Kasan was susceptible to try and fill the historic shoes of his father. Not once did he discuss college with Dodirty, or even wanting to play any sports.

The focal point of all of Kasan's conversations were about the drug game. Regardless of how much Dodirty tried to tell him to take another route in life, Kasan still wanted to know.

Dodirty had the kitchen smelling like he was a gourmet cook. Two T-bone steaks were simmering in olive oil along with onions, red peppers and mushrooms. Stuffed potatoes mingled with the fragrance of the steak. They were stuffed with provolone cheese and onions. Since he didn't run the streets, he would order cookbooks and teach himself how to cook.

Kasan strolled into the kitchen with a big smile on his face. He enjoyed Dodirty's cooking. He remembered when all they ever ate was takeout, or instant dinners.

Kasan went to the sink and washed his hands. He poured himself a glass of milk and sat on one of the round stools next to the kitchen counter. "I met a girl at school today."

Dodirty sighed and flipped over the steaks. It was just a matter of time before karate school would no longer intrigue him. He knew girls would come into play sooner or later. The girls already were paying Kasan a lot of attention.

He enrolled Kasan into a private school. The number of Blacks who attended could be counted on one hand. The school was very expensive and only the upper class went there. Kasan didn't speak with a ghetto flare. He spoke proper English. It was for this reason, Dodirty was struck with wonder. He was hoping Kasan's new girlfriend wasn't a snowflake. Whites were the majority there.

"So what's her name?" Dodirty asked with his back turned.

Kasan's eyes brightened. He dreamily grinned just from the thought of her. "Her name is Sparkle." He polished off the first glass of milk like it was a shot of whiskey and soon poured another. "We're going to the club downtown tonight and I want you to meet her."

Kasan was about to exit the kitchen to take a shower until Dodirty called him back. "I think we need to talk before you go out on this date."

"If its about sex Uncle Do, I already know about it."

Dodirty slid the steaks from the frying pan and onto two plates. He used a wooden spoon to scoop out the sauce made by the steak, olive oil and mushrooms.

"Anybody can have sex, but are you protected." Dodirty bent down to get the four potatoes out of the oven. They added another hungry aroma to the air. The cheese poured from the potato once Dodirty unwrapped them and laid them next to the steaks. "You know you're too young to get one of these girls knocked up." He leaned on the counter. "Have you two had sex yet?" Dodirty's eyes took on the hunted look. "This is man shit we're talking about so don't lie to me."

Kasan drummed his fingers on the counter. Dodirty knew this to be a habit of Don's when he was about to reveal something. "We never did anything, but we've talked about it." Kasan cleared his throat. "She's getting on birth control if we decide to do anything."

Dodirty shook his head no while his mouth was full of food. He sipped a glass of wine to wash down its residue. "I want you to get in practice with being responsible for your own life." Although he spoke in such a calm manner, his eyes were a contradiction to their conversation.

Kasan knew Dodirty's words always came with a double meaning. This conversation not only applied to girls, but life in general.

Dodirty gave Kasan a warning look. "Pussy brought you into the world, don't let that be the reason you leave." He started to cut a portion of his steak. "You have clean women and unclean women. The only way to protect yourself from the unclean is to never throw caution to the wind."

He stabbed Kasan in the chest with a sturdy finger. The muscles in his chest was hard to his touch. "Rely on no one to guard your life but you. This is the only way for you not to be tricked into a false sincerity by anyone. These niggas and bitches will cross you like Broad and Market."

Kasan gave Dodirty a hug. It was times like this he believed Dodirty was giving him the advice Don would give to him had he still been alive.

"I'll do that," Kasan said. "Thanks for the talk." He got up and was about to leave the kitchen.

"Aren't you going to eat?"

Kasan spun around. "Put it up for me and I'll eat when I get back. Sparkle will be here any minute and I have to take a shower."

He headed for the shower with his face flushed with happiness. It gave him peace of mind to be able to talk to a man about man things. At times, Kasan wondered what his father would have to say about some of the many topics he and Dodirty discussed. Everyone said his father was highly intelligent.

He recalled the first day Dodirty came to bring him back to Newark for the summer. As a child, he didn't fully understand the importance of having a man in his life. Once he grew old enough to want to learn life's lessons, he knew he needed Dodirty.

The things he spoke with Dodirty about, he would never be able to discuss with his mother. She still treated him like he was a child.

What Kasan enjoyed the most about his conversations with his uncle was Dodirty didn't try and tell him what not to do, but how to do it if he insisted on doing it. The only time he showed any signs of reluctance was when they spoke about dealing drugs. Dodirty was adamant when he said he wanted him to stay far away from it. Kasan knew these were the wishes of his father from the grave and Dodirty was doing his best to try and enforce it. Although Kasan never got a chance to know his father, he sure did miss him dearly.

While Dodirty was in the kitchen cleaning the dishes, there was a knock on the door. He wasn't expecting any company himself. Rarely did he bring anyone here. He had other places throughout the city he went to entertain his guest.

He placed a hidden camera in the hallway and one in both stairwells. There was one at the front entrance of the building and one facing his car in the parking lot. This was to make sure a bomb hadn't been planted in his car. He checked this one every time he went to get into his car.

All he had to do was turn the television to channel three and the screen was divided into four. It showed every camera he placed in certain locations throughout building.

He clicked the remote control to flip the screen and check the front door. An above average looking mulatto girl was standing at the door.

Dodirty zeroed in closer to her face. "At least the boy has his fathers taste in women?" He mumbled to himself. He made sure there were no guns in sight before he opened the door. He didn't want to scare the poor girl. She appeared not to have an inkling of what the street life entailed.

"Is Kasan here?" she asked. Her voice sounded like a soft cloud, dripping with the sweetest water.

Dodirty opened the door and stepped to one side so she could enter. Her cafe au lait complexion gleamed from the balmy lighting beaming throughout the condominium. A dainty nose was placed perfectly between a pair of delicate brown eyes the shape of a teardrop.

She fingered her long, jet black hair, which trailed down the middle of her back, as she breezed pass Dodirty. She carried herself

140

with the style and grace of a princess. As far as Dodirty knew, she was Kasan's first girlfriend and he sure picked a winner the first time around.

Immediately, Kasan rushed out of the bathroom when he heard the front door open and close. The sight of her caused his entire face to light up with an exuberance Dodirty had yet to see in the face of his Godson.

Kasan stood strong and proud in the middle of the hallway with a terry cloth towel wrapped around his waist. Drops of water glistened over his well sculpted body and when he noticed Sparkle taking notice by scanning him from head to toe and smiling, he flexed his muscles to show more definition in his physique.

"You're early," he said, eyeing the oval clock on the wall in front of him. He tightened the towel around his waist to make sure it didn't slip off. "I still had a full thirty minutes to get ready." He made a head motion for her to follow him into his room.

Dodirty blew out a stream of hot air as he watched her and Kasan interact with each other. The way she looked at him and the way he looked at her. Words weren't needed to express the connection they had between each other.

He was thankful when Kasan didn't close the door to his bedroom. Sparkle was the first girl he ever brought around, so he took it she meant something to him. The fact he didn't close his door, showed his respect for him and the house.

There were things he didn't have to tell Kasan to do. He would do it without having to be instructed to do so. Respect was natural as breathing for Kasan.

Sparkle appraised the trophies on the mantle across the entire wall of his room, as well as the family pictures he had on his desk and walls. She meticulously eyed each photo.

The picture to catch her attention was the center picture on the wall of a man who looked so much like Kasan. He wore a black suit and blood red tie and huge diamond rings on both of his pinkies.

"Who is that?" she asked pointing at the picture.

Kasan spun around to see what picture she was referring to. "My father." He searched through his closet for something to wear and spoke with his back turned. "His name is Don Starchild."

Her brows came together in doubt. "He's not the one who answered the door is he?"

Kasan numbly shook his head no. "The one that answered the door is my uncle. My father died when I was two, or three."

"How?" she asked quickly. Her father told her about how he saw death everyday at his job.

"In a car crash."

A collection of tapes were neatly arranged on a shelf on the right side of the room. It would better for her to be able to see for herself, instead of him striving to explain the circumstances of his fathers death. He wasn't ashamed by the life his father lived and didn't want to hide anything from her. Sparkle was what you would call a good girl.

Her father told her about the streets, but her life had been a sheltered one. The closes she ever came in contact with a purified gangster was when Dodirty answered the door.

Dodirty was the only reason he wasn't green to the street life. It was the life of the ones around him which gave him direct exposure to the game. Showing her the tape was his way of allowing her a free pass into the inner sanctum of his life.

Steam poured from under the bathroom door. In his excitement, Kasan had left the shower running. He finally noticed it as he was on his way back to the bathroom to get dressed. The outfit he was wearing for the night was draped over his shoulder.

Sparkle's eyes couldn't be any wider as she watched the last seconds of Kasan's fathers life. Initially, it was the staggering explosion that captured her attention. Soon after the explosion, the cameras swept over the officers standing nearby and her father's face came across the screen in plain view.

Tears and soot covered his pale face. He stood the closest to the explosion than any of the other officers, as if he was making a brave attempt to rescue his slain comrades from the burning inferno.

Sparkle came to the edge of the bed to get a closer look at the scene being played out on television. Her arms were now blossoming with goosebumps at the sight of her father on camera crying. The gold badge around his neck was a sign it wasn't for the man they were chasing, but the slain officers who died in the line of duty.

Never did she mention Kasan's last name to her father. In fact, he didn't have the slightest idea she was going out on a date. He would always tell her she was too young to date and anyone she thought to be a candidate for a boyfriend, had to first be approved by him. This included a background check. He didn't want his daughter dating a man he would have to one day arrest.

Her father was first detective Harold Scott of the Newark homicide division. On the last day of Kasan's father's life, her father was also involved in the chase.

Tears streaked the fine black powder on his face. She watched as he fell to the ground when the cars continued to explode several times over a course of seconds.

Years after the chase, she recalled her father doing several interviews for newspapers and magazines in regards to the day of the chase. There were times he would sink into depression and her mother told her once before what it was about. It was this chase haunting him and the loss of his partner.

Now she felt uneasy about dating Kasan knowing her father was involved in his fathers demise. She didn't have the slightest clue of how to break this news to him. She decided to just be straight and to the point. She really liked him and hoped he didn't harbor any ill feelings for something she had nothing whatsoever to do with.

The light from the bathroom filled the room she was sitting in. As soon as Kasan came into the room, she suddenly became withdrawn. She was trying to ascertain a way to tell him what she saw on the tape. It was initiating the conversation that was troubling her the most.

She wondered would it be easier to rewind the tape and show him the truth she found it so hard to verbally confess. She thought of how their lives were bound by much more than the like they had for each other, but her father aided in taking his father away from him.

While their lives were now openly cast into two different spectrums of the law, a overwhelming feeling of guilt struck Sparkle at the core of her being. Somehow, she was starting to feel responsible for her fathers ill deeds.

Wasn't he doing his job?

Kasan sensed a difference from when he went into the bathroom and when he came out. His mother always told him to pay close attention to a woman's feelings. Sometimes words aren't needed when she is trying to tell you something of great importance.

"What's the matter?" Kasan asked.

Sparkle tossed the remote control on the bed next to her. "This tape is depressing," she replied shaking her head from side to side. "Plus, I saw something on it I think we need to talk about."

Kasan shifted his eyes to the blue screen. He glorified the ground his father walked on. She would never be able to grasp the intricate elements of his father's life and death, because she wasn't raised with any knowledge of the grimy streets.

He gave her a dismissive wave. "There is nothing to talk about Sparkle. I don't care if my father killed millions." His voice was a lifeless monotone. "He is still my father and I refuse to allow you or anybody else to judge him regardless of whom or what; especially for the things you don't even understand."

The words she was about to say got caught in her throat. She couldn't find the words for a refined rebuttal. She clicked the off button on the television and scooted further back onto the bed. It would be better to wait to have the conversation. For all she knew, this would be their first and last date.

Kasan slipped on a dull brown, rayon suit the color of the back of a cockroach. They went shopping and he brought her a blouse and shoes to match.

"I didn't mean to snap at you," Kasan apologized. "It's just . . . "

Sparkle interrupted while brushing the thin hairs on her arm. "I'm okay," she said softly. "Who am I to talk about your father?" She didn't want Kasan to think she was trying to hide something.

After seeing her father on the tape, she thought it would be only right to inform him of the connection between both of their fathers. He had to have seen her father walk into clear view of the camera. A face he couldn't put a name to.

Once this conversation manifested itself again in the near future, she would be able to tell him, she tried to speak about it, but it was the time he didn't want to talk about it.

Hopefully by then, she would feel more comfortable to tell him her father was an officer of the law and more than likely responsible for his fathers death.

She could imagine how she would feel if it was her father who died that day. Little did she know, those thoughts would present themselves in human form.

Chapter Nineteen

After years of being abandoned, The Touch Of Class had been remodeled into a teen club called Candyland. This was the new hangout for teens in Essex county. Every Friday and Saturday the place was packed to full capacity.

Each time the front door to the Candyland opened, the vibration from the earsplitting music would rattle the windows of the cars parked on both sides of the street.

A Muslim restaurant situated in the middle of the block sent an aroma of food twirling through the air teasing the bystanders standing across the street from the club.

The fragrance was far better than any advertisement could ever be. The smell of Halal chicken and French fries always kept the teens running in and out of the restaurant for the entire time the club was open. It was jumping until seven the next morning.

Since the club couldn't comfortably accommodate everyone at the same time, the teens would make the parking lot across the street an extension of the club. Some of the kids didn't need money if they were going to hangout in the parking lot. The only time the parking lot wasn't packed was when a hot act was performing inside.

Latifah skipped over to Kasan's car when she saw him pull into the parking lot. Although, she was only seventeen, she's had the body of a grown woman since she was fourteen years old. She was Nydia's oldest daughter and had the body and green eyes to prove it.

She rushed over when she saw a female on the passenger side of the car. This was a first. She looked up to Kasan as her big brother. It was the death of her mother trying to help his father which formed an unbreakable bond. It was the pain of their loss which made them family.

"What are you doing out here girl?" Kasan asked with his head sticking out of the window. "Do Grandma know you're out here with those tight ass jeans on?" She called Carol her Grandmother since she took her and her little brother in.

She turned her gumdrop nose up at his question. When she was out of the mansion, she was a grown woman, but when Carol was around, she was the perfect grandchild.

Latifah acted as if she didn't hear his question. She was more concerned with Sparkle sitting on the passenger side. "Is she your girlfriend?" She had a sly smile on her face and tapped Kasan lightly on the jaw. "And me and Grandma thought your kung fu ass was gay." She joked and winked at Sparkle.

Sparkle couldn't help but explode into bubbly laughter at the joke. Latifah introduced herself as Kasan's little, big sister. Sparkle had a confused look on her face.

She leaned pass Kasan. "My name is Sparkle," she continued to chuckle. "How are you his little big sister?" she asked. "I never heard of that."

Latifah bent down to the car. "He's older than me, so that makes me his little sister." She spun around with her back to them and placed her hands on her hips. "But all of this makes me his big sister." She slapped herself on her heart shaped ass. "Holla," she said as car honked behind her.

Sparkle erupted into even more laughter. Kasan had a soothing smile on his face. He knew how Latifah could perform when she was around anyone of his friends. This was her way of leaving an impression on anyone she wanted to always remember her.

"How long are you staying Kasan?" Latifah asked.

"Why?"

"Because I need a ride home. You know ain't no busses going

up to West Orange until the next morning and Grandma want me home by One on the dot. I had to beg to get that."

"You better catch a cab."

Latifah took a step back to show Kasan her outfit. "Unless he is going to give me a refund on this outfit, I ain't got no money to pay him."

Kasan had to fight the laugh in his throat. "Why don't you show him why you're my big sister?" he burst out into a laugh. "You can pay him by letting him spank you for a free ride to Orange." He and Sparkle both laughed and leaned all on each other.

"Now you're a kung fu comedian," she said with a straight face. "Are you going to give me a ride or what?"

Kasan turned the key in the ignition back to switch on the radio. "I'll let you know before I leave."

Earlier, he and Sparkle had intended to lose their virginity after the club. The last person he wanted tagging along spoiling the mood was her. Sparkle was the first girl she's ever seen him with and Latifah wasn't going to stop until Sparkle was her friend also. She left to talk to a group of girls across the street directly in front of the club.

The silver moon filled the sky like it was about to fall any minute. The colorless light made the full moon appear as if it was shining in 3D and all anyone had to do was stick their hand up in the air to pull it down.

Kasan and Sparkle stayed in the car listening to music and talking, when six guys came over to his car and three plopped down on the hood with a loud thump.

The weight of the three pushed the hood of the BMW inward with a popping noise. It also made the car drop and sink forward. The three bounced up and down on the hood, making the car rock up and down like they were sitting on a ride in a amusement park.

Kasan cursed at the first thought they would put a dent in his car. He stuck his head out the window. "Can you please get off my car?" He made sure to speak with an politeness which would provoke their egos to take this matter to its final conclusion.

A dark skinned guy holding onto a golf club slid off the hood of the car and twisted his baseball cap over his leering eyes. "Ain't you Kasan Starchild?"

Sparkle's heart fluttered in her chest at the group of guys surrounding the car with predatory expressions on their faces. The fact they asked for Kasan by name made it personal and violence was what they already intended when they initially threw themselves on the car.

She locked the door on her side and quickly rolled up the window. She stared catatonically at the guys sitting on the car and hoped the trophies weren't just for show and tell and Kasan would be able to adequately defend himself against the angry mob of guys surrounding the car.

Kasan climbed out of the car and locked it before he closed the door. "Who wants to know?"

A fair skin guy sitting on the car came over to his side with a baseball bat in his hand. "We have a message for you to give to your uncle."

Kasan peered into the eyes of each of the men standing before him. He was searching for the leader. Once he had the opportune time to strike, he wanted his blow to land directly on the chin of the shepherd to cause the sheep to scatter and flee for the hills.

Had any of them known what he was capable of doing with his bare hands, the last thing they would ever want to do is provoke his wrath.

Kasan was a fifth degree black belt and could take them on without any qualms whatsoever. It was humility giving them the boisterous amount of confidence to continue their attack.

The guy with the bat came towards him. Kasan moved out of the way of the car. He didn't want his back to be pressed against the car. He needed freedom to act up like he was suppose to at a time like this. He had Sparkle in the car and wanted to show her what he was made of.

The guy held the bat over his shoulder. "Tell your uncle Terry Gambino wants the money he owes him."

Terry Gambino was the Boss of the Mafia in New Jersey. His

main reason for sending the men were to try and force Dodirty to submit to his extortion tactics and pay him a monthly portion of his drug money. As well as a slice of the profits from his lucrative businesses.

Dodirty told Terry's men on more than one occasion to go to hell with gasoline draws on, they persisted in trying to apply pressure, hoping one day he would fold. Since Dodirty has shown great resistance, they figured Kasan may be the weakest link in the chain for Dodirty to agree with their demands.

"I'll make sure to let him know," Kasan replied. He placed his key in the car door. Kasan saw Latifah across the street speaking with a group of friends from school. He called for her to go. She glanced at her watch and it wasn't even eleven thirty yet.

She stomped her way across the street ready to give Kasan a piece of her mind when she eyed grown men sitting on Kasan's car. She strolled up next to him and stood by his side.

Latifah was willing to fight with him. Although she was small, she had the heart of a lioness. She was not only a woman, but a warrior. Herself and Kasan both were trying to live up to the thorough memory of their deceased parents.

The guy with the golf club came around to the front of the car and swung the club at the front windshield until it looked like a spider's web. All Sparkle could do was throw her hands over her face to prevent the glass from going into her eyes, or cutting her. Her heart was now racing at an accelerated pace. She wasn't use to this kind of variance of violence.

Kasan lowered his head to the side of the car she was sitting on. "Are you okay?"

Sparkle's face was a mask of terror. She wanted to tell him no and she wanted to go home, but her voice was stuck in her throat. Kasan was outnumbered and she didn't want to see him, nor Latifah, who was defiantly standing by his side to get hurt.

Kasan edged his way towards the guy with the golf club since he had the audacity to throw the first stone. "Why did you do that?" he asked in a overly calm voice.

The guy with the bat crashed the other window. "Because we felt like it," he replied. "Now what are you going to do about it?" he asked with his words dripping with spite.

A female standing in the doorway of the Candyland, yelled into the club there was about to be a fight. The guys in the parking lot had to turn their loud music down and climbed out of the car to watch the event like they were at a drive in movie theater.

Kasan removed his suit-jacket and threw it inside of the car. "I'm going to show you better than I can tell you."

Sparkle finally found the nerve to get out of the car and ran over to Kasan. "It's too many and you know their not going to fight you one on one." She swallowed dryly. "Let's just go home."

Kasan gently moved her to the side of him. "Baby it ain't enough of them to handle me once I get this thing poppin." He sneered at the biggest man in the group. "They are going to pay for my windows. Either their going to pay out of their pockets, or I'm going to make a withdrawal from their ass, but I'm getting mine right now."

"The nigga got heart," someone yelled from the other side of the street.

Sparkle was searching for Latifah to help her try and talk some sense into Kasan. Latifah was busy searching diagonally across the street from the club for a bottle or anything.

Unlike Kasan, Latifah didn't have any particular warring specialties, and she was too small to fight grown men with her bare hands, but she wasn't allowing it to interfere with helping Kasan.

Kasan made his way into the middle of the street. He needed space to maneuver. The six guys were on his heels. The dark skin guy wearing the baseball cap sad. "So now you want to play super nigga in front of your bitch?"

Kasan broke all the way down in a stance. His eyes were seething and cold. His frame of mind was of a supreme hunter. He was going to a place he hadn't been in a long time. He just hoped he didn't kill all six of them.

"I'm going to show you what a super nigga can do," he spoke with brutal detachment.

Kasan leaped into the air and threw a round house kick which crashed into the dark skin guy with the bat. The kick landed square on his chin. He spun around like an out-of-control ballerina and went out cold. Kasan landed on his feet like a poised cat tossed from a high altitude.

The other five guys surrounded him in a half moon circle. "You fucked up now, partner," one of them said.

"No, you fucked up," Kasan said and broke back down into his stance. This time he had a devilish smirk on his face at what he was about to do next. It gratified him to punish the oppressor. It was the reason he first applied himself to learning how to fight. He had the instincts to kill right now, but tonight there was no reason to embrace this feeling and live it out. He set out to merely punish.

Latifah gave up her search for a weapon when she saw the baseball bat rolling towards the curb. She hustled over to pick it up and stalked over to where Kasan was holding each man at bay.

Latifah started to swing the bat wildly like she was a female version of Jackie Robinson only needing one hit to break Babe Ruth's home run record.

One of the guys swung a haymaker punch at Kasan. Kasan grabbed him by his wrist and spun into him until his back was pressed firmly against the guys chest. He briskly placed the guys elbow over his shoulder and pulled down with all of his might.

He broke the guys arm in one celeritous motion. The guy fell to the ground clutching his dangling arm in the most excruciating pain he's ever felt in his life, until Latifah finished him off and knocked him clean out with the bat.

The next guy took off running in Kasan's direction. Kasan timed his approach like a hawk would before it swooped in for the kill.

He dropped down to the ground and spun around with his leg extended. He swiped the guys legs clean from under him. The guy landed flat on his back. Kasan raised his leg in the air and gripped the ankle until he had his balance and slammed his foot down with pounding force into the guys stomach. This caused the guys bowels to burst out of his anus.

Latifah didn't see the tall, well built guy sneaking up behind her. He snatched her up into a choke hold with his forearm crushing her windpipe. He held her so tight, her feet were inches off the ground. She couldn't breath. She tossed the bat to the ground to free up her hands to scratch her way out of this predicament she was in. He was squeezing the life out of her.

Once she went limp, the tall guy threw her to the ground like a limp rag doll. He picked up the bat and was heading in Kasan's direction. His first swing was towards Kasan's legs. Kasan did a perfect back flip and landed on the hood of a nearby car.

Before the guy could swing the bat again, Kasan did a front somersault off the car and landed in the back of the guy. The guy's head went side to side trying to locate Kasan's where-abouts. It was almost as if he disappeared in thin air.

As the guy was about to turn around, Kasan dropped to his knees and punched the top of his foot like it was a stack of bricks. Pulverizing the bone into mere fragments.

He didn't stop there. He hit him in the shin and broke that, the knee cap and broke that, the pelvis and broke that, the ribs and broke that, the collar bone and broke that, the jaw and broke that. He crushed all of the teeth on the right side of the guys mouth. The guy leaned on the side of his body that wasn't broken like the leaning tower of Pisa and fell to the ground asleep.

The crowd cheered for Kasan when the guys knew there attack was futile and there was no way they were going to hurt Kasan. They all took off running like a dog with its tail between its leg.

They figured by Kasan being young, he wouldn't know anything. Also, by his meekness they didn't think he was going to put up such a good fight.

All they wanted to do was knock him around to get Dodirty's attention. Kasan swiftly turned the tables on them, and they wished they had known more about the kid other than his name. They would've at least brought a gun to make it even. They didn't know he was a Black Bruce Lee.

Kasan helped Latifah to her feet. She was still dizzy and leaned against him to get her balance. A thick film of foam was at the corners of her mouth. "I told you to stop trying to fight whenever I do," Kasan said allowing her to lean against him while they walked. "These are grown men and I can handle myself."

Latifah wiped her mouth with the sleeve of her new shirt. "They were trying to jump you." She shook her head from side to side to gain her faculties to stop the ground from moving. "I'm not just going to stand there and let anybody jump you. I don't care how well you think you can fight."

Kasan smiled down at her as he headed in the direction of his battered car. "You're just like your mother huh?"

Latifah spun into his arms and they held each other for a few moments to reaffirm the bond of loyalty first shared by their parents, had been transformed into their daily conscience.

Kasan could feel Latifah cry as he held her. She meant every word. She was young when her mother died and didn't fully remember her like he didn't remember his father. This was a touching moment of unity for both of them.

The full moon moved past the club and behind the forming clouds filling the night sky. Horns begin to honk their approval for the young brother properly regulating the situation with the greatest of ease.

Sparkle stood on the outside of the car waiting for them to get inside. The look of fear had vanished from her face once she saw Kasan's round house. She knew he could handle himself.

They had planned to lose their virginity to each other' but tonight's events had drastically changed and placed new circumstances on Kasan. He had far more important matters to attend to.

If this was merely a warning, then he could only imagine what they would do if they came across Dodirty. He had to warn him as soon as possible. Dodirty was all he had as a father figure and he was willing to do anything in his power not to lose him.

But would it be enough?

Chapter Twenty

"What!" Dodirty's voice degenerated to a guttural rasp. His eyes bulging out of their sockets. "You mean that no good bastard sent some guys at you?"

He didn't give Kasan a chance to reply. He snatched his robe from the back of the sitting chair in his bedroom and went to the extra room he used as a study. He had already heard more than enough. He hurriedly picked up the phone and dialed the number to his top man. It was imperative for him to put a end to this farce Terry Gambino was trying to pull. The entire time he counted his blessings, Terry didn't send men with guns after Kasan.

Kasan made sure to follow Dodirty from room to room listening with intensity to the conversation of how he was mobilizing the troops and preparing for war. Terry wanted to reach a bottom line he did that quick fast and in a hurry.

Kasan knew very well the severity of what had just happened to him, regardless if he came out on top or not. He dropped Latifah and Sparkle off and came back to inform Dodirty of the nights events. He wanted to be there when Dodirty had a sit down with Terry Gambino. Tonight, he believed he proved himself.

It seemed Dodirty was even more angry when he hung up the phone than when Kasan had originally told him what happened. Maybe when he was informing his top man about the situation, it inflamed him to have to tell his men Terry Gambino crossed the line and involved his family.

"I want you to drive down to your mother's tonight." Dodirty was trying to find something to wear. "I don't want you around when this shit really starts jumping around this bitch."

Kasan gritted his teeth. A spasm of irritation covered his face. "I want to be there watching your back."

Dodirty rushed one of his legs into his pants and practically tripped trying to get the other leg in too fast. "This ain't no karate match. This is guns and murder." He went to the closet and removed a case he kept a brand new Uzi in. "I don't need you to watch my back, this is what I do. You go to school and I put the work in around here."

"But they came at me and I held it up." Kasan sounded like he was whining like a child trying to convince his father to allow him to open his gifts the day before Christmas.

"Thank God they didn't have guns or tried to kidnap you. I told you what happened to your uncle Kasan. This is how this game goes. Motherfuckers will pull some trifling shit to gain the advantage. It was revenge that got your father and Nydia killed."

Dodirty's face became tight and pinched as a thought crossed his mind. "You know your father once told me it's not about dying for a cause, but living it out." He briskly filled the clips with bullets. "You have a long life to live, so live it. Now pack your things and go to your mothers house and don't come back until I call for you."

Dodirty stalked out of the condominium to the three car loads of men awaiting him. He could easily have Terry Gambino dealt with without having to be there himself, but he was a general and a good general led his men from the front line into battle.

Dodirty had every intention of just talking and explaining to Terry Gambino he wasn't the one for the madness he was trying to bring to him. He wasn't some little white store owner he was trying to extort, who didn't have any means of protection but what the Mafia could provide for him. He was Dodirty a straight gangster with an army at his disposal ready for war.

If Terry Gambino couldn't grasp he was the real deal and leave anyone he loves alone, he had every intention of killing him. This was going to be the day Terry Gambino either showed his respect, or he was going to die.

CHAPTER TWENTY-ONE

Terry Gambino was sitting in his restaurant called Umberto's enjoying a hefty plate of Spaghetti drowned in homemade Italian sauce, mixed with grated provolone and Parmesan cheese. His men were sitting at another table talking amongst themselves. No one could tolerate sitting directly in front of Terry while he ate. He smacked on his food like he was chewing cud. The food could be seen in his mouth at each stage of his chewing, because he chewed with his mouth open.

Terry made sure to always sit away from the window. Death always came to a man when he would least expect it. The window was a dangerous place for a man of his position to be sitting. It would make the job of a hitman too easy. Terry figured if he was going to die, they would have to earn it.

Each of his men were hand picked to be a part of his crew. This was after he made it to the position of Boss for the Gambino family in New Jersey. They shared a bond which went far beyond the La Costra Nostra, which meant (This Thing Of Ours.)

Terry had to make sure they weren't hungry for his position of power in the family. In the Mafia, it is usually your best friend who sets you up to be wacked. His men weren't picked to be a part of his crew for their ambition to make it to the top, but for their deficiency to want to be anything other than a soldier.

Terry had the appearance of the average Italian. His hair didn't turn gray until he was in his mid forties. He wore it like a crown of white gold. He was proud to at least see his hair turn gray.

He's been affiliated in street crime since his teens, Finally, he got made when he turned twenty-five. Many of his good friends he ran with in his younger years were dead and gone. Therefore, he wore his gray hair as a badge of honor.

Gray hair in the Mafia was a clear sign of a made man with intelligence to survive the many trials and tribulations. Living in this kind of life only few were lucky enough to die of natural causes.

Terry wiped the spaghetti sauce from the tip of his boxer's nose. The shape came from his many street brawls in his younger years. Now he was out of shape and any dish with globs of pasta was his favorite dish. The loud slurping of the spaghetti was a testament to that fact.

He was no longer concerned with the shape of his body. The women loved him for the power he held and the men feared him for the many gunslingers he had ready to do his bidding.

His men were sitting at the other table talking about how Kasan put a whipping on a group of grown men he paid a couple of hundred dollars to rough him up. They didn't expect the kid to turn into Jim Kelly.

Terry was convinced the only way for him to get the job done was to make sure he did it himself. The wheels in his head was trying to formulate a plan to really get under Dodirty's skin. He needed to find his weakness to force him to submit to his will like everyone else in the city. The last thing he wanted to do was call for outside help. It would put him in a bad light with the Commission, as if he was the wrong man appointed as the Boss of New Jersey.

He slammed a fork full of spaghetti in his mouth when he noticed three cars park in front of the restaurant. The plate of food was inches away from his face. Terry didn't glance up until he heard the numerous car doors slam in perfect unison and saw several Black men getting out of each of the cars wearing long black trench coats. It didn't take him long to figure out why they were here.

The metallic doors of the oven slammed with a dungeon cling.

The stove was the oldest part of the restaurant. It was the secret ingredient which made the food taste like it was cooked in a Italian kitchen in Scily.

A stack of logs were piled up in the far corner and cut for a perfect fit into the oven. The worker tossed a soaked log into the fire and used the spit standing against the wall to thrust the glowing logs further to the back of the oven.

He used a huge, wooden spatula to place a doughy pizza onto the stone iron inside of the oven. By the time he turned around, a team of Black men had secured the outside entrance, while a lone man was storming through the glass doors. He didn't look like he was about to place an order.

Instead of Terry having to search far and wide for Dodirty, he was coming to him. Terry felt even more comfortable because he was on his own turf.

Dodirty came inside alone. His men were standing outside waiting for him to give the signal when he needed them and they were to come in blazing. He wanted Terry to recognize there was no fear. He was demanding his respect as a man and not with the men standing behind him.

A long wax paper hung from the ceiling and stopped in mid air. It was used to catch the flies that snuck in when the door opened. Three flies were twisting trying to free themselves from an inevitable death.

Dodirty shuffled up to the counter where the cashier was nervously drinking a cherry soda. He closed the Hardy Boy mystery novel he pretended to read to give Dodirty his undivided attention.

Dodirty picked up a straw and slid off the paper sheath. He placed the tip of the straw into his mouth. "I think this would be a good time to take your break."

The cashier looked like a college kid trying to make some extra money to pay for school. He could feel the tension leaping off of the man standing in front of him. It caused the blood to drain from his pale face. He wiped his moist hands on his apron and quickly disappeared into the back.

Dodirty slid into the booth diagonally across from Terry. He snapped open the can of soda and dropped his straw inside. He was trying to do everything within his power to calm himself before he said anything. His blood was still boiling. Just the thought of what Kasan had told him happened last night, still rung in his ears. His first thought was to just walk up and put a few slugs in his head and call it a day.

Fred, who was the nephew of Terry's wife moseyed over to Terry's table. "I think he's here to talk to you."

Being the actor he always dreamed of being, Terry pretended to have just noticed Dodirty when Fred brought him to his attention. They had never met before, but both had an unwavering idea of what each other looked like.

Terry wiped the red stain sauce from the corners of his mouth and tossed the napkin into his empty plate. He had finished off an entire plate of spaghetti in less than ten minutes. The plate was so clean, his reflection could be seen at the bottom.

He squeezed his round stomach into the booth Dodirty was sitting in. "So we finally meet." He gave Dodirty a weak smile. "No disrespect on what I had to do to get your attention."

Dodirty's brows wrinkled in vexation. He spoke through gritted teeth. "I'm not here to get acquainted with you to even consider a friendship." His face hardened. "Your means of getting my attention is a violation to the highest degree of each and every aspect of what I stand for as a straight motherfuckin gangster!" He looked at Terry venomously. "Now my reasons for being here is to make sure this mistake doesn't ever happen again."

Terry held his hands up like he was pleading for forgiveness. "Lets put the past behind us. Lets talk business." He glanced over at his men. "No harm came to Kasan." He released a raspy chuckle. "In fact, he whipped the men I had hired to just scare him. They beat the pavement down trying to get away." Terry erupted into a hearty laugh.

Dodirty's facial expression hadn't changed since he sat down. He leaned across the table with his eyes blazing murderously. "My business is just that, my business and nothing concerning what I do is open for a discussion." He stood to his feet and lightly brushed his hand across his gun. "Remember you've been warned." He headed for the door.

Terry's face turned beet red and then purple from his uncontrolled anger. He slid out of the booth as if he were an in shape athlete. He could be extremely hysterical when he was angry.

"Stop right there you low life nigger!" His voice growing frenzied. He pointed a stubby finger at Dodirty. "You got some kind of balls coming into my place and talking to me with anything less than your respect you fucking nigger." Terry pretended to spit in the direction of Dodirty to further emphasize his point. His men stood up.

Dodirty had enough. He believed the only thing Terry would respect is violence. His choice of words caused him to have to react, or Terry would continue with disrespecting him and Kasan.

He faced the spacious window and touch his chin. It was a sign for his men to come in and hold him up. The temperature in the room rose to over a hundred degrees. The tension was so thick, you could cut it with a butter knife.

Dodirty faced Terry. "It was you who cast the first stone guinea nigga and if you think I have any intentions of showing you the least bit of respect, then guinea nigga you are sadly mistaken."

Terry's face was hot and pinched with resentment. "I know what I'm going to do, I'm going to wack that little nigger son of yours," he said coldly.

Dodirty gave Terry a dark, smoldering look. It was those threats which made just walking out of the restaurant impossible at this point. Now it was all coming to a head.

As if Terry's last remark was a bell ringing for two fighters, they all reached for their guns. This wasn't going to be stand off. As they drew their guns, they were ready to fire.

Terry dived to the ground and crawled like he was trying to complete a military drill in basic training. The barrage of bullets Dodirty blasted at him was missing his head by inches. Splinters of wood flung through the air.

Malik was Dodirty's right hand man. He shot twice at the Italians in the doorway leading to the back of the restaurant. He reached for Dodirty. "Lets get out of here. We're in the open."

Dodirty ducked behind the counter. "I'm not leaving until I kill that guinea motherfucker!" His face was lit with bitter triumph. He yanked the neck of his gun back to make sure it wasn't jammed. "I've seen him go to the back. Cover me."

He wasn't going to leave until Terry was dead. He had made a threat which locked Dodirty and him together until one of them was dead. By no means could he allow a threat like that to go without dealing with it properly.

Dodirty charged into the midst of the sailing bullets without an ounce of fear. The fuel in his engine was pure determination to kill Terry Gambino.

There was an enormous figure standing in the middle of the doorway and firing repeatedly. Dodirty dropped to the ground and rolled closer to the man shooting wildly. He shot him twice in the stomach.

The heavy set Italian doubled over from the two slugs to his belly, but still found the strength to remain on his feet. He got even lower to the ground trying to retrieve his gun at his feet.

Dodirty came up on one knee and slammed it into his head, and shot him again, but this time in the back of the head as he was on his way down to the ground. The man fell backwards and onto a stack of boxes dead.

Malik was trying his hardest to at least get in the front of Dodirty. When Dodirty first told him what he intended to do this morning, Malik insisted for him to stay home and let him handle matters of this magnitude. He owed this much to Dodirty. He found Malik and saved him from the lowest in his life. He was sick with pneumonia and sleeping in Newark Penn Station. He now lived in a beautiful house in Montclair.

The last thing he wanted was for something to happen to Dodirty. He owed his life to the man who cleaned him up and helped refine his dignity by getting him off the streets. It didn't matter to him if Dodirty told him he felt more comfortable on the battlefield than anywhere else in the organization. He couldn't stand by and allow anything to happen to the man he admired.

Dodirty took a giant step back. He found himself out of bullets. The trick with a Uzi, you had to make sure you made all of your bullets count. They could all suddenly disappear as soon as your finger touched the trigger.

Malik finally pushed his way in front of Dodirty and bolted to the back of the restaurant. A man leaped out from behind the door of the deep freezer in surprise. Malik picked him off. The bullet he hit him with, peeled back his skull. The blood splattered on the wall like it was splashed on with a soggy paint brush, freshly dipped into a can of red paint.

Dodirty's eyes were thoroughly scanning amongst the dead on the ground for a weapon. He located a revolver in one of the dead Italians hands. As he was making his way towards the back door, he heard a bullet hiss through the air and Malik screamed as it landed in his throat.

Dodirty flipped open the cylinder. There were only two bullets left in the gun and he had to make do with it. He had to make sure at least one of those bullets found its way into Terry Gambino. He had to protect the life of Kasan

Dodirty didn't know he was chasing a ghost. Terry Gambino had made his way out the back door as soon as he disappeared into the back. He was now on his way to his hide out, until things were safe and had calmed down.

Dodirty fired one shot around the corner when he saw a figure standing behind a wall of boxes. It hit Fred in the center of his chest, then the entire restaurant went completely silent. Dodirty could hear his heart beating rapidly in his ears and the silence only amplified its volume.

His nerves were on edge. Not out of fear, but from knowing death was literally around the corner. He didn't have any self imposed intentions of dying. He wanted to live for as long as life would allow him to. Life was only for a mere second compared to the eternity of death. This is why he lived life to the fullest.

Malik found the strength to crawl halfway down the paltry hall-way where Dodirty was standing. He griped the wooden planks in the floors to pull him along. Dodirty noticed him and laid his gun down and took Malik into his arms as a means of consoling him. The blood was seeping through a hole in his throat. It gushed out like water sprouting from a fountain.

Dodirty's heart rung with pity at the sight of his friend. The blood escaping from his throat was a clear sign his beloved friend wasn't going to make it and the least he could do was be there for him so he wouldn't have to die alone. He now accepted the fact Terry wasn't there, but he would have to continue the hunt.

Malik's eyes darted maniacally in the back of Dodirty and picked up a silhouette in the gloom creeping through the darkness. It took the last bit of strength for him to raise his hand to point in the direc-tion of the shadow, but it was too late.

A bullet whizzed through the air and hit Dodirty in the center of his back. The hollow point lodged in his lung and exploded on impact. The force of the bullet took him by complete surprise. He thought everyone had left.

Primarily, it felt like he had been kicked. As he attempted to climb onto one knee, his strength slowly slipped from his body along with the potency of air from his punctured lungs. The last thing he wanted to do was pass out.

Sirens could be heard blaring from a distance. This had to be a dream. Dodirty was thinking. A dream he hoped to awaken from, in his bed and able to relive this day all over again.

His ability to breath was slowly diminishing as his lungs filled with blood. The continued lack of air was sluggishly suffocating his ability to think and breath. His strength was depleting with each tick of the clock on the wall next to an autograph picture of Frank Sinatra.

Dodirty knew if he didn't get out of the place and he lived, he was going to prison for the rest of his life. At the moment, he refused to balance one over the other. He had to make it to his feet. By no means did he intend to give up on freedom and lay down and die.

A squad of officers burst through the front door with their guns drawn. The restaurant could pass as a war zone. Dead bodies were sprawled on every inch of the restaurant floor. A mini arsenal of guns were strewn all over the restaurant. The officers were casing every inch of the restaurant to see who could be alive. After the sight before them. It looked like a race war had taken place.

Dodirty had used the last drop of strength left in his body to raise off the floor and this caught Detective Scott's attention. Scott almost fired a shot in Dodirty's direction when he saw the sudden movement out of the corner of his eye.

Scott kicked the gun away from Dodirty's hand. "We have a live one," he said surveying the wounds. "Call for a bus. I think we can save this one." He kneeled down to make an effort to perform mouth to mouth on Dodirty.

Dodirty's eyes shot open like he just been zapped with a high voltage of electricity. He tightly clenched his teeth together to prevent Scott from being able to breath for him until help arrived. He wanted to die.

The last rays of logic were fleeting, but he did know there was no way he would be able to come out of this situation a victim. He was a known gangster and the only one alive from what he knew. They would charge him with every murdered Italian pronounced dead in the restaurant.

"Open you mouth!" Scott shouted. He tried to force Dodirty's mouth open by gripping his jaw in a vise like grip. "I'm trying to save your life."

Scott couldn't rationalize the reason the man didn't want to be saved. Little did he know, the man was able to visually see the outcome of his situation if he were to live and he wanted out. Dodirty was turning his back on life and embracing death.

The thought of Terry Gambino getting away made him want to live, but what was he going to do from a prison cell? He found himself more worried about the safety of Kasan, than death beckoning him to a realm far beyond this world.

From a distance he could still hear Scott trying to get him to open his mouth, as his mind thought about the aggravating circumstances his death would cause. He worried for Kasan.

Dodirty's eyes became wide and out of nowhere, a triumphant smile spread across his face in the last seconds of his life. The sight of a near dead man smiling caused Scott's eyebrows to shoot up with surprise. For all of the years he's been on the force and watched men die in his arms, not once did he ever see a glorious smile on their face.

It was the glimpse of seeing his friend Don Starchild living and breathing which caused him to smile. All of the answers to his life questions were answered in that flash of a moment. This was the reason the connect contacted him. The reason when the connect died the prices seem to become cheaper. Don was controlling the game.

A brisk image of the future also flashed before his eyes. He saw a encounter between Don and Terry Gambino and now he felt comfortable to die without any worry. Don was going to make him pay for what happened today.

Dodirty continued to smile as the life force slowly slipped from his being and became one with the universe. He just hoped they was going to allow him to see the showdown from hell, because he knew, hell was exactly where he was going for the life he lived.

CHAPTER TWENTY-TWO

A cocoon of sleep clung to Don until he was startled by the loud music coming from his daughter's room. At first, he reckoned it was the dreams, but its been years since those nightmares plagued him. He now had a new set of circumstances which occupied his daily life.

Don was a very rich man. The richest he thought he would ever become in his life. The drastic measures he used fifteen years ago, made the Dragon cartel the leading suppliers of cocaine all over the world and heroin in America.

He still maintained his alliances with the three men he allowed to share in his power, only because it served a greater good for his operation to go smoothly. Cecil controlled the territory he had intended to give to Felipe.

It wasn't necessary for Don to exhaust himself by sitting at the top alone. Their help aided in minimizing any and every risk. If they were hidden from the masses, then he plainly didn't exist. He was the man who lingered in the shadows of the family. All he did was make all major decisions and collect truck loads of money. He only needed to speak with the ones he allowed to live and even that was done through Hector who was the front man for the Dragon family.

The majority of Don's time was spent with his family. They were important to him. Bonita and Cecil were the only ones he shared his most intimate thoughts with, but it was only to a certain extent. There was so much he was even afraid to share with himself.

It was because of Bonita's comfort and sensitivity that he was able to rule with more compassion then he cared for. The death of his baby brother and Nydia had removed the element of care from his heart when it came to outsiders.

In the confines of his mansion, he was the most loving man, but he dealt with potential enemies with a potent form of brutality that others renamed him the gray eyed devil, especially when whisper's of how three hundred and fifty men disappeared without a trace from a party he had given fifteen years ago.

His daughter, Divine Starchild, didn't know much about his past, or present life. All she could say about her doting father was how she had him wrapped around her finger. She doesn't recall him even spanking her.

She believed her father to be a business man and owning a myriad of business throughout the world. For this reason they owned homes in different parts of the world.

Don spoiled her since she was born and this treatment continued well into her teens. She was his only girl. He missed his two sons and was trying to damper the culpability of not being a part of their lives. It was hard for him to know his sons were forced into believing their father was dead.

Silk pajamas and robe was all he would wear while he was home. He slid into leather slippers and quietly left the master-bedroom. There was no doubt in his mind Bonita heard the loud music, but she was giving Don time to hear and respond to it. She left it up to Don to verbally reprimand their daughter. Don would always say she could be entirely too hard on her for small things. Bonita was only trying to instill a sense of discipline in Divine the way her mother taught her before her life dramatically changed for the better.

The life she lived now was one she envisioned a queen would live. She mingled amongst the elite of the world, not as a maid, but as the wife of a powerful business man. Don had many identities he would use throughout the world. She would fall in sync with whatever alias they were using.

Don knocked on the door, but the deafening rap music prevented Divine from hearing her father's knock. This was starting to be a every morning thing with her before she went to school.

Standing at the door listening to the harsh lyrics of the music made him cringe at the thought she was listening to this all day everyday. He hated the lyrics, but could tolerate the beat. The gangster rappers, as they were called, were boasting about a life of crime they didn't have the slightest indication of.

A life he's lived everyday, but would never try and glorify it in the eyes of the public. The life he lived involved killing to enforce his rule. The money wasn't for show and tell, but to take care of his troops to be able to fight the wars of those trying to reach the pinnacle of the drug game he was now operating.

Divine left him no choice. He opened the door and cautiously stuck his head inside. She caught the reflection of the door opening in the mirror and spun around with a look of pitiful appeal in the gray eyes she inherited from her father. She scrambled over to the high priced stereo and turned the music down.

Don's eyes raked the room wildly. His eyes locked onto her with a withering stare. Divine knew it was just one of his tactics to pretend he was mad at her. She wasn't the least bit scared.

"I thought I told you to wear headphones, or don't blast the music," he spoke in rapid Spanish. He took a step into the room. He stared at her with cold speculation and gritted his teeth, "especially in the morning when your mother and I are asleep."

Don glanced over at her friend Lisa sitting on the bed wearing a short mini-skirt. Her legs were shaved smooth and she had them crossed like a proper lady.

She crossed her right leg over her left to give Don a little more thigh and hoped he was able to see she wasn't wearing any panties. She's had a crush on him since she and Divine have been friends. The older she got, the more she lusted for him.

It was his silent ways that made him mysterious to her. The only time he didn't wear a suit was in the mornings and she thought he had the ways and actions of a gentleman, just by the way he treated his wife and daughter.

Lisa was the one who would turn the music up every morning. She did this whenever she knew he was home after a long trip to a part of the world she couldn't even pronounce. When she couldn't take missing him any longer, she would turn the music up because it would bring him directly into the room. It would make her day to see him before she went to school.

Lisa had a coquettish smirk on her youthful face. She and Divine could pass for sister. The difference was Divine's gray eyes, but they wore their hair the same.

"Good morning Don," Lisa said with a seductive smile on her face. The only name she's ever called him by was his first name. She didn't even know his last name.

Don was humored by the way she would try to act like a grown woman towards him, but he only saw her as a child. He told her to call him by his first name, rarely did he use his last name.

"Good morning to you Lisa," he said in English. Lisa didn't speak Spanish. He pointed a finger at Divine. "You better make sure she keeps the music down, or you two will be walking to hop on that school bus in the morning."

Lisa continued to regard him provocatively. The smooth sound of his baritone voice made her writhe on the bed with pleasure. "I keep telling her you're sleep and you need your rest." She sucked her teeth and ran her fingers through her hair. "You see she doesn't listen."

Divine shifted her eyes over at Lisa and slightly shook her head. She didn't like to be used as a scapegoat. She wanted to tell her father Lisa was telling a bold face lie. She was the one turning it up so he would come to the room. The only reason why she didn't was because her father hated snitching in the least. If she did that, he would take the car from her for a month, or longer.

Don smiled politely at both of them before he closed the door and made his way through the mansion. His ears were sharp and he heard Lisa ask Divine how old he was and was he Black, or Colombian?

Don waited to see what Divine would say, but she didn't even respond to her question. She switched to another subject just as swift as the wind blowing to the west.

Divine knew to never offer any information about her father to anyone. This lesson has been ingrained in her since she was able to say Da Da and became even more relevant the older she got.

In all actuality, she didn't really know much about her father. He made it so she never really had the opportunity to ask questions. Whenever she did ask about his birth mother and father, Bonita would interject and switch the conversation to something else.

Don would rather say nothing than lie to his daughter. She didn't know the monster he was in the lives of his enemies. He was searching for the right time to tell her everything, but at fifteen years old, she wasn't ready to hear the absolute truth about her father's past, as well as his present to better understand his future.

It could take ten minutes to reach the front door of the mansion. Once he got there, he opened the door and found the stack of newspapers which would be there every morning. Don stretched his back before he bent down to pick them up.

Reading the newspapers was his only hobby. It kept him abreast of the world news. The information he read in the newspapers became a conversation piece whenever he was surrounded by legit businessmen who worked for him. He also encouraged Bonita to read the papers also. She only had a fifth grade education, and between the newspapers and thoroughly reading the dictionary, she could now past for a rocket scientist.

Don found it amusing how she was able to hold her own with people who had masters' degrees. Bonita took it upon herself to read the papers when they went on trips around the world and she would somehow weave foreign political views of what was taking place around the world into conversations. No one would ever believe she didn't even complete middle school.

Don had a ritual to reading the newspapers. He would read all of the other papers and save the Star Ledger for last. He wouldn't read the front page until he first read the obituaries of the Star Ledger. It was his only way to stay in tune with what was going on back home, who died, or who got sent to prison.

He scanned the obituaries and didn't see anyone name he recognized. He thumbed his way to the front page and gaped in silence at what he read in bold letters.

The headlines read, DRUG LORD MURDERED BY MOB. He jumped out of his plush chair when he ready Dodirty's name.

The sight of his friends name caused him to subconsciously walk in a circle around the mansion still reading the paper. He had to move to prevent himself from passing out from the shock of today's revelation. His eyes continued to blink with incredulity and became dark with pain.

The paper reported the killings between two rival crime bosses. Don didn't understand how Dodirty could've been in the game for so many years and yet he allowed himself to get killed in such a senseless manner, especially after what he watched Don go through many years ago.

Don used Hector to pry and get the information about his mother, Dodirty and his sons, whenever he came to pick up. This was the only way to find out the information the newspapers wouldn't be able to give him. He calculated business to be good for his friend. He gave him cocaine at such low prices, Dodirty could sell two hundred grams and make a profit on the entire kilo.

The telephone in his study began to ring. Don was so lost in what he was reading he didn't pay it any mind. He was confused why Dodirty was anywhere near a murder. Don made sure he was a rich man and had enough money to get anybody buried.

Don plopped down in the seat behind his desk in his study. He just couldn't make any sense out of what had happened. As he read between the lines of the paper the location of his friends murder happened to be at a mob's hangout. This only had to mean Dodirty gave his emotions precedence instead of embracing intelligence. A sin which would betray any man of power.

Don knew this to be the truth. It was how he fumbled long ago. He forgot the bottle of brandy in the window. The sight of Sosa finally dead caused him to get lost in the whirlwind of his own emotions.

After lying the paper across his desk, Don read the front page several more times to make sure nothing slipped past him in his brief hysteria. The room felt like it was spinning under his feet. He went to the middle section the story was being continued on. He had to read this disturbing story all the way through.

On the inside, there was a picture of Dodirty's coffin being carried out of Calvary Baptist church by Don's two sons and Dodirty's son. The fine print under the picture spoke of his nephew Kasan Starchild, the son of the infamous Don Starchild, would more than likely take his place as the top Boss of the illegal drug operation. The rest of the article spoke about Don's last altercation with the Newark police department and the loss of his own life in the process.

"Shit," Don cursed as he threw up his hands in disgusted resignation. "Look at this shit here."

It was the picture of Kasan that was causing him the most mental turmoil. The thought he was about to partake in the life he so desperately wanted out of. The life which allegedly claimed his life and now Dodirty's. He just found it hard to envision either of his children dying before their time, especially for a lifestyle they would be able to easily acquire through dedication and hard work.

The mantle in his study held the pictures of both of his sons. Don went over to study the picture to make sense of the time he missed out of their lives. Kasan of all people was the first to make an attempt to leap into his shoes. He could only imagine what Jewel would do, or think. The life he chose was the reason she left him. Now her only son wanted to be a part of it, what would she do now?

Don heard the crumbling of the newspaper in his hand and this forced him to take another look at the picture as if it would change from the time he looked at it before. This was far too much for him to deal with alone. He needed to talk things over with Bonita to make sure his decisions were more rational than emotional.

These were the times he needed her opinion the most. When he was entirely too close to the situation. He trusted her advice more than anything. She was on the outside looking in.

Heavy thuds of water could be heard coming from the shower

inside of their bathroom. Bonita liked the shower door to stay closed, so the steam would open her pores and better remove the dirt deeply embedded in her skin.

She came out of the shower with a pink terry cloth towel wrapped around her head and another around her body. The only reason she came out as soon as she got out of the shower was because she ran out of skin moisturizer and was coming to get another bottle. She saw Don sitting in the chair she called his thinking chair with tears coming down his almond cheeks.

The chair sat directly in front of the spacious window in their bedroom overlooking the body of water at the tip of the Florida Keys. The edge of their immense property was lined with palm trees and a plantation of wild sugar cane Don loved to eat during his frequent walks.

She rushed to the other side of the room to comfort him. She held his head against the towel wrapped around her, waiting for him to speak as she didn't want to ask him what it was that had him so upset.

The tears streaming down his cheeks alone had saddened her and she didn't even know why he was crying. Its been years since she's witnessed him crying. The last time she saw him cry was when their daughter was born. She assumed they were tears of joy. It was unconventional for him to openly display such raw emotion.

Bonita heard the newspaper ruffle in his hand as he clutched it tightly. The sight of the paper tugged at her heart. She knew it would be just a matter of time before he read some bad news in the paper. Although he didn't seem to look for it, but it was the reason why he subscribed to it. It was his only way to stay abreast of the happenings back home.

"They killed my best friend," he cried and held up the paper for her to read it for herself, but she didn't bother.

Bonita gently stroked his face and it was her soft touch that made him sob even harder. It was as if all of the years he should have cried was hitting him all at once.

He would talk about the things Dodirty told Hector as if Don and he had spoken face to face. Just the way Dodirty stepped up and helped Jewel take care of his son showed what kind of friend he was. This is after he thought his friend was dead. Sure Bonita knew Dodirty meant a lot to him. Dodirty showed his love for Don when he helped save him down Prince Street and Don was able to see the pain on his face from his assumed failure at his funeral. Because of Don's death he helped his son become a man. Don couldn't ask for a better friend.

He moved over towards the bed to lie down while Bonita got dressed. Laggardly, he was starting to gain control over his emotions. He was entitled to emotional break downs at times. After all, he still was a human being. Some would think he was a machine by some of the things he's done and continue to do, but it was times like this Bonita knew why she loved him so.

Long before he came upstairs, he heard Divine leave for school. This way, he and Bonita didn't have to speak in hush tones to make sure she didn't hear anything. Plenty of times she would tell them their lovemaking was a little too loud the night before.

Don thumbed through to the section where his youngest son was carrying Dodirty's coffin and prompted her to read the caption below the picture about Kasan taking Dodirty's place.

Bonita stared at the paper in stunned silence. Any child of Don's she considered was a part of her family also. This was her daughter's older brother.

Bonita's mouth formed a muted O. "He's going to take his place?" she asked with a agitated look in her eyes. She still held onto the paper and caught the towel before it fell from her still shapely body. "If you don't do something to stop this, they are going to kill him like they did Dodirty."

This is what he loved about his wife. She's been around the life long enough to know what the end results would be in numerous situations. She wouldn't tell him exactly what to do, because she knew he knew how to handle any situation. She knew he needed to do something and allowed him time to take care of his problem.

Don went to the phone in his study. It was untraceable and no one would be able to locate his whereabouts, also there was a scrambler on the phone to distort any conversations from being recorded.

Don searched through his Rolodex for the number to one of the mob bosses in Florida, named Aldo Vandino. Vandino didn't like Don one bit, but had no choice but to have tremendous respect for him, and the power he wielded. He just believed he came from nowhere and had it not been for drugs, he wouldn't be as rich as he was.

Vandino had heard of the other families trying to muscle in on him, but Don would always attack the core of their power and they would call for a sit down. Don would never come himself, but he would send someone in his place. No one could trace his origins and they knew nothing about this Black man, who they were led to believe was Colombian.

"Mr. Vandino, this is Don."

Vandino sounded excited to hear from him. For all he knew, this could mean some money for him and he would do anything to win favor with Don. He had a idea of what he may be worth and Vandino would be satisfied with a mere fraction of that.

"It's been a while since we last spoke Don. How's is the family?"

Don purposely ignored his personal question. He would never discus his family with known thugs of any kind. In fact, Vandino didn't even know if Don had a family or not. Not once did it ever come up in any of their prior discussions.

"I need to have meeting with Terry Gambino."

Vandino cleared his throat loudly on the phone. "From Jersey?"

"Exactly."

"About what?" Vandino asked.

"Just to have a little conversation."

Vandino ran his hand across his clean shaven face confused and he didn't like to be confused. He wondered how Don even knew Terry Gambino to want to meet with him. The situation at the restaurant crossed his mind, but he still couldn't grasp the connection.

Vandino sighed into the phone. "Why do you need to meet with Terry?" He had to ask these questions. As far as he knew Don was

Colombian. His accent was thick. This caused Vandino to consider he hasn't been in America long.

Don removed a cigar from a polished, chestnut box. "Nothing pertaining to business if that is what you mean. This is more of a personal situation I would like to speak with him about."

Don knew the Mafia weren't allowed to involve themselves with drugs and Vandino knew he dealt in drugs, but they had never done any business together. He just heard Don dealt with drugs, but he only knew him as a businessman.

Vandino was silent in thought as his mind was trying to turn over every detail before he decided what he was going to do. To not let him speak to Terry could blow this thing way out of proportion, whatever it is. But to place him in contact with Terry and . . .

"Don we've known each other for a good while, but I can't set up a meeting with Terry unless I can say for a surety he's not going to get clipped." His voice rose an octave. "I can get whacked if I did something like that." He switched the phone to his other ear. "Did he do something to you Don?"

Don chuckled to lighten the seriousness of their conversation, but his face still showed he was incurably sad. "I am trying to prevent him from doing the unthinkable to me." He bit the tip of his cigar off and lit it. "If he comes in peace, then I will do the same and we will just walk away with a better understanding of who we are as men."

"I'll see what I can do Don."

"It's not about seeing Mr. Vandino, I want you to make sure it happens." The thought of something happening to Kasan had crossed his mind. His face became pinched and tight. "I will put it to you this way Mr. Vandino, the entire existence of the Mafia in this country can and will be held responsible if boundaries aren't fully understood in advance." Don just hung up the phone.

He picked up the phone and called Hector and Cecil to get a two hundred men together and fuel up one of the planes. He let them know he was going to Newark to have a heart to heart talk with Terry Gambino.

Cecil knew something big had to have happened of grave importance. Don never spoke about going back to Newark for any reason whatsoever. When he came to the mansion to find out the particulars of why, Don just handed him the newspaper and it told Cecil everything he needed to know.

As far as Cecil was concerned, he owed Don life plus ten years, and he would leap at any and every opportunity to make good on that debt.

Don didn't show how uneasy he was about going back to the city of his youth, but he was. The thought of going back caused a knot to constrict in his throat. All it would take was one person to recognize him and it could open up an investigation.

After weighing the repercussions, he still was going back. For his son, he would do anything and if that meant coming back from the dead to make sure Kasan lived a long prosperous life, then call this day the day of his resurrection.

For his son to be safe, if a war was needed to secure this dream, he was ready to kill every Italian in the Mafia to make this one dream a reality.

CHAPTER TWENTY-THREE

The night fog descended upon the streets like a thick veil of smoke. It was cold and the streets were deserted. In the midst of the night air, a dark and gloomy feeling appeared to be etched in the buildings on both sides of the street.

The only sounds to interrupt the placidity of the night were the footsteps of Terry Gambino and his men walking from the far end of the corner. They were all wrapped in a state of confusion about tonight's meeting. In case matters got out of hand, they all were strapped with weapons in their waist under their long tweed jackets.

A flickering street light at the end of the street revealed Don Starchild standing in the middle of the block alone. He wore a pair of brown designer slacks and a black turtle neck. His two nine millimeters dangled from his shoulders from soft leather holsters.

The guns hanging from his shoulders incandesced in the night. Although the night air was chilled, Don was able to resist the force of the cold. The heat of his controlled anger was burning inside and keeping him warm.

The many diamonds from his watch ricocheted multiple dimensions of light into the inner recesses of the night. He lit a cigar and the flame from his platinum lighter illuminated the evil lurking behind his gray eyes. The man walking towards him was responsible for the death of his friend.

As Don waited for the men to stand before him, he took a deep breath to savor the delicate odor of the Newark air as it entered his nostrils. Immediately, his wrath completely dropped to a level of tranquillity.

Although he appeared to be alone, it was a smoke screen for Don to give confidence to the men coming towards him. He didn't want Terry to think he was walking into a ambush. He wanted them to enter the inner sanctum of his lair and not know it until the last minute. Don hoped his emotions didn't get the best of him and he killed Terry Gambino tonight.

The meeting was being held on a side street in North Newark. There were no houses and all of the industrial buildings had fallen into partial ruin and decay. Terry was extremely puzzled as to how would anyone from Florida know to have a meeting in the most deserted area of Newark, where police seldom traveled.

Before he agreed to the meeting, Terry inquired of Vandino to give him some insight about the man who wanted to meet him. All Vandino could tell him about Don was he was a Black Colombian who was the supplier of cocaine to America and had legions of Colombians under his direct command.

"Plain and simple Terry, he's a man not to fuck with." Those were the last words Vandino spoke to Terry and they stayed in his head.

Terry came to a complete halt when he stood in front of the man who wanted to meet him. He noticed the two guns dangling from his shoulders, but he didn't worry about that. He had no less than twenty men with him and they all had guns. The part to bother him the most about the stranger was the coldness in his eyes. Terry figured there was no need for the man to be cold towards him, this was their first time meeting.

Don's masculine cologne mingled with the moist dew of the night air. The air was stiff and the smoke from the cigar stayed perfectly still. The only time it moved was when Don blew out the second mouthful of smoke.

Terry stared into Don's face and for some reason, he couldn't recall exactly where he knew him. The man before him looked vaguely familiar.

Terry regarded his surroundings curiously and suddenly begin to relax when he glanced past Don and didn't see the legions of Colombians Vandino said was at his immediate disposal.

As if Don was reading his mind, he threw his cigar down. This was a sign for his men to come out of hiding. He diverted his gray eyes to the roofs of the buildings. Terry's eyes also followed. He saw a fleet of Colombians on the roofs and even more were standing inside of the dilapidated buildings with high powered assault weapons pointed at him and his men.

The light from the infrared beams swung through the darkness and had landed on each of the men standing next to Terry Gambino. Terry gave Don a sidelong glance. Don lit another cigar and two cars silently blocked both ends of the street. The next time he threw his cigar down, it would mean to kill everything on this street.

Terry was well known to act like he was superior to Blacks, but tonight, he was putting his arrogance in his pocket. It would only get him and the rest of his men killed. From the structure of the situation before him, he wasn't sure if it was already in the cards for it to end that way.

Not to feel confident of his fate made him feel vulnerable standing before the man who wanted to meet him. The sight of the military movement of the men positioned all around the meeting place showed Terry this man was the real deal.

Don snatched both of his guns from there holsters. The cigar was gripped between his teeth. "I want all of you to open your jackets and if you have a gun, throw it over there." He made a head motion to the other side of the street. "I expect to see twenty guns."

Terry spoke to one of his men in Italian under his breath. "Are you sure these motherfuckers are from Miami?"

Don cocked the hammer back on both of his guns with his thumbs. He thought they were speaking if they should do it or not. "No need to confer with each other if you should do it or not." His accent was thick. "This matter isn't open for negotiations. You have a half of second."

"Get rid of your pieces," Terry said to his men.

The metal from the guns crashed into the concrete on the other side of the street. Don mentally counted each of the guns as they sailed through the air and landed.

He stuck one of his Nines back in its holster. He had only counted eighteen guns. "I think we have two more and this will be my last time verbally speaking about this again." Don clutched the cigar in his hand.

Terry unbuttoned the lower buttons of his coat. "Are you sure these fuckin guys are from Miami?" he asked again.

Thomas tossed his gun to the side of the street and dropped his head to his chest. "That's what Vandino said."

While they were locked in a conversation, Don was striving to collect his thoughts and his emotions. The warehouse his brother was killed in was just down the street. Just looking at the frame of the building caused his bottom lip to quiver. The pain of his brother's death was causing the pain to resurface after so many years. Now he was here to protect his son to make sure history doesn't repeat itself.

Once the guns were tossed across the street, Don stretched his back to stand straight and proud. "Terry Gambino I presume." His accent was thick, but clear. His gray eyes were now shining with murderous pleasure. A mild grin formed at the corners of his mouth.

Terry smiled. "You must be Don from Miami." He had a huge knot in his stomach.

The grin disappeared at the sound of Terry's voice. Don's mouth tightened into a stubborn line, as he looked over Terry with a piercing stare.

Don placed the Cuban cigar in his mouth and pulled lightly to bring the fire back to life. "You may have known a good friend of mine by the name of Dodirty." Don was maliciously smiling at the first recognition of worry in Terry's eyes.

Terry swallowed the lump in his throat. It felt like his heart had been engulfed into a cold block of ice. "Yeah, I know him." His voice was wooden and distant.

Terry's mind was cloudy from the sound of Dodirty's name. He was on a back street with what seemed like a thousand guns pointed at him, and he was unarmed. He should've known Dodirty had some real power backing him. Dodirty had the best supply of cocaine in New Jersey and other states.

Don took a step closer towards him as he placed his other gun in its holster. He stood a clean six inches above Terry Gambino. He heard the quiver in his voice.

"You knew him, Mr. Gambino," Don said through gritted teeth. "He is dead now because of you." He loudly sucked in the Newark air through his nostrils. "I breath today because of my friend's loyalty and love for me." He patted his own chest to further emphasize his words.

Terry turned his head to look at his men behind of him. He was hoping by the look on his face, they would be able to sense this moment was cause for alarm. He believed his life was in danger.

Don blew out a clean stream of white smoke over the heads of the men standing before him. "Mr. Gambino, had my life been in another situation, you would have reason to worry for what you have done. But for now, please relax and don't allow your nerves to make you do or say something which has the potential to make me quickly change my mind."

He rolled the cigar between his lips with a evil smile. "Had I wanted you dead, Mr. Gambino, I wouldn't have to be here and it would've happened as soon as your feet stepped on this block. Or I could've killed you as you walked out of your house." Don gave him a manila envelope he had stuck in the spine of his back.

Terry opened it and thumbed through the pictures inside. Photo's of him and his wife and kids getting into the car were in one of them. Also, one was of his wife taking his two girls to school. Terry stared into Don's cold gray eyes numb.

"I didn't come all of this way for revenge," Don said. "My fury is completely suppressed in this matter. I am here on behalf of my son."

Don bit his tongue when he accidentally mentioned Kasan as his son. Trickles of blood filled his mouth. He didn't mean for it to slip out and hoped Terry, nor any of the other men heard him. He didn't want Kasan to come looking for him.

Don hunched his shoulders and figured Kasan wouldn't believe it anyway. He would assume the man speaking for him was Dodirty's connect and not his birth father.

"Kasan may assume Dodirty's spot. I heard about you sending guys at him. Whatever gripes you have, or had with his uncle here in Newark, it would be in your best interest to freeze it. I would hate to have to come all the way back here and scatter your blood through these streets." He pointed down at the sleek pavement. "And it won't just stop with you."

Terry was about to say something and Don swiftly interrupted him by holding up his hand. He really didn't want to hear what he had to say. As far as he was concerned, he had already done enough when he killed Dodirty. He was fighting the urge to not blow his head off, and didn't need the sound of his friends killer to trigger his emotions and provoke him.

"Sorry, but I didn't come all this way to negotiate, or hear what you have to say. I'm here to inform you of your boundaries with regards to Kasan." He stepped back so all of the men could see and hear his words. "You're going to allow Kasan to handle his business. If he dies in a car accident, I'm going to assume you did it. If he accidentally falls off of a building, or gets hit by a car, or gets set up for a murder and end up with life in prison, I am going to assume you did it, Mr. Gambino."

Don smiled and relaxed his shoulders. "If anything I just mentions happens to him, I am going to kill everything you love first, and then I am going to kill you." Don twirled his cigar between his thumb and pointer finger. His eyes became mere slits. He was ready to throw the cigar and kill them all. "It would be in your best interest Mr. Gambino to become Kasan's guardian angel." Don had a salacious smile on his face.

The only reason he opted not to kill Terry was because he didn't want it to appear as if Kasan had anything to do with it. It would be best to keep Terry suspended in terror. After doing research on him, he's heard of Terry's touchy pride and that is what made him the most dangerous. Don came to remove what others perceived as

poisonous venom from the essence of his and Dodirty's beef to provide safety for Kasan.

Don touched his right shoulder and glimpsed up at his loyal sol-
diers on the roof. They disappeared, while the ones standing in the
framed windows came out onto the streets. They lined the side of the
streets where the guns were lying, mask on all of their faces. Don was
the only one not to wear a mask.

The others who came from the roof stormed out into the streets
in the back of Terry Gambino. They also wore a mask to cover their
faces.

A quiet old Chevy marched from the far corner of the street. It
stopped directly in front of Don and two men in the front also came
out wearing a mask and carrying high powered weapons. The driver
opened the door for Don. Terry and his men could see the kevlar
steel on the inside of the door. The old Chevy appeared to be a beat
up old car, but it was thoroughly bulletproof.

Before Don got into the car, he stared Terry directly in his eyes
with one leg in the car and the other leg on the street."Mr. Gambino,
I am not assuming you are weaker than I, or less important, so if my
words have in anyway offended your honor, or pride amongst your
men, then please charge it to my emotions of not being able to get
down the way I would like at this moment."

Don smiled and showed his perfectly white teeth for the first
time. "I looked up to the Mafia when I was a child, but once I
learned I could never join, it was like a child who will never meet
Santa Clause. You just stop believing and buy your own gifts to make
you happy. So please forgive me Mr. Gambino for speaking to you
the way I have. My apology is not to fool you into thinking I'm a
sucker, or a victim for that matter, but to give you the awareness of
the breed of man you're dealing with."

Don handed Terry a cigar and lit it for him out of respect. "To
better understand the life we both live we have to study the laws
of nature, because the highest art in our profession is our ability to
distinguish the wolves from the lambs, the foxes from the hares, the
hawks from the vultures. If you make this distinction well, you will

heed my words to the letter," he laughed softly. "But if you so happen to be blind by the gift I hope you have to see me for who I am, you will force me to place a lifetime of sorrow into your life and legacy."

Don eyed Terry with a critical squint. "I'm not leaving anyone behind to protect Kasan. I am allowing the safety of his young life to mingle with the fate of your very own and the existence of the entire Mafioso." Don bent down to pick up the cigar he had thrown away and climbed into the old car and it slowly traveled down the street.

CHAPTER TWENTY-FOUR

Terry scowled at the car as it trailed down the street and made a right turn on Broad Street. A spasm of irritation crossed his entire face. It was at this moment, he allowed the anger which was gnawing at him since the first insult came out of Don's mouth to finally come to surface.

He punched his fist into his hand as he stomped over to get his gun. His men also followed his lead. Terry couldn't believe he allowed anyone to speak to him the way Don did. Thomas and the other men were also shocked beyond belief, but also grateful Terry held his tongue and intelligently prevented a catastrophe from taking place and getting them all killed.

"Who in the fuck does that Spanish nigger think he is talking to me like that? I'm Terry Gambino." He hit his chest with his fist. "I've never allowed a nigger to speak to me that way. You see what happened to the dead nigger Dodirty." Terry walked in a circle in the middle of the street. "He talked to me like I was a piece of shit!" His voice echoed throughout the night. "In my own city, he has the motherfuckin audacity to come and warn me about touching a little nigger."

Thomas came and stood next to Terry. He could pass for a Wall street businessman, instead of a Mafia Capo. "Terry you have to accept the fact he read your mind about trying to kill Kasan, and only came to give you warning." He pulled the tweed collar up to his

188

neck. "Now you can call his bluff and do as you had just planned yesterday, or you can swallow your pride and let this shit die down and not start a war."

Terry clasped and unclasped his hands together in thought. He didn't know what to do. His pride was clouding his judgment at the moment.

Terry took a hard pull on the cigar in his hand and once he remembered how he came to have it, he threw it down on the ground and stomped on it like it was Don's head.

"Did you see the maneuvers of this guy?" Thomas asked. "He's not fucking bullshitting like these two bit niggers standing on street corners. He was dead serious Terry. The fuckin guy could've killed us just for killing Dodirty. Now you are the Boss of this operation and you have to know when shit is real."

Terry Gambino stared up the street with a crazed look like he was still looking at the car leaving. Thomas was speaking with logic, but he was lost in the insults and threats Don had just verbally slapped him with, and he didn't get a chance to say not one word.

Don made him look weak in front of his men and he couldn't exist as Boss if he allowed things like this to happen on a continuous basis. As a Boss, respect was established first and foremost in the structure of the family. He's killed guys for looking at him wrong and the shit Don did would've gotten Don killed and he would've dug him up and killed him again.

Terry licked his broad lips and stared into the night with a murderous scowl. He could taste blood. "Set up a sit down with Kasan," he said to Thomas.

Thomas nodded and strolled down the street looking for a phone booth to call Kasan. He could see Terry didn't have a clue of what could happen if he made the wrong move and not the proper distinction of who and what he was dealing with.

Thomas felt something evil as he listened and watched the man who came and went. What if he would've killed all of them and thought nothing of it. His words were used to provoke Terry into doing the opposite of what he was saying.

Thomas was able to make the proper distinction of the man just by the way he led them into a death trap and used himself as bait. He knew the gray eyed man wasn't a lamb by a long shot.

Don was what nightmares are made of.

Chapter Twenty-Five

The Catholic church on Main street in East Orange was one of the only churches to stay open all night for parishioners to come in and confess their sins. It was a good thing. One never knew when a sinner would be in dire need to cleanse his, or her soul before it was ravished by evil ten times stronger than man.

Kasan's group of men were the first to arrive at the church. He had men posted across the street sitting in a car with a two way radio to inform him when Terry Gambino and his men showed up for the meeting.

He also had men hidden around the back of the church to enter behind Terry and his men. Kasan was making it appear as if their was no formation to his attack, but there wouldn't be a thread of air for anyone to escape out of the church, especially Terry Gambino. Kasan made up his mind he had to kill him for Dodirty to be able to truly be Blessed in peace.

No one was sure what the outcome was going to be. No one had a crystal ball to predict a sure win under unpredictable circumstances as this. But Kasan was making sure to strengthen his chances by being well prepared in advance and using promptness as a weapon in his arsenal. This would put Terry and his men at an oppressive disadvantage.

Thirty minutes after Kasan and his men arrived, the lookout

informed him Terry was on his way inside the church and had a miniature army trailing behind him.

Terry refused to suffer the same consequences of his past mistakes. He pondered on when he met Don, he was outnumbered and out gunned. Not only that, Don had him beaten regardless to how many men and guns he would've brought with him. It was all about the location of Don's men which ensured a victory.

Terry was just hoping Kasan didn't close his mind to reason. If he did, Terry wanted to at least have a fighting chance of making it out of the church alive.

As Terry was entering the church, Kasan was standing at the front of the church next to a statute of Mary. His gun held to his side, and his breath was short in his throat.

Kasan rubbed his fingers across the smooth surface of the gun and could feel its deadly power waiting to be unleashed. He could kill Terry from the distance he was standing, and had every intention for his gun to be the first shot fired in his war of revenge.

Death left no fear in his mind and heart. He didn't care. He just wanted to make sure the man he came to kill died before he did. Unlike a kamikaze, he wanted to live long enough to witness the death of his enemy.

Terry noticed the front doors of the church open as soon as he entered. He glanced over his shoulder and saw the men coming behind them with their guns drawn and a mask of hate spread across their faces.

Out of curiosity of the night before, Terry quickly diverted his eyes to the balcony and a team was staring back at him like snipers waiting for the command to take the shot. He had no choice but to chuckle to himself. This was the same ambush as before. The difference between this time and the last, every man was Black.

Kasan raised his gun as Terry and his men strolled past the first pew. Terry made sure to hold his hands in the air. "I only came to talk so you don't have any reason to shoot until you at least hear what I have to say."

Kasan eyed each Italian wide eyed. "Motherfucker you picked a fine time to pull some Martin Luther King JR. shit." He snapped the neck of his gun to place a bullet in the chamber.

Terry slowly walked towards him with his hands still in the air. "I give you my word, I didn't come here for any shit to get blown out of proportion."

Thomas had his hand inside of his coat like the men who came with him. They had no intentions of doing like they've done before. This group seem a little more hostile than the Black Columbian's who initially got the drop on them. He was thankful Terry was at least using his head, but he wasn't sure if Kasan was willing to ratio-nalize with him.

Terry continued. "Lets clear one thing up before you hear any-thing else. Dodirty came into my place of business shooting. I wasn't even there." The men standing along side of him shot him a glance of shock. "If I had been there your uncle would still be alive." He was now standing in front of Kasan.

Terry could now see the resemblance of the man who put the fear of God in him, in the youthful face standing before him. "Is it okay for me to put my hands down. I have a torn ligament in my left shoulder." He was looking down the barrel Kasan relentlessly held to his head.

Terry couldn't believe he was conceding to a kid young enough to be his son. He shook his head and chuckled only he and Thomas could hear. In the last forty-eight hours, he had truly compromised a great deal. Enough to last him for twenty years.

Kasan wrapped both hands around the butt of the gun for sup-port. It appeared like he was about to pull the trigger any second. "That doesn't have anything to do with those guys trying to jump me at the club. If you would have never sent them, my uncle wouldn't have come to your place and he still would be alive."

Terry took a chance and lowered his hands to his side. He had no choice. His shoulder was really killing him. "It is all a big misunder-standing. I didn't give the order."

Terry pointed to one of his men who wasn't yet made, but waiting for the books to open. He removed a twenty-two long from inside his suit jacket, and killed the man before he had a chance to protest and did not have any idea of what was about to happen.

Terry figured it was far better to provide a scapegoat and allow him to suffer for the sins of the whole, than for him to have to pay with his life for his own. It was a split second decision to lower the tension in the church.

The man fell to the floor and slumped over Terry's feet. "I brought him here to show you I am sincere. That's the man who gave the order. Now it's eye for an eye and we can let this go." Smoke slowly seeped from the barrel of Terry's gun.

Terry learned a lot in fifteen minutes from the man he met, than he did in a lifetime. In all other cases he was a wolf and treated others like a lamb. The Italian lying on the floor dead was the sacrificial lamb to bring peace before the great war could get under way.

Somebody had to die today in order to redeem the life of the one he was being held responsible for. His ploy had worked. As soon as the body hit the ground, Kasan lowered his gun. He studied the dead man on the ground in shock. This was the first time he's seen a man killed before his eyes and it wouldn't be the last.

"Why would you kill one of your own men on the account of a nigger? You were trying to extort my uncle."

"I was ordered from Chicago to let it go, but this piece of shit here reacted without my orders and almost started a fuckin war. It was he who put all of our lives in danger. Now he lost his life." Terry knew he was finally winning Kasan over. "I spoke with your father and I . . . "

Kasan cut his words short by smacking him in the face with his hand. Terry toppled over one of the pews. It felt like he had just been hit with a ton of bricks. Everyone instantly drew their guns on both sides and were now back at square one.

Kasan aimed his gun at Terry Gambino. "I'm about to arrange for you to speak with my father face to face."

Thomas jumped reflexively in front of Terry. His brows shot up at how things went from zero to sixty in a matter of seconds. He glanced around at his other men and there were red dots on all of their heads like they were Hindu priest from India. He just knew he wore one also.

Terry shook his head trying to quickly gather himself before things escalated anymore than it has. "Why would you hit me for saying I spoke with your father? What reason would I have to come all the way down here to tell you a bold-faced lie?"

Terry numbly shook his head and stood to his feet. "After killing the one responsible for killing your uncle?" He was praying Kasan didn't shoot at that instant. Now he was really puzzled why mentioning he spoke with his father immediately set the kid off, especially after he thought they were making progress.

Terry was ready to blow the whole deal and kill as many of the men he could before he died. He didn't like how he had his tail tucked between his legs to appease a kid who meant nothing to him.

A tear formed in Kasan's eyes and this emotional state was causing Thomas to bite his lower lip with worry. "My father has been dead for over seventeen years! And you think I am going to stand here and let you fuck with my head?"

Terry threw his hands high in the air. He had enough. "Forgettaboutit!" he exclaimed. "So we just spoke to a ghost." Terry squinted his eyes as he remembered the conversation word for word. "I heard the guy say once or twice you were his son."

Thomas made a gesture for Terry to keep quiet with his sly remarks. Apparently, this meant a lot to the kid with tears in his eyes. He was just searching his mind for the right words to alter the outcome of this situation. He was willing to swear on a stack of Bibles the man said Kasan was his son and if he wasn't, than who in the hell was he?

"The man we spoke to was from Miami. His name is Don and that's all we know. He didn't give us his last name, but he had a heavy accent," Thomas said. He was fighting with his memory to come up with anything on every usable fact he could remember to convince Kasan they weren't trying to pull the wool over his eyes.

A older brother named Cash knew Don well. He was with him when he first started building the empire and helped pioneer the game with Don and Dodirty when Don first came home from Trenton state prison. He knew hearing Don was alive would upset anyone who knew him. He was one of the guys on the roof killing police the day he died.

Cash was much older now, and learned a hell of a lot from Kasan's father and Dodirty. He made a few million and left the game entirely. He was willing to come out of his brief retirement to go to war with Don's son for the death of Dodirty. These were the two men who gave him so much.

Cash slid in front of Kasan to prevent anything else from happening. "What did this man say?"

Kasan put his hand on Cash's shoulder to try and move him out the way. "These crackers didn't speak to no fuckin body. Lets just do what we came to do and stop with all of this peace talk shit."

Cash removed Kasan's gun from his hand. He didn't want him to react, because this truly wasn't the place for this to go down right now.

He stepped closer to Thomas who was red in the face and trying to figure out which barrel death would come from to claim his life at thirty-seven years old.

Cash reiterated his question, as if he was convinced they were telling the truth. "What did this man have to say on behalf of Kasan?"

Terry had a defeated glare on his face. "Whatever he said I don't think the kid will believe me. I mean really. Do you really think I am fuckin nuts to come in here talking crazy unless I had my facts straight? I got balls, but they are not that big."

Thomas surveyed the situation and it seemed no one was willing to let their guard down. At the moment, Kasan couldn't be reasoned with, but believed he could talk some sense of truce to the older man. They had to get out of this church alive.

Terry felt bold in his conviction. Although he lied from the onset and killed an innocent man, he was standing firm in what he knew was the absolute truth.

"This man came down with a thousand Colombians. He's suppose to have the drug game in his back pocket. He told me to make sure nothing happened to you, or he would be back." Terry didn't care to repeat all of the harsh words Don spoke. There was no need to further humiliate himself anymore than he already had. Since the guys standing before him wasn't there to hear it for themselves. He already allowed the kid to smack him and enough was enough. His patience was starting to wear thin. It was his family he was doing this for.

Cash faced Kasan and sighed. "If someone stands up like that for you against the mob and walks away, then it's worth checking out and try to get to the bottom of this whole thing" He nodded at Kasan. "He could be the connect Dodirty was dealing with." He gave Terry a evil stare. "How did this man get in contact with you?"

Terry wiped the forming sweat from his brow. It seemed as though order was slowly coming together between the two opposing forces inside of the church. "From a made guy named Vandino out of Miami."

Kasan just couldn't come to accept what they were saying as reality. He rushed from the church knocking over every man in his path like a running back going for a touch down. He was beyond confused at this point. It took years of him watching the tape to convince himself his father wasn't still alive. The only man he knew would stand up for him is the one who already have and he lost his life doing so.

The eminently outstanding contradiction to stand out in his confused mind was the part about the accent. This counter- point alone made the Italians appear to be telling him a bold face lie.

✳ ✳ ✳

He hit the steering-wheel out of frustration. He initially came to kill the man who killed the only man he's ever considered a father. Now he was far more bewildered hearing the story his father was still alive. What kind of sick joke was this?

The sound of thunder rumbled in the clear sky. Similar to the scene at the church, the weather flipped from a sunny cold day, to a downpour of rain, thunder and lighting.

Kasan hit the wipers so he could see the street in front of him. In his younger years, he played with the thought of his father still being alive, only because he never saw him get into the car, and the skeletal remains of his father had never been found.

Don Starchild's grave was empty.

He drove at a speed which had the potential to kill him if he were to crash. It felt like he was going mad. He was heading to his grandmothers. She knew her son better than anyone. She watched his personality form as child. She knew what he was capable of. If he needed answers, she was the one for him to talk to.

He believed if his father was alive, Carol Starchild would be able to tell him so.

CHAPTER TWENTY-SIX

The thick white clouds disappeared as the heavy downpour of rain smashed into the parked cars and off of the steal gutters of the roofs.

The noise of the rain crashing against the pavement and the occasional trembles of thunder generated nature's soundtrack, along with the sweet smells of fresh rain.

Latifah and her girlfriends found shelter on her spacious porch. This was a part of her punishment. She had broken curfew the other night and wasn't allowed to leave from the mansion. She invited her girlfriends over to the house since she couldn't go anywhere.

"Why doesn't your brother stay here with you?" Linda asked while she was getting her hair braided.

Her other girlfriend named Tamara was painting her toenails. "Ain't that nigga some kind of spectacular? Do he got a girl- friend?"

Latifah eyed Linda. "He stayed with our uncle who just got killed and yeah he has a girlfriend."

"What school does she go to?" Tamara asked. "I ain't never seen him with no girl."

"You know that White school up in Maplewood," Latifah replied.

Before Linda could ask another question, Kasan's BMW darted from the main street and turned onto the long driveway leading to the front entrance of the house. Latifah hadn't seen him since Dodirty's funeral.

Linda's head jerked as soon as she saw Kasan get out of his car. "I know that ain't no Beemer he just got out of? Latifah where did your grandmother get all of this money from?"

"Hey, boy, Latifah said before he came onto the porch.

Kasan shuffled up to the mansion with an attempt to hide his heavy heart. He gave her a limp wave and slouched off into the mansion. Usually, they would joke around, but today out of all days he wasn't feeling up to playing. The girls on the porch studied him as he went into the house and hoped they made eye contact with him so through their smile they would be able to tell him they were ready for whatever.

Once Kasan came into the kitchen, his grandmother was sitting at the kitchen table peeling a pot of peas. She was watching a old Black and white television she's had before Kasan was even born. She could afford a color, but she liked her black and white television.

Although Don made his mother a millionaire, she lived as if she lived in the projects. Carol couldn't believe how big this mansion was. There were certain parts of the mansion she didn't go for weeks at a time.

Carol had enough money to buy a maid to cook for her everyday, but frugality was her middle name. Only the house got bigger for her, but her expectations remained the same.

Kasan ambled into the kitchen and sat down heavily across from his grandmother. He remained silent until she first recognized something was wrong. She could imagine how he was feeling with the loss of Dodirty. He was the only father he knew. Also, Dodirty's death happened because he was trying to protect him from the real culprits who sent grown men to attack him.

The smell of turkey swarmed throughout the kitchen. Carol had a plate of freshly fried potato skins smothered in ketchup. This was her little side dish until the main course meal was done cooking.

"What's the matter with you?" she asked. The lines in her face was now set deep. Her hair was completely gray. The vigor she's had years ago was gone and replaced with a constant feeling of loneliness.

Kasan lowered his voice to a whisper in case Latifah was somewhere close by. He didn't want for her to tease him like he had gone crazy.

"Grandma, do you think my daddy could still be alive." His brows furrowed together deeply. He wished he could take back the question, or was hoping he spoke so low, she didn't even hear him. He didn't want her to think Dodirty's death forced him to sink into an abyss of insanity.

Carol instantly stopped peeling the peas and released a bitter snort. Her laughter made him feel even more vulnerable for asking a question some would consider to be self-explanatory.

"You're just like your daddy. You don't believe anything that you hear and only half of what you see." She wiped her hands on a dish towel. "Now we've all seen him die on primetime television. I'm pretty sure Dodirty showed you the tape." She placed a mouthful of potatoes in her mouth and chewed. "If the police figure Don to be dead, then let him be, but if he has breath in his body then know your daddy is watching over all of us."

Kasan was reluctant to tell his grandmother what he heard today. How a mystery man came from out of the blue and put the fear of God into a bunch of Italians, which was unheard of in this day and time. If he hadn't witnessed their pleas of forgiveness, he wouldn't have believed it himself.

Carol released a deep laugh that rumbled in the sizable kitchen. He hadn't heard her laugh in such a long time. "I know Don like the back of my hand. He's simple, but complex to those who don't understand him."

She started to tell him some of the stories of when Don was a child. Kasan would hang onto her every word. These were the stories he worshiped. Even Dodirty couldn't provide the information Carol could. Any knowledge about his father brought him one step closer to knowing him as others saw him.

"Your daddy use to have a fire truck he loved so much. It was the only thing he asked me to get him for Christmas and the only thing I could afford." She cleared her throat as she now looked around the spacious kitchen she could put her entire project apartment in. "He would only take the truck out to show his friends, but never played with it. He just liked to look at it from a distance and know it was his." Carol smiled softly as her mind vividly took her all the way back to that day. "Well, when his baby brother Kasan was born, the one he named you after, he laid the truck in his crib as a gift the day I brought him home and never touched the truck again. He asked for the truck for Christmas just to give it away." Tears formed in her eyes. It was painful to talk about her two sons in the same breath.

Kasan placed a comforting arm around her. He knew every time he asked her questions about her father, it would bring her to tears. She knew things about him the world didn't know. How compassionate he was.

She pushed him away with the strength of a thousand men as she gathered her emotions. "I'm trying to tell you something. Sit down and listen." She wiped the tears from her face. "You know your daddy killed his childhood friend who killed your uncle Kasan?"

"His name is Sosa right?"

Carol slapped his hand for him to keep quiet. "Please don't interrupt me with the answers we both know." She leaned back in her chair in thought. "Before the police made it to Don's house, he called and gave me the combination to the safe in this mansion. I didn't have a clue of how to get in the safe. I was about to lose the mansion, and this Spanish man came from out of nowhere and showed me how to get in the safe. He didn't know no English, so I couldn't ask him how did he know to come. Your daddy had money piled up everywhere in the safe." She made an elaborate gesture with her hands.

"The man didn't try and steal nothing?"

"He didn't ask for a dime and he saw every dollar when he opened the door. In fact he laughed at the sight of all the money. He left and I ain't never seen him again," she smiled warmly. "I just knew he was coming back to steal all of that money, so I kept a gun under my skirt just in case."

Kasan lowered his eyes at the checkered place mats on the table. "You think my father sent him don't you?"

Carol hunched her frail shoulders. "I don't think nothing. I kept it to myself until now. You're the only one I told about a safe in this house." She lowered her voice to a whisper. "I could feel your uncle

Kasan was gone, but I could never feel Don missing. He's a different kind of soul.

Kasan was beginning to finally feel at ease. The wisdom his grandmother provided gave him the much needed confidence for him to push on to another day. He had been lost, but found himself in the sagaciousness of the woman who knew his father better than anyone. She was answering his questions indirectly. He was supposed to have enough intelligence to figure it out.

As he was about to get up and leave the kitchen, Carol ordered for him to sit down. "I ain't finished." She ate more of her potatoes. "If your daddy is alive, you can bet you will see him at my funeral." She rinsed her hands in the sink. "Don ain't going to miss my send off. Not the vessel which brought him into this world. I told him it was his job to bury me." She dropped her head into her chest.

"How do you know grandma?"

"Prophecy," she said. She started to beat a rhythm on the table. "Its the drums which will call him to me. That is all I can tell you. He doesn't even know I know about the drums." She started to beat on the table again. "He's the dream walker."

Kasan slipped from the kitchen feeling guilty for putting his grandmother on a emotional roller coaster. She started to lose him when she spoke about the drums, but he knew not to ask her a whole bunch of questions she wouldn't answer directly. She had already said more than enough for him to go on.

Prior to him questioning her, she seemed to be in a pretty good mood. All of this talk made her facial features become sullen and displaced with grief. The light of happiness in her eyes had vanished since she told him the story. As if there was more for her to say, but she had to keep a promise not to tell anyone.

'Prophecy?' he asked himself. What does all of that mean? Why did she say it? What does the drums have to do with anything? He seemed to have even more questions now than the answers he was looking for.

Carol called him as soon as his hand touched the knob of the front door. "That's if you don't die before me Kasan you will see him."

Kasan knocked on the framed wood of the door for good luck and went out onto the front porch.

"Where are you going?" Latifah asked. The rest of her friends were waiting with bated breath for his reply.

"Some place you're not," Kasan replied. He knew about her house arrest.

Latifah got up and threw a cup of ice water down his back. The coldness stung as it went down his back and into his underwear. "Oh you want to play water games?"

He slowly edged his way to the side of the mansion like he was about to get in his car and leave. He turned on the waterhose and folded it so she wouldn't hear the water as he was making it back to the front of the mansion.

He peeked through the bushes in front of the sun-porch. They had gone back to doing what they were doing before he came out onto the porch. They were waiting for his car to speed out of the driveway.

Kasan ran from the side of the house and released the grip of the hose and sprayed Latifah and her friends. They screamed from the cold water, also the fact he was messing up their new hairdo.

He jumped into his car before they could find water to fight back. Carol could see the porch from the kitchen. She was happy their talk helped lighten the lost expression in his eyes. She just wish she could tell him a little more to better understand his father.

She couldn't.

She sat back down and started to finish peeling the last batch of peas. "Naw Don ain't going to let nothing happen to you. He always got your back." It felt like her heart was shriveling inside of her body. "I know you will see him again." She threw the pot of peas across the spacious kitchen floor. "I wish I could lay eyes on my baby," she cried.

CHAPTER TWENTY-SEVEN

Cecil's raven colored eyes scanned over the extravagant chess board. The pieces were made out of real silver and gold. Sundays were the days he and Don would play several games of chess and discuss life.

They enjoyed long cigars and expensive wines. Bonita would cook their favorite food which was a ramen noodle soup mixed with a couple of cans of tuna and mayonnaise. This was their Sunday meal they would eat down in Trenton called a hook up. They both had everything any man could ever want. It was the simple things they enjoyed the most.

Cecil bit his lower lip in constant thought. From where he was sitting, he just knew he had Don trapped and there would be no way for him to get around his next move.

He made sure to study the board in its entirety. Don was at his trickiest when he was silent and appeared not to be playing the game so hard. He would lay traps for his opponent and allow them to think they had a sure win, but they were making the exact move he wanted them to make.

The beautiful music of Miles' Davis instrument filled the entire room. Cecil would glance up at Don before he was about to make the move he believed would finally give him a win, but Don would look away and not give him anything to go on. This was another method of him baiting his opponent.

Since their days of playing chess in the big yard down in Trenton State prison, Cecil has never been able to win one game against Don, but he was always able to beat anyone else. From the looks of this game, he finally had Don right where he wanted him. His losing streak was over.

Don would play each game as if his life depended on it. In the game of chess there was no such thing as luck. It wasn't a game of chance, but one of pure strategy. The winner was always the one who could see the most moves ahead and was able to capitalize off the mistakes and mental weaknesses of their opponent.

The winner would be the one to make the next to the last mistake. Don prided himself in being able to see what his opponent would do before his opponent even thought about it himself.

Don made sure to train his eye further than his opponent. For him, it was a game of intelligence and he wanted to always prove he was the wiser of the two, but today he was making an exception to his rule.

Don observed the move Cecil was about to make, which appeared to be one of the better moves, but it still wouldn't give him the victory he's been fighting years for.

Cecil was so focused on what he would do, he didn't consider Don's reaction to his action. He didn't see the fifth move after the one he was about to make.

Cecil moved his queen directly in front of his King and called check. He was expecting Don to move his King out of check. Don pretended to reach for the rook in the right hand corner. Cecil realized his mistake and gritted his teeth out of anger. If Don moved the rook in front of his King, Cecil would not only lose his queen, but it would be mate in five moves.

Don moved his King. "Check good."

Don moved his King just above the line of Cecil's bishop. All Cecil had to do now was bring his queen all the way down to the line of his bishop and it would be mate.

Cecil glanced up at Don and leaned all the way back in his seat. He sipped some of his beer which was in a champagne glass. The hood of his raven colored eyes narrowed speculatively.

"I know you saw your move why didn't you take it and get me for my queen?"

Don sipped his beer which was also in a champagne glass. "I guess you won."

Cecil squinted his eyes at Don. "You threw the game and for once I want to know why? I never won a game in the twenty- five years we played and I was okay with that, but I am not okay with charity."

"A win is a win my friend."

Cecil shook his head no. "Not with you my friend. I seem to know you far better than some and I am not buying it."

"There's nothing to buy."

Cecil laid his glass down on the glass table. "Don I've seen you at your best. I know you remember when that guy smacked you in the face in the mess hall down Trenton and you just walked away." Cecil chuckled to himself. "In fact, you even ran."

Don's gray eyes shined with amusement.

"I was so mad at you Don, but you wouldn't talk about it and you didn't even want me to get him. I thought you were weak and a coward, but three months later, you moved off the unit we were on and over to where the guy was and they found him in his cell dead."

"You've said all of that to say what?" Don asked.

Cecil's eyes narrowed. "You killed him didn't you?" Cecil nodded his head yes like he was answering for Don. "You had him think you were a lamb and this is what made him go to sleep and not view you as a threat. You killed him and moved back over to the unit and never told me what happened."

Don tipped over his King with his middle finger. Cecil watched the gold King fall in slow motion and land with a soft thud onto the board. The sound echoed above the jazz music. He gazed at Don over the brass lamp on the table. He couldn't see anything wrong in his friends eyes.

Since he's known Don, he was never able to grasp what he was thinking by his outward features. Don was a master of manipulation and deception. It was how he made his way to the top, as well as being able to consistently remain there.

His every move was that of a well skilled magician who could visually see into the future. Don made you look in one direction, but the real magic was happening in the place he diverted your eyes away from. Once he told you to look, whatever was there was now gone.

Cecil still couldn't believe Don was alive when he came out there to see him. He watched the entire chase on television. He asked Don how did he do it, but Don would never tell. All Don would say it was magic and blow into his hands like a white dove was about to appear. Cecil had an idea of why Don rescued him from prison. He believed Don had a greater purpose for him to stand by his side in the free world.

"Don why did you help me escape out of Trenton? I mean suppose Juan would've killed me?"

Don hunched his shoulders. His eyes dived into Cecil's soul. "After all of these years it still bothers you to be free?"

"Its not that, but I just want to know why I am here. I think it would explain why you blew the game."

Don studied Cecil's face. "You are here because you lived and that is why you are free."

"Suppose I would've died?"

Don held the champagne glass of beer to his mouth. "Then you still would've been free and you wouldn't have to wait until the insanity seeps in. Either way I was doing you a favor."

"Now that I lived, why did you come all the way to the island to get me? What is the reason. Why did you blow the game? Tell me the greater meaning Don."

Cecil never could find the right time to ask these questions to silence the loud explosions of confusion going off in his head. He wasn't sure if Don would even open up and tell him the truth of why he was here after twenty-five years.

Don even used Juan to think other wise. He had Juan thinking Cecil had done something wrong. Juan thought he was sent to kill Cecil, but in all actuality, he was aiding in an escape plot he knew nothing about, but was a direct participant in the plot.

A half lit cigar was in the ashtray. Don pulled hard on it until the simmering fire roared back to life. He blew a cloud of smoke into the air and studied it for any shape he may be able to recognize. Once he didn't see anything, he blew into the cloud and it vanished.

Don was quiet in his thoughts like he always would be from time to time. He heard Cecil's question. This chess game was only a mirror of the life he yearned for.

Don wanted out of the life he was now living. He desperately desired to live his life free of all of the killings and spreading poison to drug infested communities nationwide. He's witnessed the destruction it was causing. The main ones being destroyed looked like him.

He had no one to blame for the destruction he was causing. This is what was eating at his soul. Every dealer in the world who sold cocaine fell under his regime in some way or another. Everyone who sold heroin in America brought it from his distribution network.

If they sold kilos, or a five dollar rock in Central Park, they brought it for him. He was responsible for the massive shipments of drugs into this country and as far as he was concerned, enough was enough.

He would be fifty in two weeks. He has given over thirty years of his life to the drug game and now it was time for him to retire. He did not want to pass it on, but to destroy the means by which the large quantities of drugs was making it into the country and other countries throughout the world. He was the only one to know the way.

Financially, Don was accountable for three percent of the world's economy. He now could comprehend how Chico felt the day he openly spoke of his boredom. Don was far richer than Chico ever was. He was the richest importer and exporter of drugs in the world. He built a conglomerate of an empire and continued to kill so he was the only King of the hill.

He refilled both champagne glasses with beer. Cecil didn't bother to badger his friend to answer his question. If he learned anything from Don it was patience. If Don wanted him to know, he would have to pay close attention to Don's subtle way of teaching him the lessons of life.

There were times when Don would only pass on his messages through metaphors and similes. He always wanted the other's mind to work in discovering what he meant instead of having to always directly tell them what he meant.

Don held his glass high in the air. "Let us propose a toast."

"To you throwing the game?" Cecil asked reaching for his glass.

"A toast to the beginning of the end. A gesture of gratitude and my way of saying thanks for the years of unshakable loyalty."

"I still didn't win fair and square." Cecil tilted his glass to prevent the bubbles from overflowing.

"There is nothing more intoxicating than victory and nothing more dangerous. It should never matter how you win my friend, as long as you win." Don smiled at Cecil for he was trying to tell him something. "A win will go down in history as just that. Whether it was by accident or intentional, it will still count as a win."

"I guess we've been winning for many years." Cecil wore a huge grin on his face. "We've been at the top since the day you brought me back to the states and now look. Who would've ever thought we would be doing it like this back when we were down in Trenton State prison."

"And now we've created more enemies than we have defeated over the years." Don smashed his cigar into the ashtray. "I've stolen the game from the Colombians and a majority of them will always be my enemies. Even the babies born addicted to the drugs I import and export throughout the world would hate me if they were able to see the face of the one who has poisoned the womb from which they were born." He laid his head back on the plush cushion. "I beg to differ my friend, we have gravely lost."

Don's nose wrinkled in disgust. "I'm starting to forget exactly who I am. I've become lost in the reality I have created for myself. I don't even speak like a Black man anymore. I'm killing my people like I am a full time member of the klu klux klan. I've pushed drugs for so long, I've become a devil to my people."

Cecil brought the glass to his chin. "I think you're just being entirely too hard on yourself Don. You're living like a King, so how could you be all of those things? I've seen you give more to charities throughout the world without looking for praise from the poor people you have helped indirectly."

Don crossed his legs. "Only out of guilt. It's not done from the heart. The greatest trick the devil ever pulled on man was to prove he doesn't exist. Even the devil offered Jesus the kingdoms of the earth and he declined." He laughed to himself. "He made me the same proposition and hands down, I fully accepted the bribe."

"Sound like you're at war with yourself over your success."

"And it's the beginning of the end. I am getting out of the game."

Cecil's mouth formed a muted O. "Now you're really starting to talk crazy."

"Oh am I?"

"To be talking like that." Cecil stood up in front of Don. "I don't think Fuentes is going to allow you to get out. You've created more enemies for the Dragon cartel and who is going to deal with them? Plus, you know too much. This operation couldn't successfully run without you." He waved his hand at Don. "Do you have a death wish or something?"

Don gritted his teeth in anger. "I will never allow any man to dictate my direction in life. Any way, maybe death isn't such a bad thing. I would rather die suddenly than continue in this state of suffering." He stood up to meet Cecil's level stare. "My soul has been in this state of unrest for a long time now and I believe my death in this life would finally give me some peace."

Cecil looked back at Don with a confused look on his face. "What is that supposed to mean?"

"I want for my soul to die."

"Bullshit!" Cecil yelled. "Even you taught me the first law of nature is self preservation under every circumstance. If you wanted death then why didn't you stay in the car and die?"

"My dreams have shown me much and I saw it long before it happened. I had a way out, but if I would've stayed, only my life would've been lost. The fact I knew what to do made the first law instantly apply on impulse without having to give it a second thought. I didn't know this is what I would become."

"Your dreams?" Cecil asked suspiciously. "Your dreams told you you were going to die in that car and how to get out." He tilted his head back and laughed.

Don thought he would be able to open up to his friend about the things that have been taking place in the last days of his life. It seemed like living fifty years on this planet was preparing him for something greater then he was wiling to admit at the time. Cecil was nowhere on his level and Don was trying to save Cecil without him being aware of his true gesture.

Don laughed out loud to make light of their conversation. He just thought if he shared his feelings with his only friend, then he could give him the advice of a mortal. Instead, he had to camouflage the truth with lies. He had to put Cecil back to sleep. Now he was going to use him for the reason he initially saved him from a life in prison for.

Don held Cecil by his broad shoulders. They both had aged gracefully. Cecil had a head full of gray hair. His shoulders were strong and proud from their daily workouts. His skin was without wrinkles and he still possessed the same glow he had while doing time in Trenton Sate prison.

Don wasn't fully gray. He was gray on the sides just above his ear. His thin mustache was sprinkled with gray. His well defined body was still intact after all of these years. Cecil and he would workout like they were in the big yard down in Trenton. Neither man even considered dying their hair back to it's youthful color. They wore their crown of wisdom with pride.

"I have dreams about everything but I don't fully understand them.

"Tell me what you've been dreaming about lately," Cecil asked.

"I was just playing with you," Don lied. "I haven't dreamed in a long time. I will never get out of the game."

Cecil glanced down at the chess board and the King lying on its side. "Why did you blow the game?"

Don hunched his shoulders and held up his glass. "I caught a buzz." He lowered his eyes to see if Cecil was going back to sleep. "This will be the only win you ever get." Don's eyes watered.

Cecil playfully pushed Don back. "I knew you were fucking with me the second you threw the game." He started to set up the board. "Stop with all of these mind fucks Don."

Don laughed shortly and gave Cecil a 'if you only knew look' and said, "For years, I've never told anyone what I believe nor do I believe what I say, and if I so happen to speak the truth, I hide it amongst so many lies that it is hard to find."

"Now you're sounding like a real devil."

Don's face was as still as a statute. He tried to save Cecil for the reason why he saved him and they both could've just walked away from this nightmare, but Cecil didn't understand.

Don was playing the game of chess, but it was in real life. The pieces on the board were real people as far as he was concerned. Now it came to the point where some of the main pieces will have to be sacrificed in order to save the King.

A pain crashed into Don's heart. He was about to sacrifice a major piece and now the King will have to fight the rest of the way alone.

CHAPTER TWENTY-EIGHT

Last night's drinking had taken its toll on Don. Usually, he would be the first one up in the morning. Bonita has been up for an hour and was quietly moving around the room cleaning up. She didn't bother to wake him because she knew he had to be extremely tired.

He and Cecil stayed up talking until the orange sun was beaming in the sky before he went to bed. Bonita would rest lightly until Don was lying next to her, then she would allow herself to enjoy her sleep. Although the mansion was heavily guarded, she didn't feel safe until she knew for sure he was.

Their love has weathered many of the storms in life. They were in love as if it had just happened yesterday. They would neck like teenagers and cuddle like newlyweds. The fire continued to burn in their marriage. She couldn't envision herself with any other man.

She made a pot of coffee and sat down to read through the pile of newspapers. On Saturdays, they would stay in bed for a good part of the morning and read them together.

It felt good to be able to read the papers before Don for a change. Whenever Don would read them first, he would tell her everything before she got the chance to read it for herself. It was like him telling her the end of the movie seconds from the end while they were still sitting in the theater.

Bonita didn't read as fast as Don. Before they were married, she couldn't read a word of English. He made it his business to teach her. He used the same method he used when he taught Juan how to read down in Trenton.

She carefully slurped the steaming coffee, another thing Don hated. She didn't have to worry about that now. She took a bite of her buttered croissant. It was all she ever ate for breakfast. She found it important for her to always maintain a reasonable weight. She has seen how a lot of women allowed age to rob them of their figure.

Bonita wanted to maintain the weight that Don desired her the most. She knew she didn't have anything to worry about. Don has not once considered shattering the sanctity of their wedding vows. He had been faithful for all of the years they've been together.

Bonita eyes bulged out of her head when she skimmed down the obituaries. She rushed from the table and ran upstairs with the papers in her hand for Don to read for himself.

The room was dark and Don was still sound asleep. She pulled back the heavy black drapes and allowed the blinding rays of the Florida sun to fill the entire room with light. The light forced Don to cover his eyes with his pillow.

"What are you trying to do blind me?" Don's words were muffled by the pillow. "I've never slept this late since you've known me, and you pull the drapes open like I am wide awake?"

She placed the pile of newspapers on the ottoman at the foot of the bed. "It's time for you to wake up. There's no need for you to start any bad habits. Nothing comes to a sleeper but a dream. Isn't that what you told me?"

Don spoke to her in English for the first time since he learned how to speak fluent Spanish. "What reason do I have to get up? I am my own boss. Even if I wasn't, we could live comfortably on the jewels I dress you in." His accent was thick.

She placed his cranberry robe on the back of the door. He was right. He didn't have to sell another drug and they still would be able to live a lavish lifestyle. Generations after they were gone would be able to live the same way.

She sat down heavily in the thinking chair in the corner of the room and studied the bulge under the silk sheets. She could only imagine what Don had to do in order to make it to the top and to be able to stay there without any major threats. He never spoke to her about any of the murders she hadn't already known about.

For Don, going back to sleep was out of the question. His rest had already been disturbed and the light wasn't going to help him drift back to sleep.

Once he finally sat up in bed, Bonita stared at him like her eyes were haunted by some inner anxiety. The fact she was sitting in the thinking chair was a sign they needed to talk.

In the mornings, she allowed her hair to hang all the way down to the base of her back. Gray streaks shot across the crown of her head from front to back. Her skin was smooth and without blemish. All she had was tiny crows feet at the corners of her eyes, but they were only noticeable when she smiled.

Her olive skin was even more tanned since they've been back from Jamaica. She would also spend a good part of her days basking in the glorious sun. What else did she have to do?

Don's gray eyes beamed directly into hers with a snarl. She didn't turn away, nor did she say a word. Something was wrong. She was always cheerful in the morning. They made love daily and if they couldn't find the time in the night, they would place it on their agenda first thing in the morning. Don rarely, if ever slept anywhere outside of her presence.

"Did I say something wrong?" he asked as he yawned.

She sadly shook her head no. "You should know I don't wear my heart on my sleeve."

"Then why are you staring at me like I'm an undesirable intruder in your bed." He glanced down at the pile of newspapers. This was a first. He also noticed they were read.

Bonita got up and rushed from the room when he picked up the first newspaper. He wanted to call out and ask what was wrong, but whatever it was, it was in the newspaper.

The last bad news he discovered in the newspaper was when his best friend was brutally murdered. He wondered what was he going to read this time?

Don licked his thumb to turn the page. He wondered if this had anything to do with Kasan. He knew he had assumed Dodirty's role, by the phone call he made to Hector informing him he was on his way down to pick up.

Don hoped Terry Gambino didn't do something crazy to his son. He had warned him and maybe the warning had worn off. Its been nearly a year since the last time they spoke.

Murders in Newark were being committed at an alarming rate. From the areas where bodies were dropping, Don knew these to be drug infested areas of the city and was pretty sure Kasan was involved. He had to enforce his respect amongst the men out on the streets. Once Dodirty was killed, they were all coming for their slice of the pie. The bodies dropping, showed Don Kasan wasn't going for it.

Since there wasn't a full page spread starting at the front page, it couldn't be anything of major significance. Whatever it was he needed to know was somewhere in these papers. Don wasn't in a rush for bad news, but the anticipation was killing him.

Its been years since he's heard anything from home. He wasn't as young as he use to be and praying whatever news he came across didn't cause him to have a heart attack weeks before his fiftieth birthday.

Bonita come into the room with a tray of food and the notion he was done reading what she had read earlier. She thought she would have to give him the much needed support and to make sure bad news of this magnitude didn't push her husband out of the realms of reality. He's been acting very sensitive lately.

Don glanced up at her while he continued to leaf through the obituaries. Bonita sat down next to him and laid her head on his shoulder once she saw he was staring at what she initially wanted him to see.

Don laid the newspaper down. "Tell Divine to come here."

Instead of running all the way downstairs, Bonita called her on the telephone. She was surprise to see how calm Don was acting over the news. He was always unpredictable. When she would think he was going to do this or that, Don would always do the complete opposite.

Divine came into their bedroom like she was slogging through puddles. Coming up to their room was like going into another country. Its been years since she's been in her parents bedroom. The mansion was so large, they didn't have to be confined to the same room for long periods of time unless they wanted to. There were parts of the mansion Divine didn't go, nor did she know about.

Don patted a place on the bed next to him for her to have a seat. Now, he determined she was old enough to know the truth of his past. He had to tell her now, because things have now taken a drastic change.

Divine forced a smile as she sat down next to her father. Both her parents were silent and serious. She was wondering if they found out she had a boyfriend, or if they were going to tell her her mother was pregnant. She's heard them carrying on like teenagers late into the night and sometimes early in the morning.

The look on her fathers face was a clear sign something was gravely wrong. She could see the sadness in his eyes. She reached for his hand. "What's the matter daddy?" she asked in Spanish.

Don took a deep breath. He ran his hand across the stubble on his face. He had just shaved yesterday and the hair was growing back. It seemed the older he got the quicker his hair grew.

"My mother passed away," he finally said. His gray eyes dark with pain. He faced Bonita and back to Divine. "There are a few things you need to know about me."

Divine's face became tight and pinched. This was the first bit of news she's ever heard about her father's side of the family. She's only heard the stories of her mother speaking about her family. Don not once spoke about his family.

Her stomach was now in a tight ball as she anticipated the answers to the many questions she had in her mind for years. These were life long questions to put an entire face to her father's life.

Don cautiously begin to tell her everything he thought she needed to know. From the years he did in prison for a murder he did not commit. He removed a shoe box full of clippings at the bottom of one of his walk-in closets. He showed her the clippings of the police killings and of the three men involved with killing his brother. Divine's eyes widened when she came to the clipping of her father's death.

"They think you're dead?" she asked with a puzzled look on her face. "And you killed all of those police?" Her gray eyes became mere slits. They were identical to the controlled anger her father would exercise. .

Her mind flashed back to certain situations from when she was growing up. All of the pieces of the puzzle were starting to perfectly connect. This was the reason why he never spoke about his life before he met her mother. She knew nothing about her father and she would see him everyday, now she understood why. Not only was he dead to the world, but he kept his past life dead to her also.

Don took the clippings from her. She held onto them, but continued to stare at her father like he was a stranger and she was finally meeting him for the first time. Never would she be able to perceive her father was a killer. He just didn't strike her as a man who would kill someone.

Don could see the shock in her eyes. He's killed hundreds of men in his climb to the top, but he didn't feel he had to mention all of this to his daughter. He reckoned it would be better to allow her to digest what he told her first. Also, it wasn't like he was telling her the things he was proud of. He could feel the blood of every man he's ever killed stain his soul.

He avoided her question and held her hand tightly. "You also have two brothers back in Newark I want for you to meet."

Divine blinked with surprise at her fathers revelations. Her jaw dropped from the thought of having two brothers. At this point, the only thing which could surprise her now is if he was to tell her he wasn't her father. There were too many bombs being dropped on her this morning.

Never did Divine think when her mother called for her to come upstairs, she would hear the things she was hearing. Now, she was staring at her father with new eyes. What else was he capable of?

She covered her mouth to stifle any forthcoming cries. All of her life she thought she was the only child. She would pray for her mother and father to have just one more. She didn't want to be the only sibling. The news she wasn't the only one, rocked her even more than knowing her father was a stone cold killer. Living her life without her brothers hurt more than anything.

Divine's voice was thick with anger. "Why did you keep this from me all of this time?"

The blood drained from Don's face. "I was on the run for murders. They thought I was dead and I didn't want to wake up the police that I wasn't." Don slid his feet into his slippers. "Plus, this isn't something you discuss with a child. You weren't even born when all of this happened."

"But I had brothers you could've told me about." She ran her hands through her hair. "Why didn't you let me know about them at least."

"I couldn't tell you about them and not tell you the rest of the story Divine."

Bonita looked away when Divine glanced up at her. She knew a question was going to come to her as to why she didn't say anything, but there was no answer she could give.

Tears were streaming down Divine's face. They were out of anger and not pain. "Why are you telling me all of this now?"

"Because I'm taking you to meet my side of the family," Don replied. "I didn't want to spring all of this on you once we got there, so now you can gather yourself before we leave."

"Don, you can't go back," Bonita said standing. "What is the reason to go back and let everyone know you're still alive?"

"I am tired of just living a lie. I can't keep running from this. I have to conclude this madness."

Divine covered her eyes with her hands and silently wept. Her father's life was a complete lie. He was far from the peaceful man she thought he was. He was a killer and his sudden revelations made her wonder what else was he keeping from her.

Bonita lowered her head in thought. Why was Don going back. She thought telling her daughter would be enough, but it was almost as if his mother dying forced him to tell her, but now he wanted to go back.

Not only did Bonita calculate the risk, but she had a bad feeling her husband wasn't coming back home if he went. She knew something was bothering him by the nightmares he's been having and now this.

He was going back.

She believed he would lose his life if he went and showed his face at his mothers funeral. She couldn't put her finger on the matter, but she knew things weren't going to go smoothly and she was sure he knew it also. It was why he was explaining everything to Divine. He wanted her to know before she heard it on the news, or in school.

Bonita knew if death didn't claim her husband, it would let the police know he was still alive. Someone at the funeral would say something. The police would hunt Don down until they found him. She couldn't understand why he was even considering doing this. She overheard the conversation Don and Cecil were having last night.

She asked herself was her husband tipping his King over and about to lose this game on purpose?

CHAPTER TWENTY-NINE

Don called for his men to meet him at the auditorium he was having renovated into a multi-movie complex. The top men of his organization numbered five thousand and throughout the world the number quadrupled.

For many of the men sitting in the auditorium, this was their first time ever laying eyes on their leader. Some only heard rumors he was Black and for full blooded Colombians, this was hard to believe.

Everyone believed he had to be Colombian to run a cocaine cartel. It was the only blood allowed to occupy the upper echelons of the cartel.

Don paced the floor of the auditorium telling them his life story and exactly how he came to be the head of the cartel. Don wanted his men to know the whole story, because he was going to Newark in broad daylight. He wanted his men to know at least what they were up against.

Also, Don was thinking the worst of his situation and was using this time to tell the legacy of Don Starchild in his own words, in front of his entire organization.

"And this is how I became the head nigga in charge," Don said. Everyone bust out laughing as he completed his story.

Cecil listened high up in the balcony to the entire story, but his facial expression didn't change one bit. Don could only see the contour of his body in the doorway. Newark was the last place he wanted to go, but had to as long as his friend was going. Don has done more for him than he could ever repay at one time.

Cecil had an idea what the stakes were going to be for Don, as well as himself for showing their faces at an event which would cause people to talk. He used his hands to wipe away the sweat building in the center of his palms.

After Don concluded his speech, the room fell to a death silence for a few seconds. The men sitting down were shocked to know the life story of the man they thoroughly respected without having laid eyes on him until this moment.

"Now who is with me?" Don asked with his right hand held high in the air.

Every man in the auditorium raised their right hands high in the air. The vote was unanimous and everyone was in agreement. Don led the way out the door to the awaiting cars to the private jets he had at the airport getting fueled for take off.

Don could feel an emptiness deep in the pit of his stomach. He wished he had gone to see his mother long before she passed away. He was so caught up in his life and totally forgot she was getting up there in age, as he was also. There was no way he was going to miss the day she was laid to rest.

Don weighed the repercussions of what may happen and he really didn't care at this point. He had a way out and he was going to take it.

Regardless to whom or what, he was ready to take on the entire Newark police department to attend his mother's funeral. He owed the woman that much.

If Don only had a crystal ball to peer deep into the future, he would know there was another force waiting for their chance to not only remove him from his seat of power, but to kill Don Starchild the man they called Black Devil.

CHAPTER THIRTY

On a warm afternoon, the sun smiled through the clear blue sky with such piercing light, anyone wearing dark shades still had to squint their eyes to block its strong rays.

The tear stained faces of family members saddened all who attended the funeral of Carol Starchild. She was loved by the community for her generosity. She gave more money away to the soup kitchens in Newark, than she ever spent on herself. She just couldn't find it in her heart to splurge on the large amounts of money.

The lines to enter Calvary Baptist church trailed around the corner. The church was located in the heart of Newark and is one of the oldest Black churches in the city. It could seat a congregation of twenty-five hundred parishioners.

Detective Harold Scott was sitting in the back of the church. He really didn't feel comfortable amongst the sea of African American's who stared at him as if he was in the wrong place. He was the only Caucasian in the church. He and his wife came to show support for their son in law.

The older adults were well aware he was a part of the chase which claimed the life of Don Starchild. Why was he here? They continued to ask themselves. They didn't care if he was Kasan's father in law. He shouldn't be here. As far as they were concerned, he killed Don and sped up the process for Carol.

Scott found out Kasan was the son of the infamous Don Starchild months after he met him. The only reason he even allowed Sparkle and Kasan to get married was because he found out she was pregnant. It was too late to stop their relationship, or send her to his mother now living in Boston.

Once he got the chance to know Kasan, he forgot all about the day his father killed his friends who were trying to uphold the law. There was no need for the sins of the father to pass on to the son.

The immediate family occupied the first pews of the church. Jewel stared off into the air at the sight of Carol. She had been to more Starchild funerals than her own family. She had since married, but still thought about Don each and every time she looked into her son's face.

Kasan was sitting next to Sparkle, while she held their newborn son. He became the most powerful man in the city, seldom seen and never heard. He made sure his presence was only felt throughout the streets of Newark.

Kasan sat as still as a board. His face twisted in anguish as he watched his grandmother lying peacefully in her coffin. The coffin was all white and it looked like she was lying inside of a well kept garden. Flowers lined the entire front area of the church.

Although Carol didn't wear make-up in life, the mortician applied a foundation to her face to make her look twenty years younger. There wasn't a wrinkle on her face. Her skin was smooth as ever.

Carol wore an all white, silk dress. A red rose was placed in her hair. It matched the red ribbons on her all white alligator pumps. This was an outfit Carol wouldn't wear in life. Latifah was the one who picked out the clothes and she wanted to send her grandmother off in pure fashion.

Kasan continued to stare at the coffin lost in his emotions. She was all he had left, the only true link to his father's past. This was the womb which brought his father into the world. Now she was gone and there was no one to tell him the stories of his father.

Her words repeatedly echoed in his head like a skipping record. He recalled when she said if his father was alive, he would definitely show up to send her off. His grandmother had never lied to him. This day he hoped her words were the truth.

It pained him to know he will never hear his grandmother's angelic voice again, but it was the anticipation of the revelation she made while she was still alive bouncing around in his head. It forced him to pay more attention to anyone coming through the front door, than to the beautiful sermon the preacher was preaching for his grandmother.

Kasan was paying attention for any lone man to show up and sit quietly by himself. All of the pictures he's ever seen of his father were plastered into his memory, but aged by twenty years. If his grandmother was telling the truth Don would show, he figured he would attend her funeral incognito. He just had to pay attention to all who were there, who he had never seen before.

Kasan's bladder started to fill from all of the wine and beer he was drinking to aid in getting over the loss of his grandmother. Jewel saw how he his legs were going up and down like a piston.

"What's the matter with you boy?" Jewel whispered in his ear.

Kasan gritted his teeth. "I have to go to the bathroom."

Jewel nudged him with her elbow. "Get your ass up and go to the bathroom before you mess around and pee on yourself."

Kasan sat perfectly still. He didn't want to miss anything. He calculated if he was to leave to go the bathroom, his father would slip in and out before he got a chance to see him. He really needed to pay close attention to see if his grandmother knew what she was talking about.

Jewel nudged him again once she saw his leg bouncing up and down again. "Do you have a diaper on or something?" She pushed him again. "Go," she ordered.

Kasan didn't want to tell her why he needed to stay still. Once he felt the urine start to spill from his body slowly, he knew he had to get up and go to the bathroom.

As he walked down the red carpet, the church doors swung open like they've been struck by an eighteen wheeler. A mighty force of men dressed in all white suits and a red rose on the lapels of their suits, barged into the church from every entrance with their hands stuffed inside of their suit jackets. It didn't take a genius to know what they were holding on to. The sight of the men caused everyone in the church to freeze, even Kasan who was standing in the middle of the isle about to pee on himself.

The heavy footsteps of the men sounded like thunder as they all filled the church. As if each movement was well scripted, they surrounded the people in the pews and every other entrance leading inside the inner sanctuary of the church. They did all of this as if they were up all night rehearsing. No one was given instructions, they knew exactly what to do. Every move they made was with knife-like precision.

Everyone in the church blinked with surprise. They had the entire church surrounded. Detective Scott's eyes widened with alarm. He didn't have the slightest idea what was going on. Today was supposed to be a funeral, but the men standing inside the church seemed to be robbing the place.

Out of instinct, Detective Scott automatically unsnapped his thirty-eight which he had strapped to his ankle. He leaned back in his seat and crossed his arms as he observed the spectacle of Spanish speaking men covering every square inch of the church.

Once every entrance of the church was heavily secured, a young girl and a older woman maneuvered through the open space made just for them to be able to walk through.

They slowly strolled down the red carpet to the all white coffin. The wore white silk business suits and a red rose in their hair.

The young girl peered down into the coffin at the woman who was her grandmother and begin to sob into the red handkerchief. This caused everyone to eye each other with surprised looks on their faces. They shook their heads in thought, they had never known Carol to have Spanish speaking people in her family. As far as they were concerned, this entire scenario had to be one big mistake.

The tall dark skinned preacher finally found the nerve to question what was taking place in his church. He waited until the older woman's attention shifted in his direction.

"I think you have the wrong church," Reverend Smith said. He glanced around at the men with their hands still inside their coats. He closed his Bible and held it in his hand. "As a matter of fact, I know you got the wrong church." He had known Carol since she first joined church and she wouldn't allow anyone in her family to act this way.

The older woman cleared her throat. "This is my husband's mother." She pointed to the coffin. "This is Carol Starchild?" She spoke as if she wasn't sure.

Kasan was just making his way back from the bathroom when he heard the woman say the word mother. He ran to the bathroom at the time the men were coming in. He almost peed on himself in the center of the isle. He had to hurry to the bathroom and hurry back.

Kasan made an attempt to try and make his way through the wall of men to the woman to ask her what did she say, but one of the men placed a hand firmly on his chest and said something in Spanish.

The preacher tried to leave through the entrance where the ushers would take the collection of money. The Colombians were standing in the doorway and wouldn't move, nor did they say a word to the frightened preacher. This incensed the people sitting in the pews and everyone stood to their feet.

Someone yelled from the crowd. "They can't stop all of us from leaving."

Before anyone could try to leave, the swinging doors to the front entrance of the church swung open as a mighty force swooped into the room.

Don came in with a all white and red pinstripe silk suit. A red fedora hat with the brim turned up and the crown creased from front to back. He wore a pair of red alligator shoes and a red rose in the lapel of his suit.

All of the Colombians in the middle of the isle stepped aside. Cecil and Hector walked alongside of Don. His presence seemed to compel the church to become deathly silent. For some odd reason, everyone knew he was the cause of this chaos by the calm which came as soon as he entered the inner church.

Don came to a complete stop in the middle of the church as he saw the woman who carried him under her heart for nine months lying there. The one woman he could never replace in his life. He had to be still just for a moment.

He called the funeral director and asked what was his mother wearing and coordinated everyone around what she was wearing. She was the queen of the kingdom. The rose was his idea. Only his mother and he fully understood its meaning.

Don took a deep breath as he took a few more steps in the direction of his mother. He felt his knees buckle under the weight of depression. This was the hardest walk he's ever had to make in his life, the walk to the coffin of the woman he loved more than any other woman in his life.

Frank stepped out into the isle with tears streaming down his eyes. His fist balled up out of anger at his brother still being alive and the guilt he felt for being the only son alive.

Don paused as he took his brothers entire being into view. He knew there was no words for him to say to his little brother. He held out his arms and Frank's fist opened and he walked into his brothers arms with the embrace of forgiveness.

"I'm sorry, little brother," Don said with his accent heavy. "I only did what I thought was best."

"I know," Frank said as he cried into Don's shoulder. "I wish mommy would've known you were alive."

"She knew," Don said. He broke his embrace from his brother. "Let me go and talk to her."

The choir director was named Lori and she was Don's first cousin on his mother's side. She was the one who made the three way call for Don at Sosa's club.

Once she got a good look at Don, she made a gesture for the choir to stand up. The choir begin to sing Amazing Grace. Don made his way down the isle listening to the song his mother would always sing to him since he was a child..

Don couldn't fight back the tears. Divine stood at the top of the church waiting for her father to stand next to her. This was the first time she's ever witnessed him cry. She didn't know her father had a regimen of men under his command until she saw the three planes of Colombians riding along with them. It was at that moment, she knew her father was a powerful man.

Don turned around and stopped a few feet away from his mothers coffin. He needed strength to take him the rest of the way. This was the longest walk of his life.

Don touched his mother's silver hair. This was the first time he saw his mother with gray hair. His mind flashed back to every memory he's ever had of his mother and the moral lessons she tried to teach him. A smile formed on his lips. He could hear every word she's ever said to him in his head. It was like he was hearing her voice in his head.

"Hey mama." A chill shot through his entire being. It has been a long time since he said that. "It's me. Your bad ass son coming to say hello. I know you knew all along I was still here. I remember you told me a mother can feel when something happens to her child. I've been here acting all crazy and shit. I finally had a girl." Don reached over for Divine. "She can get on my nerves, but she reminds me so much of you. I wish I would've come earlier, but I didn't have the heart to face you once you knew the things I've done. I had to kill them mama. They killed Kasan."

The thought of his brother lying in the same place his mother was now lying flashed before his eyes. "I know I've done a lifetime of things mama you didn't approve of. I can't take it back. I know you didn't blame me for Kasan's death, but I blamed myself and I still do."

Don's voice started to quiver. "I . . . just . . . miss you mama!" Don just lost all composure and tried to take Carol into his arms. This caused everyone to gasp.

Cecil and Hector did all they could to try and restrain Don from doing the unthinkable. This was the first time either of them has ever witnessed Don displaying such primitive emotions. Don was slow to anger and never showed emotions of pain in front of his men. They could only understand this was his mother and they just turned their head the other way. They finally were able to see Don was a true human being.

Kasan scrutinized the man's features for clues. He heard the heavy accent of the man. Immediately, the words of Terry Gambino filled his ears. The man who came and warned him had an accent. This was the man, Kasan said to himself.

The man quickly shifted his eyes in the direction of Kasan. Kasan got a clear glimpse of his gray eyes which shined like a set of brand new marbles. A rush of heat caressed his cheeks and in a instant, he knew this was his father. The man the world thought was dead, but was very much alive.

He tried to force his way through the bodyguards, but they were doing a good job not allowing anyone anywhere near him and the family. Instead, Kasan screamed at the top of his lungs.

"Daddy! Daddy! It's me. Kasan." The guards still refused to allow him near Don. Kasan became hysterical. "Get the fuck out of my way. That's my father." He hit the guard closest to him with a gut shot which caused him to fall to the ground.

The next guard went to reach for Kasan, Kasan snatched the man by his wrist and pulled him towards him. He reached into his jacket and ripped the gun from his holster.

Anthony and Latifah repeatedly blinked at each other at the sight before them. This man couldn't be the man Kasan was saying he was. Not the man they would lay flowers on his grave and their mothers grave. They stood to their feet ready to fight with Kasan.

Divine's gazed shifted from her grandmother to the face of a younger version of her father. She ran into Kasan's arms and draped her other arm over Anthony's neck. "You're my big brothers."

Divine escorted her brothers up to where Don was being calmed by Cecil and Hector. Don turned his attention to his two sons. He wiped the tears from his eyes, once he saw his daughter hugging two men he knew was his blood.

The sight of all three of them together prevented his tears from drying. Today was the saddest day of his life, but yet the happiest. He brought all three of them to his chest and finally heard the majestic sounds of peace silently echo in his heart and soul.

"Forgive me," Don said through his tears. "Please forgive me for leaving. This is why I came back."

Kasan tightened his grip on his father. "You never left. I always knew you were there protecting me."

Anthony patted Don on the back. "We're together now and that's all that counts."

Lori quietly led the choir from the choir box and down into the pew on the right side of the church. Once the preacher saw things were under control, he took a seat behind the altar.

He had preached at the memorial service for Don. His eye brows shot up once he saw the gray eyes of the man even he thought was dead. His wife thought this was the resurrection of the dead, but he corrected her.

"This is the resurrection of the devil himself."

Don stepped away from their embrace and said a few words in Spanish to his men. Kasan grinned from ear to ear at the way his father eloquently spoke in a another language. This was the man who put the fear of God into the Mafia. His father may have died to the world, but at the same time, he recreated himself into a man of supreme power.

Streams of sunlight poured through the stained glass windows. The well polished silver on Carol's coffin deflected the light and caused it to shine on Don's white suit as he climbed the steps to the pulpit.

Don tapped the microphone to make sure it was working. The squelching sounds reverberated through the sound system. "Don't worry," he said smiling. "I'm not a ghost. I am Carol Starchild's first born son. I am Don Starchild."

Everyone in the room sucked in a mouthful of air at the same time. They pulled a draft of air in the direction of the church where a exit sign hung over the swinging doors.

The women sitting on the hard wood bench shook their heads in disbelief. They recalled when Carol would tell them she don't feel her son Don is dead and she hoped to see him before the lord calls her home. They thought Carol was going senile in her old age, but now they knew she spoke with more sense than they could ever have the potential to grasp.

Don noticed Latifah standing up at the edge of the stage with tears of confusion and tears of joy in her eyes. Her younger brother was also standing next to her. Don was the only father they recognized. The man their mother loved so much, she gave her life for him.

Don stared down at them for a long moment. He reflected on the times with their mother and how she laid down her life for him. He was the reason they grew up without their mother. This was what he was trying to explain to Cecil about the life he was living and why he wanted out.

"I can see your mother in the details of both of your faces," Don said. "Your mother was everything any man could ever imagine a woman to be." His voice choked. "I'm sorry you had to live your life without her. Come on up here. You're my children as if you came from me."

The crowd sat with their mouths wide open at the sight of Carol's family standing up on the stage. This wasn't a funeral, but a family reunion for the Starchild family.

Don brought Kasan close to him and placed both hands on his shoulders. "I've always watched over you."

Kasan lowered his head and said just above a whisper. "I know daddy."

Sparkle came through the crowd carrying a bundle of joy. She held him up to Don. "Who is this little fellow?"

"This is my son," Kasan replied. "This is Don Starchild."

Don kissed his grandson on the forehead. He looked into the eyes of everyone on the stage. "I want to bring everyone with me. Grandma is gone, and I will look after you now."

Anthony knew he couldn't leave. He had a full scholarship to a division one school for basketball. He wasn't about to change his plans in the middle of his junior year. It was his dream to play in the NBA. His quest was one of fame and legit money.

Scott's head was about to come off his neck as he strained his neck to peer over the crowd at the man he knew was dead. He was staring directly at public enemy number one.

Deep within the recesses of Scott's mind, he was begging the Gods for him to be an impostor. He clearly heard the accent, which raised the bar of doubt in his mind. His mind suddenly begin to search every technicality for any of the familiar features to distinguish him as the cop killer Don Starchild. He had to presuppose what Don would look like at the age of the man before him.

Over and over again, Scott re-played the day the man standing before him was assumed dead. He just couldn't fathom anyway the occupant of the car would be standing before him today, without even a burn mark on his smooth almond skin.

It was the cold gray eyes which convinced him. Everything about his face can change, but the windows to a man's soul will forever remain the same. He could see in the eyes of the man before him, this man was in fact Don Starchild.

The thought of all the officers who died at the hands of the man standing before him continued to race through his head. The sight of the man responsible, clinging to his children, to Scott's grandson, caused his blood to boil.

The officers couldn't hold their children, because they were dead and gone. They were denied the privilege to have the same opportunities Don was experiencing today. All because of the man before him. Scott found it hard to grasp the sight before him. He just couldn't believe he was looking directly at Don.

He reached for the his gun strapped to his ankle. His wife read his mind and gripped him by his bicep and whispered in his ear. "If you are about to do what I think you are about to do, then I strongly suggest you not do it."

Scott's eyes raked the scene in front of him. He turned red with anger. He replied to his wife speaking out of the corners of his mouth. "I'm still an officer of the law and this man killed police and there's no telling how many more. He has to be stopped. I can't just let him walk out of here a free man after knowing firsthand the destruction he caused in the lives of the women of my friends." Scott gritted his teeth and faced his wife. "Suppose it would've been me who died that day?"

Hector glanced down at his watch and said something to Don in Spanish. Don quickly stepped down from the altar. "Grab her."

Four of his men lined up on opposite sides of Carol's coffin. They raised it up and started to follow Don out of the church. Don was taking his mother to be buried in a special place where he can be close to her.

Before Don could cross the next to last pew, Scott leaped in front of Don with his gun drawn and his badge held high in the air for the rest of the Colombians to take in view.

"Don Starchild you're under arrest for multiple counts of murder." Scott pulled back the hammer of his gun. "Put your hands up and make this easy for yourself."

Don released the buttons on his pin stripe suit. "Please put that Lone Ranger badge down Detective Scott. It carries no weight at this stage of my life." Don's face became a dark mask. His gray eyes became cold and indifferent. "You stake out my mothers funeral and pull some shit like this? I ought to kill you where you stand." A venomous grin found its way to his lips. "What would one more dead cop mean to me?"

The vein in Scott's neck was pulsing and swelling dangerously. He aimed the gun at the center of Don's chest. "I'm not the slime bucket you are. Your son just so happen to be married to my daughter that's why I am here."

Everyone stood and turned to see what was about to happen. Ruth, Carol's friend for over sixty years, glanced at the four men carrying Carol out of the church and wished Carol could witness the public spectacle taking place. This would give them years of conversation.

Don's eyes hastily glanced over Kasan and Sparkle and their child. He locked Scott into his frigid stare. "I don't care if you call it a hog or a pig, it's still swine." He boldly stepped up to Scott and placed the barrel of his gun to the center of his chest. "If you want this child to lose both grandfathers in one day, then pull the trigger pig." He faced Cecil. "Before my body hit the ground I want you to kill him." He aimed a sturdy finger at Scott's wife, "And Kill her." He swung his arm and pointed it at Sparkle. "And kill her."

All of the guns the men held in their suit jackets now came out into plain view. The sleek metal of the guns reflected the sunlight from the stained glass windows and cast a luminescence silver light throughout the entire church.

Innumerable sounds of clicking filled the church all at once. Even the men holding onto Carol's coffin placed one in the chamber without lowering the coffin.

Kasan's brows raised up in the air in complete shock. "Didn't I tell you this is my baby's mother?"

Don eyed his son. "Don't blame me blame him." He pointed at Scott. "We are doing three for one." He walked closer into Scott's gun. "Check."

Cecil's raven black eyes sunk low as he stared at all three of them. He was trying to see if Detective Scott was willing to go one step beyond his friend and if so, he would enjoy watching all three of them die.

Scott's hand trembled as he held his gun. It felt like he was holding four hundred pounds with one hand. He heard two voices sounding off in his head and wasn't sure which one was making the most sense under these circumstances.

Sparkle recalled the events on the tape and placed her hand on her father's wrist. She applied enough pressure to lower the gun pointing at Don. "Daddy please let Kasan's father go." She placed his grandson in his arms. "Do it for him."

Don kissed his grandson on the forehead. His face was now inches away from Scott's face. "Two enemies' blood flows through this precious vessel," he grinned. "Fate and destiny can be a pure bitch at times." He strolled past Scott and his men followed.

CHAPTER THIRTY-ONE

A row of limousines were idling in the dry cleaning parking lot across the street from the church. There was an eighteen wheeler parked in the school parking lot across the street from the cleaners.

Kasan's brown eyes flinched at the sight of the battalion of Colombians waiting outside. Don said something to them in Spanish and they proceeded to climb into the back of the carriage. The also carried Carol's coffin inside as well.

Kasan was witnessing the true essence of power in the purest form. His father had come well equipped and well prepared for this trip. It seemed his father didn't leave anything to chance.

Don opened the car door for Bonita and Divine. He faced his children "Ride with me to my plane."

"You have a plane?" Anthony asked as he climbed into the limousine.

Don leaned back and rode in absolute silence. He just wanted to see the faces of all of his children together. The sight of them chatting away was worth all the money he had scattered throughout the world. He was taking a mental picture of this moment a million times over.

At one of the main intersections, a middle aged woman held a bag of groceries in one hand and was being pulled across the street by a eager pit bull. Although the weather man had made a forecast there was going to be no rain, she wore a pair of bright yellow rain boots.

The preacher pointed in the direction of his office and showed Scott where the telephone was. Once he flashed his badge, Reverend Smith had to accommodate an officer of the law.

He made sure to call for every unit in Essex county to make their way to the Newark International airport and stop every limousine and arrest each of its occupants.

He warned the dispatcher to tell every officer to be on the look out for Don Starchild and spit out a quick description of him. Also, he warned them everybody was armed and dangerous. He repeated it twice for her to get the point.

The dispatcher paused before she repeated the message to everyone out in the field. She was working the day it was reported Don had died along with other officers, but now he was alive? She figured it would fall on the head of the reporting officer if this was a farce.

Ten minutes later, Hector called Don on the car phone. "There are some White guys following us."

"Police?" Don asked in Spanish.

Kasan and Anthony didn't have the slightest clue of what was going on, Bonita and Divine did. Bonita begged Don the night before not to come back to Newark, because she had a bad feeling about the trip.

Once they exited the church and got into the cars, she thought everything was going to be okay, but all of the nervous feelings she had prior, were now coming back with force.

"I don't think it's the police, or there would be sirens on. They look like Mafia boys," Hector said.

Don slammed down the phone and picked it up to make another call. He called his men he left at the airport and informed them of the current situation. They had some unwanted guest who needed to be taken care of.

"You have men at the airport?" Kasan asked.

Don smiled at his quizzical look. "The first psychological requirement of strength is to prepare for your enemy before he attacks, and never take it personal. In order to have ultimate victory against your enemy you must be ruthless in your dealings with him." His gray eyes were intensely staring at Kasan. "Do you understand?"

Kasan nodded his head yes. "Were you serious about killing my wife? Is this the ruthless part you're speaking about?"

Don eyed his daughter and knew the way he spoke and the things he's done thus far was overwhelming to her. He faced Kasan. "Just a ploy my son. It wasn't real."

Bonita knew it was. Once Don gave the order and he was killed, Cecil would've done just what he said. If his blood didn't flow through their veins, they were subjected to death by his hands.

Divine watched the road through the side window. Had she heard her father speak this way prior to his telling her of his contemptible past, she wouldn't have believed what she heard. Her father's words back at the church and just now convinced her there was far more to her father as a man of power than he was willing to reveal to her. She was intrigued to know more about him.

Don held both of his sons by the hand. "I want you two to stay in the car when I get out."

Bonita shook her head no. "Don why can't you come with us?" Her voice sounded like she was seconds away from dissolving into tears. She didn't want Don out of her sight. She was willing to die with him if the case may be.

"Because whoever it is wants me and I'm not going to sit in this car and allow them to riddle it with bullets just for me." His eyes fell to his lap. "Everything I love in the world is sitting in this car. It would destroy me as a man if anything went wrong. I have a better chance on foot."

He removed a leather briefcase and slipped his holsters onto his shoulders. He removed the clips in his guns to make sure they were full and placed them into each holster. Divine was repeating the stories her father allowed her to read in her thoughts. This was almost like deja vu to what was about to take place at any moment.

Don strapped two belts of clips to his waist. Every movement was mechanical. He twirled two sliencers in his hand and watched the traffic out of the cars moving around in a trance like state. It was as if he was mentally preparing himself to do battle. His mind was converging on the dangerous task ahead of him.

Kasan picked up the car phone. "Cash, have everyone available at the airport with enough heat to blow up this fucking world. My father is alive and we think Terry Gambino is trying some bullshit."

Cash's legs almost gave away from under him. "Put him on the phone."

Kasan held the phone out to Don. Don pushed it back towards him. "This isn't the time for a reunion. Tell Cash I send my regards and do as you say. I'm going to need as much help as possible." He pointed to Kasan. "But you're staying in the car."

Kasan gave Cash his message and slammed the car phone down. "Daddy, if I am willing to die with you, there's nothing you can say, or do to stop me." He paused. "If I ain't got you, then I have nothing."

Don snatched Kasan by the collar of his suit-jacket. "You have a son and wife to live for," he said in a huff. His eyes smoldering. "Whatever happens to me are the repercussions of the bad decisions I made long ago without even considering you. Maybe if I had, then I would've settled for a job shoveling horse shit, than trying to gain the whole world and missing the lives of my sons." Don's voice choked, "Please don't make the same mistakes I made trying to fill my shoes, they're too large and too dangerous and the price is too severe."

Divine bowed her head and said a silent prayer in Spanish. She was struggling to come to grips with what was happening at this very moment. All of this time, she had taken her father for granted. Never did she ponder on the thought of having to live without him.

The cars simultaneously arrived at the airport. Cecil was sitting in the front seat listening to the entire conversation which nearly caused him to break down. His life was identical to Don's, he had no where to go. He was stranded on the same deserted island.

Cecil was the first to get out of the car and he tapped the window for Don. "We're here."

Don hurriedly got out of the car. He bent down to the window and eyed his wife. He spoke in Spanish. "I love you woman. I wish I could say everything is going to be all right, but we've always been honest with each other."

He stuck his head into the car and gave Bonita a passionate kiss. "Whatever the future holds, I want for you to know you've made me the happiest man on earth." He kissed her again. "Take my mother and bury her where I told you."

Bonita's voice was lost in a abyss of pain and hope. She wanted to speak, but nothing came out. All she could do was wrap her arms around her husband and pray this wouldn't be the last time. She was praying he was able to create another miracle.

Divine held her father and instantly she respected him for the decisions he made past, present and future. Just because she didn't understand them, didn't mean they weren't the right ones.

Don gazed into the eyes of all three of his children and if he died today, then at least he got his last dying declaration to see his sons and daughter together. Now they would know each other for the rest of their lives.

Don was searching for Cecil as the limousine drove off. He was just standing right next to him. He didn't have time to try and figure out where he ran off to, but he had to make it safely back to the planes.

Don took off running through the main ramp leading to the air strip. He came to a barb wire fence and climbed over to the other side. Once he landed, he noticed a line of cars pulling up on the other side of the airport. This convinced him Hector was right on point with his observations. The sight of eight carloads of men had to be the Mafia. By no means could they pass for police.

The roaring sounds of the plane engines coming to life caused the ground to shake. Don was standing several yards away from the plane, but he could feel the acceleration of the engines as if he was standing directly in front of them.

Don kept his eyes open as he trotted across the tarmac towards the private jets. He placed silencers on both of his guns, the entire time keeping both eyes on the group of Italians inching their way between the planes in the direction of his private jets. Once he saw the men removing guns from their coats, he knew they were after him.

The high noon sun seemed to be attracted to the pitch black

concrete. Whenever a plane was rearing to go, the heat would overcome the cooled atmosphere and cause the workers to momentarily start to sweat.

The black concrete gripped the wheels of the speeding plane as they burst down the airstrip as if they were about to break the sound barrier. Crew men were moving about and transporting luggage and refueling commercial planes preparing for takeoff.

Don removed his tie and rolled up his shirt around his wrist. The diamonds from his presidential Rolex glittered from the abundance of the shimmering sun. It shimmered like a mirror reflecting light from the beaming sun. Don took it off and placed it in his pocket.

The Italians had broken up into splinter groups in different locations of the airport. Don saw one of the Italians squatting down beside one of the planes. He edged his way behind him and as the man was about to turn around, Don fired two shots into the back of his head. He fell flat on his face and the blood trailed down the concrete and stopped at the wheel of one of the planes.

Don turned the dead man over for a look of identification. It was one of Vandino's men. Don had a troubled look on his face, a look of confusion. Why was this happening? Why would Vandino send men all the way from Florida after him?

He didn't have time to wait for an answer to pop into his conscious mind. He had to make sure he made it out of here alive. This matter would be better dealt with if Vandino was standing in front of him. Not to explain, but to die.

Don dropped down to one knee to scan the ground from under the planes. This was just to see if any of the men were close. He heard a shuffle of feet three feet away from where he killed the first man and noticed another man crash to the concrete with a death mask on his face and blood trickling from his ears. Kasan had hit him with a death blow to the temple instantly killing him.

He blazed a trail in the direction of his father. "You died once and I'll be damn if I sit back and let you die again. I've waited too long for this." He surveyed the surrounding planes on the ground. "I saw a squad of police on the overpass and two cars full of Italians, they looked like Terry Gambino's men."

As Don was about to say something, Kasan placed a finger to his lips for him to remain quiet. He pointed East for Don to go around the plane and made a thumb motion west, he was going the opposite way.

Don sucked in a mouthful of hot air which tasted like he had just inhaled fumes from the gas tank, as he shrunk to the other side in silence.

It angered him Scott couldn't leave well enough alone. Also, the fact his son was now sharing in the danger and was directly in the line of fire. He needed to stay focused on making sure Kasan at least made it out of this situation alive. He didn't have to worry about the Mafia killing him, but he definitely had to make sure the police didn't get their hands on him. At least not alive and kicking.

He tiptoed in the direction of the group of men as they were standing in a circle discussing matters in a whisper. He quickly shot one in the heart and the other two directly in the neck. He had to make sure they didn't get a shot off since they held guns.

Next, he circled in the direction Kasan had gone and watched as he moved with the speed and force he's never witnessed a man move before in his life. He shook his head with surprise to see Kasan kill two men with his bare hands.

A plane's engine came to life and made speaking a simple word impossible with the high volume of noise. A crew man wore a bright orange vest and swung two globe lights at the pilot to give him directions to head to the runway.

Don ran behind his son. Kasan drew his hand back ready to deliver a death blow. Don held both guns up to his face. "Wait a minute boy!" He shouted leaning back. "It's only me." He shook his head at the close call of nearly losing his life at the hands of his son. "Where in the hell did you learn to hit like that?"

Kasan didn't have time to reply. He was trying to save his fathers life and at this point his own also. Shots rang out fifty feet away in the direction of his planes. A group of Italians were firing at the windows of the plane.

Don swung around the piston of the massive tire of the plane, he released both clips of his guns into the bodies of the men. He watched each of them fall one by one. Kasan picked up one of the guns and mowed down the remaining men.

The last man standing was none other than Terry Gambino.

CHAPTER THIRTY-TWO

"Don't kill me!" Terry screamed out of fear with both hands held high in the air. A hot stream of urine poured out of his brown slacks and formed a puddle at the heel of his shoe.

Kasan snatched him by the back of his neck, like it was the fat around the neck of a puppy. He dragged him onto the plane with his face flushed with indignation.

Don slid one of his nines into its holster. "They say the greedier a man gets, he becomes so stupid, he makes such enormous mistakes." He slapped Terry with the neck of his gun. A white gash appeared and in moments it filled with blood.

Terry held his hands to his face to block the next oncoming blow. "It wasn't my idea. The call came from Chicago. They want you out of the way." He lowered his arms just enough to see how close Don was standing next to him. "The family wants to get into the drug trade, but you're in the way."

The scent of the leather seats filled Don's nostrils. It smelled like a new car just driven off a car lot. The rows of seats were endless as they went all the way to the back of the plane.

"It really doesn't make a difference at this point," Don said glancing out of the front window of the plane. "I told you what would happen if I had to lay eyes on you for any reason whatsoever." A soft smile formed at his lips. "Now my life has taken on another set of circumstances. I gave you the best advice a man could give a potential

245

enemy at that time. You didn't manifest the intelligence I thought you had in your favor."

Kasan snatched the gun from Don's hand. He aimed it at the center of Terry's head. "You might as well say your prayers. This is for Uncle Dodirty." Without a second thought, he pulled the trigger and blew Terry's head off. The blood splattered onto the white shades over the plane window. Terry slumped down in his seat dead.

Don felt a rush of heat shoot across his face at the sight of Terry and then his son. His son could be as cold blooded as he was, if not more ruthless.

Don was trying to figure out where did it all come from. Jewel wouldn't allow for him to be raised in a climate of violence to breed this kind of man and Dodirty wouldn't show him the way of the streets. It had to be in him and not on him.

Don knew what had transformed him into a cold blooded killer. It was the death of his little brother, but he still couldn't understand what happened to his son. If he would've asked, Kasan would've told him it was the death of his father.

Kasan was about to say something, but Don held up his hand for him to be silent. He cocked his head to one side to listen close to some far away sounds.

"Do you hear that?" Don asked. Sirens could be heard blaring in the distance.

"I told you they were on their way. I guess my father in law couldn't leave well enough alone."

Don raised one of the shades to eye exactly how close the cars were to reaching the tarmac. He pivoted once he knew the time would be soon before the entire fleet of police showed up and the helicopters.

"I guess this is where you and I depart my son." Don checked the clips of his guns to make sure they were full and ready to fire. "They're here for me and there is no reason for you to go down on a sinking ship, when you can leave on a life raft."

"I'm going all the way," Kasan said. He balled up his hands into a tight fist. "All the way." He repeated for his words to sink into his fathers head.

Don went to the cockpit of the plane and checked the dials of the radio. He called Hector by his code name. "You might as well take off. The police are on their way and things can only go from bad to worse."

"Don, we're not leaving here without you," Hector said over the radio. "Remember what you said from day one. We never leave a soldier behind."

"Where's Cecil?" Don asked in thought. This was to see if all would be lined up like he thought.

"Where else," Hector replied. "He's in the last plane waiting on you. We can hold the police off until you get here. There's a few Mafia boys running around, but once they see the cops are here, they will go the other way."

Don pressed the button on the side of the hand held device. "If you stay any longer then you won't be able to take off. The police will assume I am on the plane. I'm going to have to be careful. I won't make it before the swat team sets up."

Don released the button and wiped the sweat from his brow onto his shirt. The plane was hot enough to fry a egg on the seat. "Just take off and tell Cecil I said to wait for me."

Hector's voice came back sounding nervous and unsure. "Are you sure about this Don?"

Don laughed into the mic to relax his friend. "When did you start doubting my word? Now take off and I'll see you back in Colombia." Don switched off the radio. He had matters of more pristine importance to deal with before he played his last game.

"So what do we do now?" Kasan asked alert and ready.

Don regarded him curiously and stepped off the plane. Kasan was dead on his heels. Don saluted one of his planes as he watched the nose of his plane pointing towards the clouds. It now would be just a matter of seconds before the swat team made it onto the tarmac. He was determined to get to where Cecil was waiting for him.

Don climbed the stairs of another plane and Kasan followed. He took the machine gun from Kasan and strapped it onto his back. He sat down to reload his two nine millimeters. Kasan watched as his father was preparing for battle with the police. He didn't care his father had taken his gun from him. He had his hands and they were proven 44 magnums by themselves.

Don placed both guns in his holster. "I can't allow you to go any further with this than you already have. I have money to set you up for life in a Swiss bank account. There's no way out for me. I'm going to try and make it, I need for you to stay put Kasan."

Don embraced his son and held him close to him. He could smell the sweat overpowering the faint smell of his cologne. He was only trying to place all of the years his son presumed him to be dead in one embrace.

"I love you and I am thankful for everything you've done for me thus far. But you must do this one thing for me." He stared Kasan in the eyes. He used his thumb to trail his chiseled features. "You look just like me. I would hate for you to leave this earth so young."

Kasan had tears falling from his eyes. "I hear you, Daddy, but I'm with you all the way. All the way," he repeated.

Don kissed his son on the cheek and handed him his ring without him knowing it. "Then so be it. You may hate me for this, but I am doing it to save your life."

Don pushed Kasan down into one of the seats and shot him in the crown of both of his feet. Kasan convulsed with pain in the seat. He couldn't hold the scream in his throat. His hands balled into a fist so tight, his knuckles turned white.

The breath was knocked out of his lungs by the excruciating pain coursing through his entire body, but starting at his feet. He had never been shot before, so he never felt pain like this before. His screams was so loud, it filled every space inside of the plane and vibrated in both of their ears.

"I'm sorry," Don said. "Not for shooting you, but not for being there to show you a better life." He paused before he climbed off the plane. "I need for you to live to tell my grandchildren the legacy of Don Starchild. Please don't tell the story in a manner to glorify me, but so they will know to become everything I wasn't."

Don shot and killed two more men as he stepped away from the plane. They were running in the direction of Kasan's screams. Don eyed his son who was sitting near the window crying with pain.

There were tears streaming down Don's cheeks. He raised his right gun to his brow as a sign of saluting him with high honors of a five star general.

He mouthed for his son to see the words coming out of his mouth. "I want for you to live Kasan. Let me die." Don took off running.

Kasan shook his head still trying to fight the pain. "I can't, Daddy," he said and made an attempt to stand, but fell back down.

CHAPTER THIRTY-THREE

The swat team was positioned around the last plane left on the tarmac. Cecil remained inside. He could see out of the pilot's window, but he didn't care how many cops there were.

Don slyly edged his way in the back of the sea of police officers. He was searching the crowd for Detective Scott. If it was in the cards for him to die today, then it will be very much justified if Scott died also, a selfish act, but one which would make dying a little more pleasant.

In order for him to make it to the plane, he had to divert the swat teams attention away from the plane and towards him. He needed to do all of this, with the hopes of being able to circle back around, and try to get the plane in the air.

Don could hear the drums beating with the rhythm of his quick beating heart. He would only hear them while he was asleep. It was as if the memory of the drums were filling his head.

He had no choice at this point. He removed the machine gun from his back and sprayed the crowd of police with a barrage of bullets, not only to kill as many as he could, but to get their undivided attention. He smiled as they ran for cover like cockroaches when the lights come on. Cecil followed up by firing out of the window of the cockpit. He could see Don in a distance and his hopes were now replenished.

As Cecil sat on the plane waiting, he thought about what Don had told him over the game of chess. It all started to make sense. This was his only way out. The reason he freed Cecil from a life of mental torment was because he knew Cecil would be the one to stand with him in his final hour of life.

Whose final hour of life?

✳ ✳ ✳

"Where are the shots coming from?" Scott yelled at one of the officers as they ducked behind a squad car.

Before the officer could reply, a bullet landed in the center of his throat. Along side of him, two more officers fell dead. Scott shook his head at this moment of deja vu."

Scott ducked down beside a blaring squad car. The sirens on top of the cars swung red and blue lights across the air strip and against one of the planes.

Scott swallowed the lump in his throat at the sight of the dead bodies sprawled on the ground throughout the airport. He shook his head in commiseration at the sight before him. There were more dead the second time around than there were the first time the force tried to apprehend Don.

Scott asked himself how many more bodies had to fall before they were able to finally stop public enemy number one? For him, this was like being trapped in a never ending nightmare. Since the time at the church, Scott wondered would this be the day he dies? He had less than a year to retire from the force.

Armored trucks were driving in circles around the airport for the location of where the shots were initially fired. Don traveled in the opposite direction of the moving cars like he was being attacked by two forces. The Mafia wanted him dead and the police wanted answers as to how was he alive.

Occasionally, Cecil would release a few rounds out of the cockpit window whenever he figured Don needed a distraction. The police refused to fire on the plane until they received a report of the passengers. They didn't know it was a private jet.

An officer had Don within his direct view. His mind was telling him to radio back and let his superiors know he had him within range, but he didn't want the crackling sound from his radio to alert Don to his position. There were officers on the ground dead, therefore, the man he was hunting had no regards for the life of any of the officers.

Don felt a biting sting to his face and the cool air of the bullet kissing his cheek as it continued through the open air.

His face twisted in pain. The exact location of the shooter was lost by the sound of a rumbling plane at the far end of the airport. Don spun in every direction to try to focus on any movement. Anyone on the tarmac was to considered an enemy.

Don heard another hiss sing through the air and miss his head by inches. In rapid rotating motions, he glanced in every direction. Apparently, the shooter could see him, but he couldn't see the shooter. This was the second bullet and he didn't want to wait for the third. He may not be so lucky.

In his peripheral vision, he saw a frightened officer ready to fire upon him again. Don quickly released two bullets into the officer's chest. The officer dropped his gun. Don ran in the direction of the officer and hit him two more times.

The officer only staggered, but leaned against one of the planes he had first used as a shield. Don took a circuitous path to the officer. The officer grimaced as he fought to breathe. Don grabbed him by his shirt and snatched him to his feet. He checked the heavy padding of the officer's shirt and now knew why his bullets didn't penetrate the officer's chest. He was wearing a bulletproof vest. The kevlar plate prevented any of Don's bullets from touching flesh.

Don pressed his gun to the officers temple and fired. The blood from his brain splattered onto his face. The officer fell to the ground like a limp rag doll. Don removed the vest from the dead officer. He was going to need as much protection as possible.

Bullets continued to fly around the airport in every direction. Don didn't want to get hit by a bullet of a gun not pointed directly at him. It would be just his luck to die from a bullet that ricochet off a plane and hit him. He wanted to be able to see the gun it would come from and this would give him a fighting chance.

The armored car located Don and informed the officers. They stuck their guns through the firing holes of the truck and fired at him. The other squad cars screeched as they made their way through the airport where the sighting was originally reported. They fired upon him as if this would be their only opportunity to stop and kill him.

Don felt the first bullet hit him in the center of his back. The force of the bullet knocked him forward and also pushed the air out of his lungs. He gasped as he tumbled to the ground and used the wheel of the plane for a moments' cover. The police were everywhere and every cop was firing in his direction.

While he was down on the ground, Don heard shots being fired not at him, but at the officers. Kasan was standing a hundred feet behind the fleet of squad cars. He was limping towards the officers and firing at the same time.

This gave Don a chance to roll under the nearest plane and roll again under the next one to confuse the officers of his last location.

Slowly the air was trying to find a way back into his deflated lungs. The pain in his back was pounding like he was being hit with a million sledge hammers. The officers had lost any sense of where he was, but turned their guns on Kasan.

Don snatched the silencers off his guns and jammed them into his pocket. He ran directly out into the opening and began to fire upon the officers. This time, he was not trying to find a cover of safety. He wanted them to see him and exactly where the shots were coming from so they would come after him. He would rather have his own brains blown out, than to see his son get killed for trying to save his life. By no means could he have a front seat to watching his son die.

The drums begin to pound in his head and heart. The chanting suddenly began to magnify in his ears. Mental images shot pictures to his brain of faces as if he was looking through a photo album. The faces were clear, but yet unrecognizable to Don. These were people he had never met.

Or did he?

A bullet hit him in the chest knocking the new air out of his lungs and depleted his breathing. He fought to suck in as much air as he could through his nose to expand his lungs and fill them back up. He blew air out of his mouth and repeated the process until he could breath regularly.

A loud siren from one of the traffic control towers rung to alert all of the pilots oblivious to the firing, not to move, or try to reach the runway, as well as all workers to exit the tarmac and get inside of the terminal for safety.

Don had nowhere to hide. He was now in the open. His white suit was now covered in huge patches of beige from the dirt. The rose on the lapel of his coat was no longer lustrous and vibrant. Don still held his guns, but appeared to have been defeated. For the sake of Kasan, he was giving up.

Kasan couldn't believe the horrific scene taking place in front of him. Suddenly, he realized he wasn't saving his father, but he was placing him in the greatest danger. He rushed to a nearby plane which was rushing passengers on before the all out war had taken place.

Before the stewardess could close the hatch, Kasan hobbled up the stairs and onto the plane. He could've won a Oscar when he acted like he had accidentally got caught in the crossfire.

He took a seat by the window to watch the conclusion of the gangster show taking place right before his eyes. His father was playing the leading role for the second time of his life.

Kasan watched as his father took another hit to the chest and his father dropping to one knee. Don pressed the tip of his gun to the ground and used it as a crutch to hold him up, until he got his breath. He discovered the technique for breathing from the impact of each bullet hitting him. He just prayed none hit him in the face. There was no technique to overcome a blast to the face.

Kasan's hand brushed his pocket and felt a bulge. He dug inside and came out with a ring. He gave the ring a long searching look. This was the first time he's ever laid eyes on it.

He turned to the window and didn't see his father. "This has to be his," he whispered.

"What did you say?" A red hair woman asked in the seat next to him. "Can you see anything?"

Kasan shook his head no and went back to studying the ring in his hand. The ring was engraved with the insignia of a dragon. It's weight was heavy in his hand. The fit was perfect as if it had been sized for him.

The freshly cut diamonds sparkled brightly. He flipped the ring up to see the round holes behind the diamonds for them to freely breath. They were set in rich platinum which made the ring heavy and thick. It almost felt like stainless steel.

Another shot rung through the air from the sea of officers and hit Don in his left arm. His shirt instantly turned crimson. He grimaced as he tried to get to his feet. It felt like the bullet hit a nerve, because the pain traveled through his entire body at the same time.

Don noticed Scott standing in the crowd of police as they aimed and continued to fire at him. All he wanted to really do was locate Kasan and make sure he was no longer in danger. He was willing to sacrifice himself for the safety of his son.

Blood was now dripping from his face and the sleeve of his arm. He placed his hand over the bullet wound with pressure to try and stop the bleeding. The officers were screaming orders for Don to get down on the ground. He had no intentions of giving up. He just needed to buy more time.

Scott picked up the bullhorn from off the hood of the squad car. "Don its all over. You've done enough damage. Throw down your guns and get on the ground. I promise to make sure you get fair treatment."

The pulsating pain caused Don to clamp his teeth. In his eyes, he was wounded, but he wasn't giving up. This was just check, but he had to do everything in his power to prevent mate.

Don slipped his gun from his other holster. "I don't need to wait for you White motherfuckers to stick a needle in my arm!" he screamed coldly. "We are holding court right now." He raised his gun and aimed it at Scott. He had a clear shot.

Cecil noticed from the plane Don was stuck in a ambush. He used the butt of his gun to knock out the window close to where they were and begin firing at the officers. They quickly turned away from Don. This gave Don the split second he needed to now run to the opposite side of the plane to climb aboard.

The entrance of the door was on the other side of the officers, so Don was momentarily safe from any gun fire. Cecil held them at bay for the entire time it took Don to run between two planes to make it to the door.

Cecil eyed Don standing at the door. "I stayed for as long as I could." He switched on the engines to the plane. "I don't think they're going to allow me to get this thing up in the air, especially with knowing you're on it."

Don slipped on his parachute and tied a sharp double edge blade to his ankle. His gray eyes shined from the light on the dashboard of the plane. "So what do you want me to do now? Its too late to turn back and ask for a do over. We have to take it up Cecil."

Cecil smiled down at Don sitting on the steps. "And you're not one to tip the King over and give your opponent an easy victory. Everything is done for a reason isn't it Don? The sign always come before the reality. That's what you always told me."

Don laughed for the first time that day. Him tipping over the King stuck out in Cecil's mind. "An opponent is considered an enemy at all cost. You have always been my best friend, my brother since the day I walked into Trenton." Don chewed on his lower lip. "Why would I free a enemy when I have many out in the world to deal with?"

"This is the meaning of the game," Cecil said. The look on his face became dark and cold. "You would never allow me to beat you in a game of chess. When you did tip your King it was only a meta-phor for this moment right here. The only way for me to win is if I save my King from being captured by the opposing side."

Cecil stared straight ahead at the open field next to the plane. "I was the piece you lost, but got back once your pawn made it to the other side of the opponent's board. Everyone has to know how to play their part. Some pieces are more important than others and some must be sacrificed, but all must know their place and that is to protect the King."

Don tried to wipe the sticky blood from his face. As his hand wiped at the open wound on his face, the temporary scab opened and caused blood to seep out and spread to the other side of his face. "What are you talking about?" Don asked. "Where is all of this coming from?"

Cecil snatched the forty-five automatic from his waist and aimed it at Don. "I think you know this already. Now you are going to get off this plane and allow me to win."

"Nigga are you crazy?" Don said through gritted teeth. "How dare you pull a gun on me?"

Don was about to climb the stairs. Cecil used his thumb to take the safety off. "One more step and you will die at my hands." Tears filled his raven colored black eyes. "It's not about the destination, it's about the journey. I would've never beaten you at chess, because I always attacked with the same moves," he smiled. "Now my unpredictability has startled you and now for the first time I can see I've beaten you fair and square by the look of checkmate in your eyes, but who is to say who really won, Mr. Starchild? This is your game."

Don tucked the straps of the parachute firmly on his shoulders. He pulled his pants leg down over the knife attached to his ankle. He didn't care. He ran up the stairs and threw his arms around Cecil and kissed him on the cheek. This moment was just like the day Don was going home and leaving Cecil behind, but now Cecil was telling him to leave and it was okay.

"I love you, Brother," Don said into his neck. This was the game he's been playing for all a along. "Thank you," he cried. He knew this would be the last time they would see each other again.

Cecil kissed Don on his cheek also. "Checkmate, my brother, and thank you for everything," Cecil said with tears streaming down his face. "I finally beat you." He smiled at Don. "My King is still on the board."

CHAPTER THIRTY-FOUR

Scott watched as the airplane begin to bolt down the runway for takeoff. There was no way he was going to allow Don to escape this time. He had a major decision to make without a chance of contemplation. It was either going to be now, or never.

"If the plane goes up, then shoot it down," Scott said. He locked the sight of the plane in his intense gaze.

A Captain from the swat team came up next to Scott. "We can't shoot the plane down with civilian passengers on the plane. We have to wait for the report."

Scott stared at the plane. "This is Don Starchild. If we have to kill a thousand to stop him then so be it Captain."

The nose of the plane moderately begin to raise up into the air. Scott watched as Don Starchild was getting away for the second time. He had to make sure this thing was done right.

No mistakes allowed.

Scott nodded at the man standing in the open on the airstrip. "Shoot it down!"

The Captain understood exactly what Scott meant when he got off the phone with a higher authority. He also nodded his approval at the officer with the rocket launcher to shoot the plane down. He tried to protest Scott's command, but it was confirmed Don wasn't to leave alive for any reason whatsoever. Anyone on the plane who died along with him, whether it be a civilian or criminal, was to be considered as collateral damage.

The officer with the rocket launcher fell to one knee. He had the rocket launcher stationed firmly over his left shoulder. One eye was closed and the other measuring the distance of the plane through a scope on the bridge of the rocket launcher.

He was waiting for the plane to reach a high enough altitude before he shot it down. The group of officers on the ground were too close to the explosion. Also, if the fire was to fall back to the ground and ignite the other planes and engulfed the entire airport into fire, it would be a monolithic, catastrophic disaster.

For the officer to secure a sure shot, he had to take aim at the back engine which held the most of the plane's gasoline. This would make sure the entire plane would completely disintegrate into tiny particles while it was still in the sky.

Kasan watched as the officer was taking aim to shoot the plane out of the sky. When he had observed the plane going in the air, he was reeling with unfettered joy. His father had gotten away.

Now the officer was taking aim to shoot the plane down, his eyes were enthralled in terror at the sight before him. Don and Cecil was about to die.

The rocket sang through the air, as fire shot from the back of the gun to propel the rocket from the launcher. It hit the target the officer was aiming for. The back engine exploded into a orange ball of fire. Small pieces of the plane fell back to the ground, but the majority of the plane crumbled into shreds of dust in the sky.

Kasan leaned back in his seat in shock at the combustion of his father before his eyes, dying in a fire similar to the first time. This time it was in mid-air.

The red head woman sitting next to him noticed the tears flowing down his mink colored cheeks. He stopped the stewardess as she was strolling past with a tray of beverages.

"Where is this flight headed?" he asked.

The stewardess glanced down at him in her uniform with a

puzzled look. She wasn't the one to let him aboard. She thought if he brought a ticket, he was supposed to know where he was going.

"We're headed to Miami Florida," she replied.

Kasan reached under his seat for a set of pillows to place under his throbbing feet and stuck one in the back of his head. His feet was in pain, but nowhere near comparison with his heart at what had just seen with his own eyes. There was no need for him to rewind a tape. The video was now firmly implanted in his mind.

The blood from both wounds in his feet had turned to a scab of dried blood. He didn't know how to explain how they got that way to anyone without suspicion as to how he was hurt. It may look like wounds from a gun battle on the outside, but he knew they were wounds of love from his father to keep him alive.

Slowly, he turned his head towards the window to prevent the woman sitting next to him from seeing him still crying. He thought he saw a figure running through a field of tall grass with a backpack on. When he blinked to try and focus his eyes on the fast moving white figure again . . .

It was gone.

He wiped his tears and blew out a stream of air for the sake of relief.

The woman next to him asked. "Are you going to be all right?"

Kasan allowed the plush seat to wrap around his body in comfort. He closed his eyes with a smile on his face. "If I believe my lying eyes, I am going to be just fine." He twirled the ring on his finger as the plane finally took off down the runway.

TO BE CONTINUED
BAPTISM BY FIRE PART III (PANTHER)

Epilogue

The Boy sat in silence at the conclusion of the story. He gazed over at the Bum with a look of uneasy puzzlement. The Bum appeared to be in a trance like state. Tears filled the orbs of his gray eyes.

The Bum sucked in heavy mouthfuls of air as if he was trying to calm himself. He removed a handkerchief from his pocket with initials stitched in the corner, but the Boy couldn't see what they were.

He wiped his eyes first and then blew his nose. "I'm sorry," the Bum apologized to the Boy. "I always seem to cry when I just think about this part of the story."

"Why?" the Boy asked standing to his feet. "How well did you know Don Starchild?"

The Bum shook his head slowly. "I knew him well. I've come to fully understand what he continued to lose each time he died."

"They think he's dead again right?"

The Bum nodded yes. "A piece of him dies every time someone he loves dies."

"Is he dead?" The Boy dug his hands in his pockets. "He wasn't on the plane when the police blew it up was he?"

"I thought we had an agreement on the questions."

The Boy rubbed his hands across his baby soft face and shook his head from side to side in thought. "That Don Starchild was strong in his spot like no man I've ever known. I can tell you that much." He faced the Bum and his brows wrinkled. "Where were you when all of this was going on to know the story of his life so well?"

The Bum's eyes burned into the Boy. "I was on the outside looking in."

"You sure know a lot."

The Bum smiled and then began to laugh loudly. "I'm learning something new every time I even think about the contents of the story. It's like I'm seeing it happen all over again."

The sun which once illuminated the clear sky had now descended behind the doughy clouds. A refreshing breeze drifted through the gigantic oak trees and circled the entire park, before it boomeranged back in the direction it initially came.

The Boy glanced up into the trees searching for the Panther. Its rich black coat was slowly transforming into a cloak and dagger disguise as the night fell.

"I can't see the Panther."

"She's there," the Bum said something in a language the Boy had never heard.

The Panther came down to one of the sturdy lower branches. She hissed at the Boy as if she understood his remark to the Bum. She settled lazily back down on the bench like she was lost in the contents of the story.

Once the sun finally disappeared from the sky, the Bum opened and tossed eight hefty bags of ground beef onto the ground in the back of the bench. The Panther bolted from the tree and begin to feast on the meal. The Bum and the Boy released the baby Panthers and they ran to join their mother to suckle while she ate.

"I think you had better start making your way home." The next breeze which flowed through the park carried the aroma of a well kept garden. "It's night and you're too young to be running the streets like you're a grown man."

"But I am a man."

The Bum removed his jacket and stuffed it inside of his duffel bag. He rolled the bag up into a pillow. "Being a man is far deeper than just being born one." He lightly tapped the Boy's temple. "A man is one with divine intelligence and pure in discipline. It takes a lot to be a true man in this world and until the strength of your manhood has been confidently tested by what has the potential to destroy you, you will never grasp the underlying laws of what it takes to be a man of intelligence and discipline."

"If you know all of this, then why are you living like a bum?"

"Are you wasting another question?" The Bum released three buttons on his shirt. "Or do you want to ask something about life and I will answer freely, but any questions pertaining to anything about the story or me, will waste one of your three questions and the story is a long one."

The Boy sat in silence for five minutes in thought. He stared into the quietness of the night. He felt the baby Panthers playing around his feet, so he raised his legs to make sure he didn't accidentally step on one of them.

"How can I be a man?" the Boy asked breaking the silence. "What do I have to do?"

The Bum leaned all the way back onto the bench. "I know you're expecting a mysterious and profound answer, but it is quite simple." He hunched his shoulders. "Always do what is right. There are no shortcuts to anything worth its weight in gold. Sometimes you have to know how to make bricks without straw. Always look to go the long way when you don't know something because..."

The Boy swiftly cut him off. "It's not about the destination, it's about the journey." The Boy had a broad smile of triumph on his face. "That's what Cecil said to Don."

The Bum nodded with a smile. "So you are listening." He placed his bag to his side. "The more you see on your journey, the more you will come to understand once you finally reach your destination."

One of the Panthers took off running in the direction of the middle of the park. The mother hissed at the Panther and it stopped dead in its tracks.

"You listen to your mother, because she will never tell you anything wrong."

The Boy lowered his eyes. "All I have is my mother. I never got a chance to meet my father."

The Bum reached under his seat and brought one of the Panthers into his arms. "Don grew up without a father."

"Where was his father throughout all of this? He didn't even show up for Carol's funeral."

"The answer to that question comes much later in the story about Don's father."

"Why last?"

"It explains his dreams." The Bum stared off into the darkness. "His mother knew what he was. She gave birth to him."

"I understand, I think."

The Bum stretched his arms. "I am going to get some rest. I have a big day tomorrow."

The Boy stood to his feet cheerful. "What time do you want me to come and see you?" The Boy stood up once he realized he was sitting on the Bum's bed for the night.

"Don't," the Bum replied lying down on the bench.

The Boy felt his breath get stuck in his throat. "I thought you said the story was a long one."

"It is, but I won't be here for awhile to tell you." The Bum used his forearms to cover his eyes. "I have other matters of importance to tend to."

"So when do you want me to come back, the day after tomorrow?"

The Bum fixed the pillow under his head to add support to the base of his neck. "Come back on your eighteenth birthday."

The Boy's face twisted in anguish. He was really enjoying the company of the Bum. He looked forward to meeting him in the park everyday and was learning things from the Bum he couldn't learn any place else.

The Bum's knowledge astounded him to say the least. He knew as much about Don as Don Starchild himself. This is what puzzled the Boy the most about their encounter. Just from the way he told the story, the Boy was learning about himself.

"But five years is a long way," the Boy said. His chin sunk

dejectedly into his chest. He rolled dried leaves under his feet. "How do I know you won't forget about me after being away for so long?" The sadness could be heard in his voice.

"I won't forget," the Bum said and turned his back on the world like he did when the Boy first threw the bottle at him. "Just be here on your eighteenth birthday and I will tell you the rest of the story."

The bad news struck the Boy like a crippling blow from a hammer. "But I want to know did Kasan really see his father running through the field, or was it just his imagination?" He dug his hands into his pockets like he was about to bring out a ring. "Did Kasan go to Miami and take Don's place?"

The Bum sat up on the bench. "Five years and I will be right here."

The Boy walked away from the Bum with his body wracked with convulsions of grief. He was lost and didn't understand why the Bum wanted to wait for five years to tell him the rest of the story.

He wasn't sure who was on the plane at the time the swat team blew the plane out of the sky. This is why he was eager to hear the rest of the story.

He sauntered out of the park and came to the light at the corner. As the light turned red, the traffic came to a complete halt. The Boy was about to cross the street, but stopped dead in his tracks. A thought shot across his mind, how would the Bum know when was his eighteenth birthday? He had to run back and tell him.

He darted back into the park at full speed. A cramp found its way into his right leg from him extending his stride too far. His eyes tried to focus on the bench before he reached it, but the Bum was gone.

He fell to his knees to have a look under the bench and was hoping at least the Panthers were still there. This would mean the Bum would have to eventually come back to get them and then he could tell him his birthday.

The Panthers were gone also.

The Boy heard the crushing sounds of dried leaves. He spun around on his heels to eye every direction of the park, just to make sure the Bum wasn't leaving from another exit of the park.

He saw nothing.

He wanted to walk away, but flopped down on the bench and clamped his eyes shut to stall the tears before they fell. His grief was growing like Cancer. He heard a sound above him. He glanced up into the trees for the mother Panther.

All he saw was darkness.

The Bum had vanished into thin air as if he never existed. The Boy knew he was never going to see the Bum again. The Bum didn't know his birthday and would have no reason to show up.

The Boy's eyes scanned the entire park. He hunched his bony shoulders and headed back to the front exit of the park. The Bum had been full of surprises. The Boy had every intention of showing up five years from now.

He was praying the Bum would also.

ACKNOWLEDGMENTS

I would like to thank God for giving a wretched soul like me a second chance to figure it all out. I thank you God for not allowing me to die in my own iniquity. I would like to thank only those who played a pivotal part in making Michael Stanton a success, especially to those who believed in me and took the time to help me climb the charts better known as statistics. To Hakeem, Tyson, Kenny from Black and Nobel; to my man Dexter from Source of Knowledge; to my man Nate from Urban Knowledge; to Chris B who was the only one pushing my books when I first came out of the gates of heaven; to my man Divine from Books in The Hood, Sidi from Harlem Book Center and Sosi; to my little brother Shawn, CC, Justice, Khalil and Khaleemah, Daymaris, and Daystar. To the outlaw family holding it all the way up in the life we lead, if daytime be for suckers then tonight we breathe!!! To all the real right dudes and to Sweets for properly understanding who I am as a man. I cannot begin to thank you enough for your support and encouragement in everything I do. It is your belief in this movement that strengthens my desire to strive for the unknown stages of success awaiting me in life. You are such a freak (SMILE).

Starchild Publishing Presents an Excerpt of

Game Player

By
Michael Stanton
Available wherever books are sold
in September 2012

The Livingston Mall was packed to full capacity. It was like this every Saturday afternoon. Families would come out to the mall in droves searching for a sale, or out to hurry and see the newly released blockbuster movie before a long line would make the most enthusiastic movie buff wait for it to be released on DVD.

Aromas from the nearby food stands filled the air with intoxicating fragrances. The sweet smells made it almost impossible for anyone to just walk by without their mouths watering from the scent of the many different foods mixing together and forming an aroma of one well cooked meal.

Khalil Jones leaned up against the wall and was trying not to seem obvious amongst the sea of shoppers. He was not here to shop or see a movie like the others. He was here to make money in only one of his many hustles.

His hazel eyes scanned the crowd coming from the store. He was searching for his little brother whom he had sent into the store with a hundred dollar bill and a cab number written across the face of the bill. It was a tactic to make his job a little easier. This was going to be his last score before he finally went home. He has been out all day. It was close to five o'clock and he could tell his little brother was now exhausted and needed to rest.

Quran strolled out of the store carrying a small paper bag in one hand with the store's logo on it and clutching a receipt in the other. He stopped at the exit and glanced around trying to locate his big brother. At nine years old, it was hard for him to see over the crowd of tall adults blocking his view. He just had to wait until the crowd dispersed in order to see where his brother was waiting.

Khalil waved his hand in the air to signal his brother. Quran's hand shot up in the air with nothing but extreme happiness and loyalty for his big brother. He enjoyed the fact that Khalil would spend a lot of time with him and would buy him anything he wanted when they went out on the days he did not have to go to school.

Khalil sat down on the bench next to the water fountain. It was a safe place to duck down. The bench was enshrouded with a family of evergreen eucalyptus trees and well kept palm trees from California in garbage can size plant holders.

His brother handed him the change from the hundred dollar bill he had just cashed. He had a bag of candy worth five dollars. He took the candy out of the store's bag and placed it in his bulging backpack with the rest of the candy he scored from a day's work. In his little mind, he called it a sweet victory.

Khalil slipped a charms lollipop into his mouth. "What register did you go to?" he asked.

Quran wrinkled up his gumdrop nose and his fox colored eyes glanced down at his brand new sneakers his brother bought him last week. He was trying to make sure he told his brother the right one. When he first started going out with his brother, he had made a mistake and did not like it when his brother was angry with him for making this mistake. Now he paid attention to the details.

"I went to the lady with the brown hair and glasses," Quran replied. "She's near the end of the counter and has a black shirt on and a cheetah colored scarf around her neck."

Khalil tapped the bench next to him for his brother to have a seat. He wrapped his arms around his brother. "You are doing well Quran." He eyed a shapely girl as she passed by. "I'm going to get you the new X-box when we get out of here."

Quran tossed a piece of butterscotch candy in his mouth. He was pleased to be hanging out with his big brother. Khalil was the only father figure he had ever known and the only one who took care of him. His mother has been in and out of psychiatric hospitals ever since he could remember. This was the longest she had been away. He knew it had something to do with his oldest brother who killed himself way before he was ever born, but he was glad Khalil was twenty four and able to take care of him until his mother got well.

Khalil thumbed his aquiline nose that was pointed like an eagle's beak. He licked his thumb and index finger and used them to smooth his pencil line mustache and to fix any out of sync hairs. He was very anal about his appearance. In his line of work, he dressed in order to put his mark at ease. It would be hard for an ill dressed bum to be convincing in his line of work. He was a con man in every sense of the word.

"You stay right here until I get back," Khalil said. He tucked the shirt into his tailored suit. He was 5'9" but with his gators on he stood and even six feet. "Don't talk to anybody until I get back and if someone bothers you, then you come in the store immediately and let me know."

Quran scooted backwards until his back was pressed firmly against the bench. He was more focused on his candy than what his brother was saying at the time. He's heard this speech a million times today and it was the only part of the day that made him sick with his brother saying the same thing over and over again.

Khalil would say the same thing every time he was about to leave his brother out in public. He would end up like his mother if anything were to ever happen to Quran. He was trying to make sure they had a roof over their heads and food to eat. It was summer and he had to take his brother with him whenever he could. He did not fancy someone else watching his brother. He was afraid of . . .

Khalil sauntered through the crowd and spun around before he was about to walk into the store. Quran glanced up from his candy bar just in time to see his brother point a stern finger at him to further emphasize his lecture, to make sure he understood how important his parting remarks were.

As Khalil entered the store, his eyes searched for the description his brother had given him. He noticed the woman at the end of the counter taking care of another customer. He picked up a bag of Vicks cough drops and got into line behind an elderly man who was wheezing like he had a bad case of asthma.

Khalil slid the cough drops to the woman and she scanned them to ring up the price. He handed her a ten dollar bill and watched as she punched in the digits and gave him his change. She placed his cough drops in a bag and handed it to him.

Khalil searched the bag. "Can I have my receipt please?"

The woman smiled down warmly at him and tore off his receipt from the slot in the cash register. She placed it in the plastic bag and handed the bag to him. Khalil made his way to the door with his change in his hand.

He stopped at the door and glanced all the way to the back of the store. He was checking to see if anyone in management knew him from any past dealings. When he saw the White man in the back with a colorful shirt and tight slacks strutting about like the manager, he knew he was in the clear.

Khalil spun around and headed back for the register. He patiently waited for the cashier to finish with the customer who was standing behind him and then he made his way towards the register.

He placed the bag and receipt on the counter in front of the woman. "I think you made a mistake. I gave you a hundred dollar bill, but you gave me change like I only paid you with a ten." He handed her the receipt and bag to give her a closer inspection of its contents.

The woman's name tag said her name was Frances. She raised her glasses up to her forehead as she studied the receipt. "You didn't hand me a hundred dollar bill," she eyed the last ring up. "You only gave me a ten," she said with extreme confidence. She had never made a mistake like this before.

Khalil fixed one of his shoulder length braids that fell out of place. "I don't want to sit here and argue with you over matters that are apparently confusing to you." He straightened the knot in his tie. "Can you please call the manager so we can solve this minor inconsistency over my change?"

The woman called for the manager over the intercom and Khalil watched as he zoomed his way through the aisles and to the front counter. Khalil took a step away from the counter so the cashier could help the next person in line.

The manager went behind the counter to speak to the woman. They spoke in hushed tones. Khalil knew they were discussing his matter when the manager's eyes glanced in his direction.

Khalil eyed himself in the mirror just behind the counter. His rich brown skin was shining from every angle of the mirror. As he was about to go to the counter, he saw Olivia standing at the next register waiting for someone to help her. Khalil was in love with her ever since he could remember, but she did not reciprocate those feelings to him. She was deeply involved in the church and only knew Khalil to be a street hustler. Although she never knew him to have a job, he always had large sums of money in his pocket.

Khalil tried to focus on the manager and cashier. He knew it was just a matter of time before Olivia wondered what he was up to. She was starting to understand his patterns. He didn't do business dressed like a thug. He wore suits and ties when he was out hustling.

The manager called Khalil up to the counter. Olivia stood by within ear shot of the entire conversation. Khalil continued to stare straight ahead like she was just like any other stranger in his midst. He was too far into his game to just walk away. He had to play it for all it was worth.

"What seems to be the problem?" the manager asked.

Khalil had control over his inner emotions but his stomach felt like it had a swarm of butterflies locked inside. "I can't say what your employee's problem is and I don't know if her mistake is intentional or a sincere accident but she gave me the wrong change."

The manager took his receipt and studied it like he was going to be able to recognize the mistake at first glance. "I don't see how," he said.

"She gave me change back like I gave her a ten dollar bill." Khalil noticed Olivia shake her head in disbelief. "I gave her a hundred dollar bill."

The manager rocked on his heels. "I don't know how we can prove that. You are holding eight dollars and if you deduct what you bought it would equal the change you now have."

Khalil glanced at the manager with his hazel eyes that were flecked with a touch of green. His pearly white teeth beamed in the direction of the manager. "Then I guess my poor ability for remembering numbers has finally come to my defense in that case." He cleared his throat, "before I came over here I called a cab and the only thing I had to write the cab number down on was the hundred dollar bill."

The manager blinked with surprise. He hurried to the register and raised the tray where they kept the big bills and came out with the hundred dollar bill that Quran had made his purchase with. The manager's eyes scanned over the numbers on the bill.

"I'm extremely sorry for the mix up sir," the manager said. The cashier was about to say something but he swiftly cut her off. "Thank you for handling this matter with respect."

Khalil handed the manager the bag with the cough drops. "Just give me back my bill and take back the cough drops. I don't like to be doubted over matters that only I seem to know is the truth. If I didn't write the cab number on the bill then I would've had to suffer the loss for her innocent mistake." He reached for the hundred dollar bill in the manager's hand. "Thank you for your doubt. I won't be shopping here anymore." He took the bill and wrapped it with the stack of money he had in his pocket and left the store. Olivia shook her head at the sight of him running one of his many scams in her ear shot and eye sight.

Khalil waited where he had left his little brother for Olivia to come out of the store. He knew he had blown his chances of ever being with her.

One time she had called him a drug dealer because he always had large sums of money but he would swear on his brother's grave that he was not. Now she knew what he did for a living to pay for that money green Jaguar he drove.

She had known Khalil's family since they were children and knew he did not have legal money to support the lifestyle he was portraying. He was one of the poorer families in the projects back when they were growing up.

Khalil divided the rest of his day's money into two separate piles. He placed one in his shoe and kept the other in his pocket. The money was bulging out of his front pocket too much and he did not want to get robbed for even a dime, not that he was expecting it to happen but he was always prepared for any calamity that could befall him and interfere with his hard day's earnings.

He played the game and would never allow the game to play him.

OTHER BOOKS BY MICHAEL STANTON

Promise, Part 1: The Chosen One

Baptism by Fire, Part 1: Empire

Other titles coming soon by Michael Stanton

Baptism by Fire Part III: Panther

Baptism by fire Part IV: Trial by Death

Baptism by fire Part V: The Prophecy

Baptism by Fire Part VI: Birth of a God

Promise Part II: The Dream

Promise Part III: The Awakening

Double Or Nothing

Illuminate

Game Player

SHHH You Scream You Die

Outlaw Gangsters

Chase

Shining Evil

World's Greatest Hoe Catcher
(The Autobiography of Prince Darby)

Silk

Black Jack

Murder Game

Ultimate Revenge

Terror Dome

From Promise

Promise was born in the South and didn't find out he was a foster child until the day of his foster mother's death. He had heard whispers throughout his young life that he was a 'tricks' baby and was ashamed to tell anyone about the origin of his birth or his birth parents.

Upon his foster mother's death, Promise escaped the system of numerous foster homes by migrating to Newark NJ. It was his foster mother's last dying declaration for him to live with a couple who gave their word to raise Promise if anything happened to her.

Promise arrives at the infamous Lincoln Motel and is immediately exposed to the world of players and women. He instantly becomes fascinated with the life of a player and yearns to be a full time member of its street fraternity.

Promise is taught vital secrets of the game by Silk who becomes Promise's mentor to the art of being a true player. Promise shows he has an innate ability to grasp the essential elements of the game and meets a woman named Ming who helps him rise to the top. She exposes him to an ultimate danger that possesses the potential to rob him of his life but not before he takes the pimp world by storm and elevates the game to another level right before the eyes of the entire world of players. He simultaneously discovers the mystery of who his mother and father really are.

PRINCIPLES OF WAR

Without unity the heart of one's being will cease to beat, when you don't know the other, or know thyself, you shall meet defeat. Before a war is waged all should make a declaration of their grievances. If your comrades pledge death before dishonor, you know where their allegiance is. For a warlord there is nothing more important than having loyalty amongst his warriors, behind enemy lines you are either carried off the battlefield, or you walk off victorious. On dangerous grounds rivals that come within firing range automatically become target practice, the ambush, the quick strike and any sneak attacks are the harshest tactics. Since I refuse to lose against any opposing forces, or stand still, my adversaries get beaten like scrap metal between a hammer and an anvil. On many occasions I have been in hand to hand combat where my opponents fought valiantly but when it was all said and done by my hands they died violently. To me size matters because the bigger they are the harder they fall to the floor. Anyone who sacrifices his or her life for a cause dies a martyr of war. I learned the best way to avoid being hit is by hitting first. People say everything gets greater later, nevertheless sometimes they keep getting worse. You have an edge on life if your mind is your sharpest weapon, but what makes some people succeed while others fail is the hardest question. Think before you speak, plan before you move and listen before you answer. Happiness keeps the body healthy, but envy deteriorates it like an awful cancer. Abraham Lincoln said, "You destroy an enemy when you make him a friend." I say it is best to keep it real than to be a fake or pretend. In due time I feel who is real will be revealed. In war the first rule of engagement is to kill or be killed. Any so called friend found seeking to betray will be the very first one I slay. Since tomorrow is not promised everyday my enemies pray they don't become prey. Anyone who lives by the sword will die by the sword, yet when someone suddenly meets death he or she still has the audacity to cry to the Lord. To live in fear is what those scared to meet their demise must want, consequently a coward dies a thousand deaths, while a soldier only dies but once.

By David "Outlaw" Franklin

ATTENTION WRITERS

Writers looking to get their books, movie scripts or stage plays published and produced can view our submission guidelines by visiting our website at: www.starchildpublishing.com

What are we looking for? contemporary, urban fiction in the tradition of our author Michael Stanton. The plot and characters must be captivating. We are looking for groundbreaking mainstream stories and movies like a *Menace II Society,* or *Waiting to Exhale* or Stage plays in the genre of Tyler Perry.

We prefer email submissions to Star@starchildpublishing.com in MS word, PDF or RTF format only. For a book, we only need to see three sample chapters and a synopsis. For screenplays and stage plays we need to see a detailed synopsis. However, if you wish to send submissions via snail mail, you can send them to:

Starchild Publishing (Acquisitions Department)
PO Box 6068
Newark NJ 07106

****By submitting your work to Starchild Publishhing you agree to hold Starchild Publishing harmless and not liable for publishing similar works as yours we may already be considering or may consider in the future.****

Submissions will not be returned without a SASE.

Do not contact us for status updates. If we are interested in receiving your full manuscript, we will contact you via email, telephone or letter.

Do not submit if the entire manuscript is not complete.

Due to the heavy volume of submissions we receive, if requirements are not followed, we will not be able to properly process your submission.

ATTENTION MODELS AND PHOTOGRAPHERS

We are in search of models for our book covers and upcoming magazine. We would like to establish a working relationship with models looking to break into print and video. We will also work to get jobs for other magazines, fashion shows and videos.

We are looking for models not only with a pretty face and nice body, but with another talent for them to capitalize on. Modeling should only be used as a vehicle to break into the entertainment industry. Therefore, we are looking for models with other talents such as but not limited to acting and singing.

Go to our website and read the submission guidelines. Please submit pictures to Star@starchildpublishing.com in jpeg format. Send pictures in sexy style of dress, bathing suits but no nude photographs. Send a daytime phone number and list other credentials in the entertainment industry you would like to be involved with.

We are looking for photographers to submit photos of models they are working with as a proof of their skill as a photographer. It would make it easy for a photographer to have a team of his own models, but we will be willing to set up photo shoots with photographers in different locations where we have models who need to be photographed.

ABOUT THE AUTHOR

Michael is the bestselling author of *Baptism By Fire Part I Empire* and *Promise Part I The Chosen One*. He is also a freelance writer for major mystery, horror and romance magazines throughout the country. He writes movie scripts, stage plays and music. He sings and plays the piano. For him, writing is always going to be cheaper than therapy. You can visit him at his website www.Michael-Stanton.com.

In Memory Of

Helen Stafford my grandmother, the woman I miss like crazy. I can't wait to get to heaven and for you to tell me how happy I have made you for changing my life and heart. I wish you were still here to see all I have done in my life.

My uncle Nelson, you always told me I had to watch those who profess to love me in life, because in death they will quickly forget you. I see how they did not want to help pay for you to have a proper burial. For this I turn my back on all of those suckers.

Dayshawn Swinton, I did not find out until years later that you were gone until I bumped into your nephew. He and I hit it off just like you and I did. I was hurt as if I had found it out the day it happened. I missed our laughter and your jokes.

Q Gumbs, I am completely at a loss for words. I have learned so much from you about the life we lead. You always told me to watch these niggas, because they are not for me in the least. I know you always said you were going to read my books. You bought one but did you read it? When I get there, I want you to tell me all about it.

Last but not least, Krissy. I tell you every day how sorry I am for leaving you. If I had known then what I know now, I would not have left. You have made me look at life differently. I am ten times the man I was because of you. I have strength and endurance in me which I learned from you. I love you and I thank you.